What readers are .

DEATH IN DOOR COUNTY

and

The Val & Kit Mystery Series

FIVE STARS! "When meeting an old friend for coffee and a chat, do you think to yourself 'Wow, I really miss them. Why do we wait so long to catch up?' That is exactly how I feel every time I read a Val & Kit Mystery. Like I just sat down for a hilarious chat over coffee and cake followed by wine and chocolate. These girls are a hilarious mix of Laurel and Hardy with a dash of Evanovich sprinkled with Cagney & Lacey. Comedy, love and mystery: a brilliant combination."

FIVE STARS! "I really enjoyed this book. Not only was I in Door County at the time that I was reading it and Door County has always been one of my favorite places, I am also a homeowner in Downers Grove, IL, which is where Val and Kit also live. I did read the first two books in The Val & Kit Mystery Series, which I also thoroughly enjoyed. Being from Downers Grove, I got quite a kick out of the real names of most of the streets being used in the stories because I could just picture where the events were taking place."

FIVE STARS! "Another page-turner in the Val & Kit Series! What a great story! I loved learning about Val's family. These stories stay with you long after you have finished the book."

FIVE STARS! " . . . I was reading in the car and laughing out loud. My husband looked over and just shook his head. Thanks again for another good one."

FIVE STARS! "I love these Val and Kit books. Fun to read, and I feel like they are girls I can totally relate to."

FIVE STARS! "The girls have done it again . . . and by girls, do I mean Val and Kit, or Roz and Patty? The amazingly talented authors, Roz and Patty, of course. Although Val and Kit have landed themselves right smack dab in the middle of yet another mystery. This is their third adventure, but don't feel as though you have to (albeit you SHOULD if you haven't done so already) read *The Disappearance of Mavis Woodstock* and *The Murder of Susan Reed* in order. This book and the other(s) are wonderful stand-alones, but read all . . . to enjoy all of the main and supporting characters' quirks?/habits?/mannerisms? I can't seem to express how much I love these books. . . . Speaking of characters . . . This is what sets the Val & Kit series apart from the others in this genre. The authors always give us a big cast of suspects, and each is described so incredibly. . . . It's like playing a game of Clue, but way more fun. . . . The authors make the characters so memorable that you don't waste time trying to 'think back' to whom they are referring. In fact, it's hard to believe that there are only two authors writing such vivid casts for these books. So come on, ladies, confess . . . no, wait, don't. I don't want to know how you do it, just please keep it up."

FIVE STARS! "Whether you are a mother, daughter, grandmother, great-grandmother or best friend . . . this is a heartwarming and hilarious read. . . . I loved getting to know Val and Kit better. Their relationships with their loved ones had me laughing and weeping all at the same time!!!"

FIVE STARS! " . . . This series is a fun read. There's friendship, suspense, mystery, humor and a bit of romance for good measure. I can't wait to read what happens next."

Death
in
Door County
A Val & Kit Mystery

Rosalind Burgess
and
Patricia Obermeier Neuman

To Jan –
I know from our long
friendship that you will
relate to Val + Kit's!
Thanks for your support!
Love,
Patty

Cover by

Laura Eshelman Neuman

Copyright © 2013
Rosalind Burgess
and
Patricia Obermeier Neuman
All rights reserved.
ISBN-13: 978-0692303979
ISBN-10: 0692303979

Blake Oliver Publishing
BlakeOliverPublishing@gmail.com

Also by
Rosalind Burgess
and
Patricia Obermeier Neuman

The Disappearance of Mavis Woodstock
A Val & Kit Mystery

The Murder of Susan Reed
A Val & Kit Mystery

Lethal Property
A Val & Kit Mystery

Palm Desert Killing
A Val & Kit Mystery

Dressing Myself

Acknowledgments

It takes a village to write our books—to catch the mistakes in the forest that we can't see for the trees and to enhance the fun! So thanks again to our beta readers, Kerri Neuman Hunt, Jack Neuman, John Neuman, Laura Eshelman Neuman, Betty Phelps Obermeier, Sarah Paschall, and Melissa Neuman Tracy. Special thanks to Michael Gerbino for sketching Val & Kit, thus infusing our girls with still more life:

The Val & Kit Mystery Series

To my sister, Jill Reeves. My hero.
Love, Roz

To my family, my reason for being.
Love, Patty/Mom/Grandma

Death
in
Door County
A Val & Kit Mystery

The Val & Kit Mystery Series

CHAPTER ONE

I'm coming with you, Val," I heard, as soon as I put the phone to my ear. It was Kit, my friend for more than forty years. I looked across the small apartment at my daughter, who was stretched out on the couch in her pajamas, reading the back of a Honey Nut Cheerios box.

Emily caught the look on my face and mouthed, "What's wrong?"

I put my index finger to my lips, warning her to remain silent. "Are you sure you want to, Kit? We're staying two nights."

"Of course; it will be fun."

"But it's Mother's Day on Sunday," I reminded her. As if she would forget *that*.

"Don't they have cute shops and stuff up there in Door County?" She said it as if we were planning to visit Istanbul or someplace equally far away, instead of merely visiting the state that borders ours to the north. And she'd ignored the mention of Mother's Day.

I knew her son wouldn't be coming home from Texas for the occasion, and her husband, Larry, was in Florida for a golf tournament. I felt a stab of guilt that she would be alone for the weekend. But not enough guilt to actually invite her to accompany Emily and me on our visit to my mother's.

I grimaced into the phone. Sure, they have cute shops, cute restaurants, cute everything in Door County. None of which, by the way, Kit admires in the least.

As far as I'm concerned, Door County is a little stretch of paradise nestled neatly between the Bay of Green Bay and Lake Michigan. But the last time Kit dragged herself from Chicago to visit my mother, she was bored and tiresome. I think I made some secret promise to myself at the time to never take her there again.

"Okay, if you're sure," I said. But trying to hold on to my vanishing promise, I scrambled for the next reason why she absolutely should not accompany us. "Remember how tiny my mom's place is? You'd have to sleep on the couch, Kit."

"Fun, fun, fun," she said, as if I'd suggested she sleep in a tree house.

I felt certain she didn't mean it, but I produced a fake laugh in return, anyway. I saw Emily roll her eyes and knew it was time to put the lid on Kit's plan. "And you really think you can spend two whole days with my mother?"

"Are you kidding? I'm looking forward to it. I haven't seen Jean for two years."

"It's been five."

"Two, five, what's the difference? I'm coming with you, Valley Girl. So break out the snakebite repellent. Wisconsin, here we come!"

Kit has been my best friend since we met as kids in our cozy Chicago suburb of Downers Grove. She's that one person everyone should have in life, the go-to friend, the one you share everything with, the one to call in case of emergency.

But even though we're so close, I can't bring myself to just *tell* her that my mother is no big Kitty Kat fan. Why doesn't she get it? She's the smartest woman I know, and my mother's never made any secret of her feelings for my pal.

"So now what do we tell Grandma?" I asked Emily, after fiercely punching the disconnect button on my phone—the current equivalent of slamming down the receiver. Sometimes I miss the old technology.

Emily sat up, cradling the cereal box in her lap as if it were a sleeping baby. "Tough one, Mom. Not sure."

Emily gets it. She knows how my mother feels about Kit. Heck, everyone knows except Kit.

"Why can't she see that Grandma doesn't like her?" I asked.

"And why *is* that? I never really understood it. Kit's so awesome."

"It probably stems from when we were young. Grandma always felt Kit was the instigator who led me into all kinds of trouble," I said, dismissing any collusion on my part. "Nothing serious, just kid stuff," I added, lest my daughter think I lived a life of crime before she was born.

"I guess she can be a little headstrong," Emily said.

"Exactly." I joined her on the couch and snuck a Cheerio out of the box.

"Well, she's not gonna change at her age, so we should just roll with it and enjoy her." Emily continued rocking the cereal box a little.

"*Her* age? She's the same age as me."

"Mom, I'm talking about Grandma, not Kit."

We both laughed, as I reached across and ran a hand through her blond hair. I guessed we would get through it. Somehow.

"Have you ever noticed," Emily asked, shaking the sleeping baby/cereal box, "how Grandma and Kit are so much alike? They could be mother and daughter."

Wow. Why hadn't I ever realized that?

Emily is my only child—an actress, although not a famous one (yet), and married to Luke, her adorable husband who does something clever with computers and thereby supports his wife. Her acting roles are few and far between, but her determination to succeed remains as strong as her talent (in her mother's opinion). Luke and Emily have an outrageously high-priced two-room apartment in Los Angeles (three rooms if you count the bathroom that is the size of those found on most planes). Her trips home to Chicago are rare and precious and very dear to me. Just like she is.

Her father and I are divorced, and I live in my own small apartment. The huge home she grew up in is solely occupied by David.

After the split, Emily acted as if I'd been unfairly forced to downsize, even though I tried to convince her I love my new little apartment and it was my choice to let her father keep the house—along with the enormous mortgage, high utility bills, and assorted costs that go with maintaining such a place.

***

"So I guess we should break the news to Grandma," I said. Emily and I were scrunched up on either end of the couch, both still in our pajamas, a pizza box between us. It was seven o'clock on a perfect Thursday evening.

I'd taken the week off work for Emily's visit. My boss, Tom Haskins—the owner of Haskins Realty—had readily agreed to the vacation. Not so much because I needed or had earned it, but because he loves Emily nearly as much as I do. He'd already taken us out to dinner twice that week, both times to pricey restaurants where he showed Emily off to his cronies as if she were his own daughter.

"Want me to do it?" Emily daintily wiped her mouth with a napkin.

"Of course." We both knew it was the logical solution.

"Wimp," she said.

"Show-off."

Emily did a superb job of preparing her grandmother for the additional visitor, but my mom wasn't pleased. After the initial blow had been struck, Emily and I remained huddled on the couch with my mother on speakerphone between us.

"Well, for heaven's sake, at least don't let that Katherine drive. I mean it, Valerie. Especially with Emily in the car."

Emily put her hand to her mouth to suppress a laugh. I immediately conjured up a vision of the grown Emily strapped into a baby's car seat in the back of my Lexus.

"I'll drive, Mom," I said. "Everything will be great. Emily will survive, and Kit is really looking forward to seeing you."

"Hmm. I don't know what all I'm going to tell William Stuckey."

Emily and I both smiled. William Stuckey is my mother's closest companion in Door County. Although she has known him for most of her life, she always refers to him by his full name. He was a good friend of both my parents in Chicago and moved to Door County after his wife died.

A few years after my father passed away, my mother moved up there too, and I was so glad William lived nearby and seemed to like watching over her.

"Grandma, how is your boyfriend?" Emily winked at me.

"He's not my boyfriend, for Pete's sake."

"*Man* friend?" Emily tried again.

"I don't know what that is, Emily. Is it European?" My mother often assumes that if she doesn't understand something, it must be European.

"No, Grandma, it's just . . . well, I know William is your friend, and he's a man—"

5

"Good heavens, of course he's a man. What did you think he was, a cocker spaniel? I don't like that kind of talk, Emily. That's exactly the kind of thing that girl Katherine would say."

I thought it a little unfair that Kit was being blamed for Emily's choice of words. But on the other hand, I knew she would have loved being referred to as a girl.

And with the news broken to my mother, I was kind of glad she was going with us. Having just listened to my daughter tell one funny story after another about her crazy life in California, I recalled Kit had not seen her only child for a long time. I could share, couldn't I?

***

My mother's house, a two-bedroom one-story, is situated on the edge of Egg Harbor, a charming town that offers all the amenities anyone would ever need. And she has enough yard to satisfy the gardener in her that insists on growing tomatoes every year, a passion she took with her from her former life in Downers Grove. When my car pulled into her driveway shortly after noon on Friday, she was waiting for us outside.

At seventy-eight years old, the honey-blond woman with clear blue eyes and a small-but-curvy figure caught me off guard, and I was struck by how pretty she still is. She wore blue pencil pants and had a soft-pink wool cardigan casually wrapped around her shoulders over a short-sleeved cotton shirt. She could easily have been modeling for an L.L.Bean catalog.

She waved and smiled as Emily bounded out of the car to run toward her grandmother, the way Emily has done since she was old enough to bound anywhere. I took a moment to watch the two of them embrace.

"Jean looks fabulous," Kit said from the backseat. She had removed her Versace sunglasses and placed them on top of her head. The tortoiseshell frames blended perfectly with

6

her shiny auburn hair, and I noticed her lipstick had not diminished during the five-hour drive up from Downers Grove, even though we'd stopped at a Wendy's for hamburgers to eat in the car.

Emily had chosen the fast-food place, and Kit proclaimed the food surprisingly good, although I know she secretly hates fast food of any kind. As a gourmet cook, she often lectures me that the words *fast* and *food* are like oil and water. Never to be used in the same sentence, much less digested. But I was pleased that she was making an effort.

"She does look good, doesn't she?" I felt proud as I looked at my mother.

Then I made the mistake of pulling down the visor in front of me to take a look at myself. I hadn't worn any makeup for the drive and had pulled my short blond hair into a ponytail the size of a walnut. I looked as if we'd driven across the entire country without a stop. As I caught Kit's reflection over my shoulder, I realized she looked as if she'd been at a spa all day, getting the full treatment.

I started digging around in my purse for a lipstick, before my mother could ask why I wasn't at least making an effort, when her tapping on the window made me jump a little. "Open the door, Valerie," she said.

When I did as I was told, my mother leaned into the car. Her familiar scent of a gardenia-based perfume filled the space, wiping out the smell of French fries and pickles. She reached in to hug me and at the same time peered over my shoulder at the backseat.

"Hello, Jean," Kit said brightly.

"Hello, Katherine." My mother kept one arm wrapped around me, but reached out the other and took Kit's hand in hers. "I'm glad you girls all got here in one piece," she said, as if we'd beaten impossible odds by reaching Egg Harbor without falling into Lake Michigan.

"Well, of course, Mom." I released myself from her grip and stepped out of the car. "We had a fun drive, didn't we, Kit?"

"Yes," I heard my friend reply. "I counted more than a hundred cows."

"Well, you girls come inside and relax for a while. We'll go into town for lunch in a little bit, and then William Stuckey is taking us to dinner this evening."

"Fun." Kit clutched her brown Louis Vuitton overnight case as she stepped out of the car. "This will be fun."

What wouldn't be fun, I knew, would be telling my mom we already *had* lunch, from a fast-food restaurant, no less. She finds them even more distasteful than Kit does.

"Uh, how about we just go shopping this afternoon?" I asked. "Then we can save our appetites for dinner tonight."

"How *thoughtful* of you," my mother said, eyeing the two wadded-up Wendy's bags on the front seat. She flashed an accusatory look at Kit, as if she'd force-fed me a double cheeseburger. At least *I* was off the hook. And then she just had to add, "Valerie, you look like the dickens."

I followed my three favorite women into the house, carrying Emily's backpack and my overnight case. I've never really known what the dickens are, but it has been one of my mother's pet phrases all my life. Whatever they are, they aren't good.

***

William Stuckey had a home in the Lake View Coves Retirement Villas. After we stopped at the gated entrance and my mother greeted the guard on duty as if he were an old friend, I noticed there was no lake view. Nor any coves. And the one-story condos made of stone could hardly be classified as villas, although they looked luxurious. William greeted us at the front door. His home had a light, airy feel, with a lot of glass and chrome and a view of the swimming pool (apparently a substitute for the implied lake).

A tall man with a shock of white hair and a still-handsome face, William wore a gray suit and red bow tie. His eighty-two years were well concealed by his straight posture and broad shoulders. He and my mother made a dashing couple, and seeing them together made me a little lonely for my father, who hadn't been as lucky. William bent down to kiss her on the cheek and then opened his arms to give Emily and me big hugs.

"You remember my friend Kit James," I said.

"Of course." William opened his arms and gave a third hug to Kit. "I never forget a beautiful redhead."

My mother was ahead of us, farther inside the "villa," and I wondered if she'd heard William's flirty comment.

"You'd forget your own head if it wasn't attached to your neck," she said, without turning around. Okay, so she'd heard.

William's taking us out to dinner consisted of walking out through the sliding glass doors at one end of his living room and around the swimming pool to the restaurant on the other side, conveniently called the Lake View Coves Restaurant.

He'd made a reservation, which must have been mandatory, judging from all the full tables. Only the one reserved for us stood empty, a table by the window with a view of the pool (and William's home). Since it was only six o'clock, both were still visible.

"Ah, Edmundo," William addressed the waiter who appeared at our table as soon as we were seated. "I must be the luckiest man in America to have four such beautiful women at my table, don't you think?"

"Yes, sir, Mr. Stuckey." Edmundo whipped white linen napkins off our plates and landed them perfectly in our laps. "You are, indeed."

As soon as our drinks arrived, wine for four of us and a margarita for Emily, William led us in a toast. "To a wonderful weekend. May you find our little corner of the world as peaceful as Jean and I do."

If only William's toast had come true . . .

CHAPTER TWO

Oh crap! I thought, once I realized where I was. I didn't know if it was because Emily and I had stayed up too late talking after turning in the night before or if it was the third glass of wine I'd let William order for me; but I'd been so sound asleep, it took me a minute to remember I was in one of the twin beds in my mom's spare bedroom. Emily was still asleep in the matching bed a few feet away, which only confirmed the bad news: the muffled conversation I could hear coming from the other room must be Kit and my mother.

I bolted out of bed but slipped out of the room quietly. Emily was still on California time, and I felt certain she wasn't ready to wake up. I glanced at my watch, wondering what time it was, but of course couldn't see the hands because my glasses were somewhere in the bottom of my purse, or wherever I'd left my Kindle.

When I entered the combination living room and kitchen, I could see my mother talking on the phone. She was wearing a light-pink robe, and a matching pink net affair covered her hair. In a 1950s sort of way, she looked pretty.

"Shh," Kit said, even though I hadn't uttered a word. She came toward me with a cup of coffee. "Jean's had some bad news."

I ignored the coffee and walked past Kit to my mother. She was in the center of the living room area, a pale-blue telephone held up to her ear; the curly cord stretched all the way back over the counter into the kitchen area.

"Is there anything we can do?" I heard her ask. She held up her index finger to me, indicating I should remain silent.

I moved to the kitchen part of the room, and Kit followed me, still extending the coffee cup. This time I took it from her. "Who is she talking to?" I asked.

"One of her friends. I think someone had an accident."

"Not William, I hope." I took a long sip to cover my alarm. I don't know why I said that, but he was the first person I could think of.

"William Stuckey?" Kit said so loudly that I shushed her. "Why would you think it's him?" she continued in a noisy whisper.

"I don't know. He's her closest friend up here." I shook my head, glancing at my mother. She was nodding as she listened to the caller, one hand placed over her heart. "No. Not him," I said. "She'd be more upset. Right?"

"Perhaps." Kit looked over my shoulder at my mom, as if considering my suggestion. "No, definitely not him. I think she likes him, by the way."

"Well, of course she likes him, Kit. Who wouldn't? He's charming."

"Yeah, right. He's very charming."

"What do you mean by that?"

"I'm agreeing with you, dum-dum."

"But you don't mean it. I can tell. Kit, what are you thinking?"

"I'm not thinking anything. He's totally delightful."

11

"What does *that* mean?" I don't know why it was so important to me for Kit to approve of William.

"It means he's got it all. Looks, money, *charm*. He's got charm coming out of his ass."

"*Girls*. Stop it this minute."

We both turned to watch my mother hang the blue telephone back on the wall. I was suddenly thrown back to my thirteen-year-old self, in a different kitchen, a different house, with my mother catching Kit and me in the middle of some mischief (which had been totally Kit's idea).

"Is everything okay, Mom?" I pulled out a kitchen chair, as if she needed to sit down. But instead, she went to the refrigerator and took some homemade biscuits out of the freezer.

"No, it's not. That was Virginia. Remember her, Valerie?" Before I could respond, she continued. "She's the one who lost all that weight, and we thought she was sick; but it turned out she'd actually gone to the Cities to have that ring-band surgery."

"Lap-band," Kit interjected.

"Ring, lap, whatever it is, she had it." My mother opened the oven and put her biscuits on the middle shelf. "And now she parades around like she's Lauren Bacall." She flipped the dial on the stove to the temperature she wanted (without having to put on reading glasses, I noticed).

"Hmm . . . what movie was Lauren Bacall in?" Kit asked.

My mother looked shocked. "Well, a lot of them. *To Have and Have Not*, for one, which come to think of it, would be perfect for Virginia—"

"What happened, Mom?" I cut in, before we were treated to a recitation on movie stars from the fifties.

"Bad news. I'm afraid our dear friend Doris Dibble had a terrible accident last night. You remember her, don't you, Valerie?"

I sat on the vacant chair I'd pulled out for my mom, racking my brain. But I didn't remember Doris Dibble at all.

"Are you serious, Jean? *Doris Dibble*?" Kit sat down next to me.

"You didn't know her too, did you?" My mother reached onto the top shelf of her pantry and pulled down a jar of dark-purple preserves.

"No," Kit answered my mom, who had her back to us. Then, in one of those stage whispers she does so well, she said to me, "Doris *Dibble*? Are you kidding me?"

"Katherine, no one kids about a serious accident." My mother's hearing was obviously as good as her vision, and I wasn't convinced she had missed the point of Kit's observation.

At that moment Emily, bless her, emerged from the bedroom. She looked sleepy, with her blond hair tousled, and she wore an oversize Lakers T-shirt. "Who's Doris Dibble, Grandma?"

"She's a friend of mine, sweetheart. She had a bad fall last night. Nothing for you to worry about."

I watched as Emily put her arms around her grandmother. "I'm sorry," she said. "That's so sad."

For the first time since she had heard the news, my mother actually *looked* sad. But I suspected it had more to do with Emily's concern than poor Doris's misfortune.

"I know," my mom said. "I hope this isn't the beginning of the end. You know what they say about falls. But the good news is, she's youngish, close to my age. Seventy-five."

I resisted the urge to look at Kit, as I felt her gazing at me over the coffee cup she held to her lips.

"So," my mom said. She gave Emily a gentle swat on the behind. "You sit down, and I'll fix you girls breakfast. How do you want your eggs? Valerie, check on the biscuits. We have a lot to do today." As she spoke, she took a tiny notepad from the pocket of her robe and flipped it to the first page.

"Okay," I said, opening the oven door. "What's to be done?"

"Lunch with a couple of my friends at Al Johnson's—I want them to meet Emily. You know, Valerie, the place with goats on the roof."

I realized my mother was reading from her prepared itinerary for the day. "Yes, of course I know it, Mom." I closed the oven door. We have lunch at Al Johnson's every time I go to Door County. (I would recognize any one of those goats if I saw it shopping for dress pants at Target.) And ice cream at Wilson's in Ephraim always follows our lunch.

Sure enough, she continued, "Then we'll visit a few more shops and stop by Wilson's for some ice cream."

"Wait; shouldn't we check in on Doris?" I asked.

"We'll be seeing Virginia at the restaurant. She'll update us."

"Who's Virginia?" Emily asked.

"Door County's answer to Lauren Bacall," Kit said.

"Good heavens, Katherine." My mother poured fresh coffee into our cups. "Emily doesn't know who Lauren Bacall is."

"I certainly do, Grandma. Very beautiful. Married to Humphrey Bogart. *The Big Sleep.*"

"Correct." My mom looked as proud as if Emily had just aced her entrance exam to Harvard.

"Well, Grandma, she was an actress like me, don't forget."

"She was nothing like you." My mom kissed the top of Emily's head. She's seen Emily act in ten million school plays, a television commercial for diapers, and nonspeaking roles in both a movie and a short-lived sitcom. I knew she thought Lauren Bacall would have had to get up pretty early in the morning to outact her granddaughter. "Valerie, why don't you start fixing the eggs? I have something to do."

She disappeared from the kitchen so suddenly, I felt a little unnerved.

Kit caught my look and jumped up to begin breaking eggs into a glass bowl.

I waited a few minutes and then followed my mom down the tiny hallway to her bedroom. I tapped on the door. "Mom? Are you okay?"

By the time she opened the door just enough to let me in, she seemed to have shrunk, and I felt like a giant. Her eyes were moist from tears she had just wiped away. "Now don't go making a lot of fuss, Valerie. I'm okay. It's normal to shed a few tears when a friend has a serious accident."

"Well, of course it is." I put an arm around her shoulders and led her to the bed, where we both sat down. "What did Virginia say?"

"She stopped in to see Doris last night—they're both a couple of night owls. And she saw poor Doris lying at the foot of the stairs." My mother took a tissue from the pocket of her robe and blew her nose softly. "Seems she was crumpled up like a rag doll. Oh, Valerie, it's such a long, deep staircase; it goes all the way down from the landing at the top to the hallway at the bottom." She looked at me as if for some clarity.

I nodded, confirming I totally understood the intricacies of how a staircase works. "Was Doris home alone?" I asked.

"Her husband returned home just as Virginia was calling 9-1-1. Oh, Valerie, I pray she'll be okay. She's such a good person. When I first moved here, she went out of her way to make me feel welcome. It wasn't easy for me then, you remember."

"I certainly do. I think you were very brave to move all the way up here without any family."

"Oh, my girls are always with me." She patted my knee. "In here." She tapped her chest over her heart with her other hand.

"Mom, tell me about Doris. Have I ever met her?"

"You'd remember her if you did. She has that big house on the water. It really is a mansion, full of beautiful things. She's got a lot of money, and I've never met anyone more generous with her friends."

My mother paused and looked thoughtful. "I think her most precious possession is her computer. She really loves that. She even bought me one for my birthday last month. Well, it's not a regular computer. It's an iPad. She promised to teach me how to use it . . . so let's hope she recovers soon, eh?" My mom smiled, but her lips quivered.

"Tell me about her husband," I said, moving on quickly. I couldn't believe Doris gave such a lavish birthday gift to my mother, when I'd just sent her an Edible Arrangement (she claimed the kiwis upset her stomach). I was feeling like the biggest cheapskate in the world.

"She was widowed when she was in her fifties; then eight or so years ago she up and married that Stan Dibble."

"Stan?"

"Yes. He's fifteen years younger than her if he's a day. Comes from New York, or somewhere out East. He's got that funny accent. Not all of Doris's friends care for him, but she was so taken in by his charm."

Was every *man in Door County considered charming?* I wondered. "Does she have children?" I asked instead.

"Only one, a grown daughter, Margaret. She lives in Minneapolis and doesn't visit Door County often. I don't think she likes Stan that much. But Doris goes to Minneapolis about once a month."

"Margaret must be upset."

"Yes, I'm sure she is. And Stan too. He looks after Doris very well. Has her on all sorts of vitamins and stuff. Makes sure she walks every day. That sort of thing. He even bought her a bicycle that never goes anywhere. You know what I mean?"

"A stationary bike?" I thought of my own bike that had more than lived up to its stationary status in my spare bedroom back at the Big House. It was a great place to hang clothes, though. Maybe I shouldn't have let David keep it in the divorce.

"Right. We all think Doris is in amazing shape."

"And Virginia said she thought the fall was serious?"

"Yes. She said they took Doris to the hospital, and she's in critical condition."

"Are you sure you don't want to call Doris's husband?"

"Not yet. We'll see what Virginia has to say at lunch. What I really want to do is enjoy the day with my girls. I think that's what Doris would want too."

"Then you got it, lady."

***

After breakfast I was the last in line to use the tiny bathroom. When I came out, my mother was reading from her notebook again.

"Tonight William Stuckey is taking us to a new art gallery and then to dinner, so you'll want to dress up for that." As she said it, she gave my jeans and plain white T-shirt the once-over.

I opened my mouth to remind her that Door County is the typical vacation spot, where people feel free to dress casually just about any time, any place. But I know her generation has never quite accepted that, and so I kept quiet, racking my brain for how I could make the outfit I'd brought for that night seem a bit dressier. No doubt Kit would have something I could borrow, a Chanel scarf or a Prada blouse stuffed into the bottom of her bag.

"Tomorrow, of course, we'll go to church." As she said it, she glanced down at my feet, and my Skechers suddenly felt like clown shoes. It made me realize I don't come visit my mother often enough, if I didn't even know what clothes to pack. "And William Stuckey is going to make Sunday dinner for us," she continued, "so I don't have to cook on Mother's Day."

"Good," I said. And then I added, "You and William seem to be seeing a lot of each other."

"What on earth do you mean by a remark like that, Valerie? William Stuckey and I are friends and nothing more. He was a friend of your father's."

I didn't bother to explain that I would hardly consider it cheating if she chose to have a relationship with one of my father's friends. My dad's been gone for nearly a decade, for Pete's sake. I waited for her to return to our weekend plans, worrying what else she would present that I wouldn't have the right clothes for.

But instead, she said, "You're as bad as Minnie Ebert."

"What do you mean? What's wrong with Minnie Ebert? Or *me*?"

"Oh, that one is always insinuating there's something going on between William Stuckey and me. But I know full well *she's* the one with a thing for him. Not to mention half the women on this peninsula. For heaven's sake, he's not *that* great a catch." She set her coffee cup down hard on the table, as if for emphasis, but the look in her eyes didn't match the opinion that had come out of her mouth. It was a look of . . . what? Pride? *Ownership*?

"Ya know," Kit said, "it doesn't seem like there'd be any reason for you *not* to have something goin' on with William, if you wanted. Unless—"

"Are you not listening to me?" my mother all but yelled. "I *don't* want. Now this subject is closed."

CHAPTER THREE

We arrived at noon on the dot at Al Johnson's Swedish Restaurant & Butik in Sister Bay. The exterior of the one-story building was made from wooden logs capped with a sodded roof of bright-green grass. It looked as though it had been transported whole from Sweden.

Like a small child, Emily clapped her hands in delight when she spotted two goats grazing on the grassy roof. Kit took one look up and then lowered her head as she quickly entered the restaurant. It was as if she were exiting a helicopter and afraid she'd get whacked by the blades.

My mother's friends Virginia Huntley and Ruth Greenway were already seated at a table in the back of the restaurant, and both rose when they saw us. They waved across the crowd of diners, many of whom turned to check us out.

It was hard to guess the ages of these two women, but they looked older than my mom. Virginia was rather glamorous, for a woman over the age of eighty (I was guessing). Her chestnut-brown hair was cut in a style that suited her, and she wore khakis and a red polo shirt. I noticed her makeup was subtle but doing a great job, and her skin looked good for her age. If she had indeed undergone lap-band surgery, it was a success.

Ruth, on the other hand, wore no makeup. A red sequined baseball cap covered most of her gray hair, which was cut very short, almost like a man's. Huge glasses with heavy black frames the size of hubcaps partially obscured her twinkling blue eyes. To finish off her bizarre ensemble, she had chosen a hand-knitted sweater with a big cat stitched into the front. The cat appeared to be decimating a ball of yarn.

While I grasped Ruth's hand in greeting, I looked down at the cat's yellow eyes, one of which appeared to focus on its prey and the other on me.

Virginia brought us up to date on Doris. She was still in critical condition. The hospital wouldn't allow any visitors other than family. Her daughter, Margaret, had arrived from Minneapolis and was at the hospital with her mother, along with Stan.

"Of course," Virginia went on, "we'll go over later and see if they'll let us visit. I'm so worried about Margaret." She grew quiet for a moment and then, sounding only a little forced, said, "But right now we didn't want to miss meeting Emily."

"I'm so sorry to hear about your friend," Emily said, and was suddenly engulfed in an embrace that squashed the yellow-eyed feline between her and Ruth. I prayed Emily wouldn't come away with scratches.

"Thank you, toots." Ruth released my daughter. "Doris is only seventy-five, you realize." She looked at each of us for confirmation that seventy-five was indeed far too young to sustain any serious injuries from a fall down a flight of stairs. We all nodded in agreement. In that group, seventy-five appeared to be the new fifty.

"Healthy as a horse," Ruth continued, as we all took our seats at the table. "Her husband too. Of course he's a lot younger than she is. He ran in the last Door County Half Marathon. Didn't your William run in that?" Ruth turned and fixed her giant frames on my mother in the seat next to her. Her tone dripped admiration.

"That was years ago, and he's not *my* William Stuckey."

"Hmm." Virginia looked a little sad. "He sure looks like he could still do a marathon." *Geez,* I wondered, *is William Stuckey the only available man* on *this peninsula?*

The pot that was suddenly presented to Kit proved more than she could resist stirring. "Just who does William Stuckey belong to?" she asked. "He seems *quite* the eligible bachelor."

"He is that, all right," Ruth said. I could see her eyelashes fluttering behind those big glasses of hers.

My mother was definitely the best- and youngest-looking of this trio of senior women, especially taking into account Ruth's wacky appearance, but she seemed to be the least interested in a romance with William. "For Pete's sake," she said. "Let's order."

***

As we ate, the three of them talked about Doris. How smart she was. How kind she was. A great and generous friend who had devoted boundless energy to various charities, not only in Door County but also Green Bay.

"She has plenty of dough," Ruth informed us. "Left to her by her first husband. He died of a heart attack years ago. He invented some cockamamie doo-dad for the aerospace industry that made him millions."

Virginia nodded in agreement. "Why she married Stan, I'll never know. Uff da."

Kit gave me a weird look, no doubt unfamiliar with the Norwegian expression. Well, she'd soon get used to it. "Why do you say that?" she asked.

"She could have done much better. He didn't have a penny to his name. Or so I heard. I'm not one to spread gossip, but sometimes you hear things. Doris, of course, won't listen to a word against him, so we all keep our mouths shut."

"Where'd she meet him?" Kit asked, sounding nonchalant. She held a coffee cup up to her face, but wasn't drinking.

Virginia leaned into our circle, as if she were about to impart a great secret. "She met him on one of those dating businesses they have on the Internet. Doris is a bit of a computer whiz."

"Darn tootin'," Ruth confirmed. "But that computer stuff comes easily to younger people. She loves playing solitaire on that machine of hers. And of course she does a lot of other stuff . . . way too complicated for me. But I really do think you are wrong about where they met, Virginia. I thought she met him when she and her daughter were on that cruise."

"I prefer to use real cards myself," Virginia said. "You're right about Doris being very knowledgeable when it comes to computers, but you have it all wrong about where they met, Ruth." She didn't add *as usual*, but her tone and raised eyebrows clearly implied it.

"Dating business, my foot." My mother emptied a packet of Equal into her iced tea and whipped it with a long spoon. To her, finding a husband on such a site is equivalent to picking him out of a police lineup. "I'm sure Doris told me she met Stan at a bridge tournament. You know how she loves her bridge, and she's an outstanding player. No one can beat her."

"And no one is more generous than Doris," Ruth informed us, choosing to ignore Virginia's earlier look of indignation. She couldn't have *missed* the look since she was wearing the world's largest spectacles. "She helped me set up a shelter for lost and homeless cats. And she didn't just help with computer stuff; she also donated a lot of moola."

"Really?" I tried hard not to look at the yellow-eyed cat covering her sweater. It seemed to be staring me down with its one unoccupied eye, daring me to challenge the wisdom of donating to homeless cats. I had no choice but to blink first.

"You're darn tootin'," Ruth said again. "Doris understands the need. People don't realize how tragic—"

"Uff da," Virginia said. "These girls don't want to hear about your stupid cats. Emily, tell us about all the famous people you've met."

Ruth tried again. "I was only saying—"

"Have you met George Clooney?" Virginia asked Emily. "He's so handsome. Reminds me a bit of . . . what's his name?"

"Gregory Peck?" my mother offered.

"I was going to say Burt Lancaster, but Gregory Peck will do."

"Hot diggity dog." Ruth slapped a thin knee.

The three of them giggled, and I realized there is no age barrier when it comes to liking handsome movie stars.

"I met Ben Affleck once," Emily said.

The three of them stopped giggling instantly. "Who's he, dear?" Virginia asked.

Okay, so maybe there is a slight age barrier.

While Emily went on to explain who Ben is, we were joined by another lady. The infamous Minnie Ebert. She was wearing a lot of foundation, too much blue eye shadow, and a thick coating of red-orange lipstick. I knew she was in her late eighties, but she still had a trim figure and pretty good legs. Although personally, I would have worn slacks, not shorts.

"What do we have here?" She pulled a chair from the vacant table next to us and seated herself at the head of ours. "Jean, why didn't you tell me Valawee was coming up this weekend?"

I smiled at hearing Minnie's childlike way of speaking and rose to give her a hug. When I returned to my seat, I noticed my mother's exasperated look. She was no more a fan of Minnie than she was of Kit.

"What are you doing here?" she asked. I thought she sounded rude.

"I was just over at Doris's," Minnie said. "Luckily, I caught Stan. He'd just returned from the hospital for a change of clothes and a quick shower. He's devastated, poor man."

"What's the latest?" my mother asked.

"He's not happy Margaret's in town."

"He can just get over himself," Virginia said. "Poor Margaret."

"Yes, how awful for her," I said. Even though I'd never met Margaret, I felt a twinge of pain at the worry she must feel.

"Very much so," Minnie said. "Especially since she and Stan can barely be in the same room without arguing." She put a bony hand to her glossy blond curls, which surely had to have been manufactured in China, and began twisting a strand with her fingers.

"I just went over there to offer my support," she continued. "Actually, I thought maybe I'd find you girls there at the house too, but of course I see now you had more important things to do."

"You better believe it," Ruth said. "We don't often get to have lunch with a genuine film actress." She beamed across the table at Emily.

"Yes, I see that," Minnie said. She put her elbow on the table and cupped her chin in her hand in a coquettish gesture. "It's always about celebrity with you, Ruth Greenway."

"Oh, please," Emily said quickly. She looked concerned, as if she might have to break up a fight. "I'm no celebrity. I'm barely an actress."

"You are, too, an actress," my mother disagreed. "One of these days you will be discovered. Why, you just wait and see—"

"*Please*, Grandma, let's not talk about me." It was the curtest tone I had ever heard Emily use with her beloved grandmother, and I was a little shocked.

"I don't see William at this little soirée of yours." Minnie removed her hand from under her chin and nonchalantly waved it around the table at us.

I turned my attention away from Emily, thankful that Minnie had butted in.

"A soirée is held in the evening; this is lunchtime," Virginia corrected her.

"And why should William Stuckey be here, for Pete's sake?" my mother asked.

"No reason, other than you two seem to be joined at the hip. When I spoke to him this morning, he told me you'd all be here—"

"Wait! You spoke to William Stuckey?" my mother asked.

Minnie fanned her face with a napkin. "Have I said something wrong?"

"Don't be ridiculous. Where did you see him?"

"He was over at Doris's place, offering a neighborly hand to Stan when he returned from the hospital. We all do what we can. And William used to be a doctor, after all."

"And you hightailed your caboose over here as soon as you found out where we were," Ruth said.

I felt Kit kick me under the table, a sure sign she was having fun.

"Let's get the check and leave," my mother said. "We have a lot to do today." She turned and waved at the waitress who had served us, beckoning her to our table.

A pretty, young blond woman, wearing what I assumed was a traditional Swedish dress covered by a red-and-white-striped apron, approached us, smiling. "Was everything okay, ladies?" she asked.

"Yes, it was wonderful," Kit said. "And please bring *me* the check. It's my treat," she insisted, as my mom's friends started to protest.

"No need for that," Miss Sweden said. "A Mr. William Stuckey called and gave us his credit-card number. The lunch is all paid for."

"Oh my," Minnie said. "Your boyfriend is so generous."

"He's not my *boyfriend*," my mother said wearily. Clearly, she'd had to say it ten million times to this crowd. But again, I noticed that glint of happiness in her eyes at the suggestion. It was as if we were all sixteen, sitting in the school cafeteria, and she was toying with the affections of the star quarterback.

Before we left the restaurant, Kit grabbed my arm and pulled me toward the restroom.

"That was great," she said, as soon as we were alone. "Seriously, when I said we'd have fun, I didn't mean it, of course. But we've got a great gang of gals here." She began applying fresh lipstick.

"They are a hoot, aren't they?"

"Hell yes, they are. I thought we were gonna have to break up a fight." She put her lipstick away and picked something from the sleeve of her navy-blue raw-silk blouse. "Look at this, Val." She held something miniscule up to my face, but I couldn't determine what it was. "Cat hair," she said. "Next time we gals get together, I'm not sitting next to Cat Woman. And what was up with Minnie and the shorts?"

"She's still got good legs," I said, in answer to Kit's question, not as a justification for a near-ninety-year-old woman to wear shorts.

"Yeah, she likes flashing those gams." Kit burst into a gale of laughter. "Seriously, Val, these women are hilarious. Why did I wait so long to come back for a visit? Really, I secretly thought we were in for a dull time with a bunch of old biddies. By the way, I'd forgotten William was a doctor."

"Yes, family practice. But he's been retired about a million years." I took my own lipstick from my pocket and reapplied my Raisin Rum.

"So whaddya think?" Kit asked.

"About what?"

"About Doris, of course. Falling down all those stairs . . ." She looked at me in the mirror and then continued. "Boy, it's a bit of a mystery where she met this Stan. Everyone seems to have a different opinion."

I jammed my lipstick into its case and stuffed it back into the pocket of my jeans. "Let's just concentrate on having a nice visit."

"Say no more." She tweaked the ends of her perfect haircut. "Ya know, I think this weekend is gonna be very interesting."

As usual, Kit was right on the moola, as Ruth Greenway probably would have said.

CHAPTER FOUR

The four of us were buckled into my mom's Escalade, waiting for her to start the engine. She didn't seem at all sure where we should go next. "Wilson's? Ice cream?" I reminded her.

But she had other plans by now. "Valerie, I think we should first drive over to Doris's house. If they won't let us see her in the hospital, at least we should see if Stan is home and needs anything."

"Of course we should. Will it be all right if we all go?"

"Why wouldn't it be? Friends visit friends, and sometimes they bring family. And besides, we won't stay long. Just see if he needs anything."

Kit spoke up from the backseat. "William might still be there, and he could fill us in."

"Katherine, that's not why we are going. We can see him anytime."

Just then a ring sounded from the console of my mother's car. It was such a shocking occurrence that no one made a move to answer it, but finally she reached over and pushed a button. William Stuckey's name appeared.

I couldn't have been more shocked at her high-tech action if she'd hit an ejector button and we were all thrown through the sunroof. As far as I knew, the only cell phone my mother had was the one I insisted she have, the one she kept fully charged on her kitchen counter, where it never moved and remained totally unused.

"Way to go, Grandma," Emily said. "Look at you. You're like all high-tech."

"Doris had this installed for me. I've used it only twice." My mother sounded nervous.

"Well, it's William. Shouldn't you answer it?" I asked.

"HELLO, WILLIAM STUCKEY," she yelled into the dashboard, after hitting a connect button.

"Jean? Bad news, I'm afraid. Doris passed away this morning."

We were all silent, until William's deep voice boomed through the vehicle. "Jean, did you hear me?"

"Yes, yes, William Stuckey. We heard you. I'm here with the girls." From my vantage point in the front passenger seat I could see two fat tears roll down her powdered cheeks.

"Are you at the hospital, William?" I asked, more to break the silence than because I needed to know.

"No, I'm at the house. Stan just called me from the hospital. He's with Margaret. They've just been told Doris's neck was broken."

We were all silent again, until Kit spoke. "How did her husband sound?"

"Devastated, of course. I gave him a strong brandy when he came home to change. He still hoped she'd pull through."

"Lucky you were there," I said.

"Why *were* you there?" Kit asked.

My mother turned to face her. "What sort of question is that, Katherine? Why wouldn't a friend stop by—"

"Actually, I've been here since last night," William's voice interrupted what might have been an awkward exchange. "I drove over here after you ladies left. I knew Stan would be awake, and we had some business to discuss. But he'd been out running and just got here himself, and then the ambulance came—"

"So did you actually see her fall?" my mom asked.

"No. When I got here, Stan and Virginia were both kneeling over her at the bottom of the stairs."

"How terrible," I said, picturing the horrific scene.

"Yes, terrible," he said. "I didn't want to have to spoil your fun by worrying you until—"

"Could she talk? Did she say anything about how she fell?" Kit scooted toward the speaker as far as her seat belt would allow.

I gave her a *let it go* look, and she sat back in her seat, her arms crossed over her chest, with a return look of *for now*.

There was another long silence, and then William spoke in a much quieter voice. "Jean, I wish you would hurry and get here; I really need to see you."

"We're on our way, William Stuckey. Two shakes of a lamb's tail."

My mother, who usually drives at least ten miles an hour below the posted speed limit, rammed the gearshift into drive, and we zoomed out of the parking lot as if we were in a high-speed chase. We all heard the tires squealing, but the goats seemed oblivious as they continued happily chomping on the roof.

As shocked as I was by Doris's death, I was more shocked by Emily's sudden change in behavior, although I was sure it had nothing to do with the bad news we'd just received. I'd been vaguely aware of her texting after we'd all commented on my mom's car phone and Doris's demise. And I certainly didn't think anything of it. Most of her generation has a phone in hand at all times, with one or both thumbs in motion more often than not.

30

But then suddenly she leaned over my mom's shoulder and said, in a voice barely above a whisper, "Would you mind terribly taking me back to your place, Grandma? Before you go to Doris's, er, Stan's? I . . . I feel like I just need to lie down a while. I have a headache."

My mom flung her own head around, as if to see for herself how Emily was. I felt nervous, my eyes riveted on the road, until my mom returned her attention to her driving. "We can all just go home, Em," my mom said.

"No, Grandma; you guys go ahead. It'll be better for me to have quiet."

"Okay, but we don't *have* to go to . . . where William Stuckey is."

"Isn't anyone going to call Doris's house *Doris's house* again?" Kit asked, and I would have glared at her if I hadn't been so preoccupied by concern over Emily.

I could almost hear my ex saying *if Emily gets a hangnail, you're sure it's cancer,* but I still felt troubled about the sudden onset of her headache. Assuring myself there were at least several reasons she might have just a mere headache, I decided to follow the advice David had always dispensed so freely and not fear the worst.

Still, once we'd swung into the driveway and watched Emily let herself into my mom's house, I felt a moment of panic. "Wait, Mom. I gotta go get something." I opened the passenger door just as she was putting the car in reverse, and I was probably halfway up the sidewalk before she returned it to park.

I didn't mean to enter the house quietly. I wasn't trying to sneak up on Emily. I just wanted to dig the ibuprofen out of my cosmetics bag in case she wanted it, and then I'd be on my way.

But obviously, Emily didn't hear me enter the house behind her because she was making no attempt to keep her voice low as she spoke on her cell phone. "No, I haven't said anything to her. I told you, I was hoping I wouldn't have to." There was a brief pause before Emily continued, even more loudly, "I'm going to wait until we're back in Downers Grove; I don't want to ruin her Mother's Day." I heard Emily heave a huge sigh, and then she said, "Yes, yes. Okay, I will."

As much as I wanted to stay and learn more—didn't I?—I couldn't bear the thought of Emily thinking I'd been eavesdropping, however accidentally.

I turned and crept out as quietly as any cat burglar.

"That was quick, Valerie," my mom said. Was she eyeing me suspiciously?

"Yeah." Obviously, she wanted to know what it was that I had to get out of the house and where it was. Mothers want to know everything. Whether it is good for them or not.

***

Talk about depressing. Not that it wasn't appropriate, but the scene at Stan's house—or Doris's house, as Kit apparently preferred to call it—felt oppressive. When we let ourselves in after my mom rang the doorbell, I wasn't surprised to see Ruth and Virginia already deposited on the white L-shaped sofa, a Kleenex box on the oversize glass table in front of them.

A man, who I assumed was Stan, sat in one of the striped armchairs on the other side of the table, his eyes red and swollen and a crumpled white linen handkerchief in his hand. He rose when we entered the room.

Stan Dibble looked a lot taller sitting than when he stood up. His lack of height was a little surprising, but it did not diminish his attractiveness. Although I knew he was about sixty years old, he actually looked younger. He had one of those boyishly handsome faces that stick with some men as they age. His blond hair looked freshly cut, with no sign of gray, and his body was lean and athletic. He wore a checkered shirt tucked into black pants, as if he were dressed for casual Friday at an upscale office somewhere. I had no recollection of what Doris looked like, but she'd certainly had a nice-looking husband, even if her friends didn't seem to think he was much of a catch.

"Jean, thanks for coming." He approached my mom for a hug.

She quickly introduced Kit and me and assured him we wouldn't intrude for long.

I felt a great relief at hearing that. Selfishly, my thoughts were all on Emily. Doris was dead; I could be of no help to her. But Emily . . .

"Stan, I'm just so sorry." I heard my mother's voice crack, and that got my attention.

I scooted closer to her and put my arm around her shoulders. I looked to Kit for some comfort of my own, but I saw her roving eyes taking in the immense room with its plethora of paintings and unique furnishings. One thing the women had been right about: Doris Dibble had some money, along with a terrific sense of style. The thought idly crossed my mind that Stan might have been one of her accessories.

"I know. And I appreciate your sympathy, Jean." Stan took a deep breath. "Here, come sit, ladies. Can I get you a drink?"

My mother couldn't help herself. She looked at her watch, as if to remind Stan that it wasn't five o'clock yet, so of course we didn't want a drink. Not one with alcohol, anyway. I could almost hear her thinking that we weren't in Europe, where a person could have some booze any old time of the day.

Not caring what country she was in, Kit said, "I'd like some wine." I tried to hide my amusement as my mother glared at her and Kit gave a sweet smile in return.

"Of course," Stan said. "Anyone else?"

"I'll join you," Ruth Greenway said, from her place on the couch.

My mother switched her disapproving glare from Kit to Ruth.

"Virginia?" Stan asked, and when she didn't seem to hear him, he asked again. "Virginia, would you like a drink?"

She shook her head wordlessly.

"I'm okay," I said, although that was far from the truth.

After Stan returned and delivered the two glasses of wine, he sat back down, and my mother joined him in the matching striped chair. Kit and I declined Stan's invitation to sit, feeling like the intruders that we were.

And then Stan began to recount his horrible night, and of course we listened—everyone else intently, me with half my attention focused on what could possibly be going on between Emily and, I assumed, Luke.

" . . . I came in through the back door," Stan was saying, "and called her name as I started to make my way through the kitchen and dining room. I got really worried when *you* answered me, Virginia, instead of Doris. I could tell by your voice that something—"

He stopped and sobbed for a few minutes, which felt like hours.

My mom rose from her chair to pat his back, although Virginia was crying even harder than Stan.

At last he blew loudly into the hankie and then continued. "When I saw her lying at the bottom of the stairs in a ball, she looked so little, so broken. But she was breathing."

"Wait! Where's William Stuckey?" My mother looked alarmed, as if she'd just realized her purse was missing.

"Margaret called." Stan's words were clipped in irritation. "She wanted him at the hospital with her. Said I should stay here because someone should be at the house. Which is ridiculous. Why does someone need to be here?"

He rose from the chair and fumbled in his pocket for his car keys. "I'm going to the hospital to see just what the hell is going on. I don't see why either Margaret or William needs to be there. Doris is dead, for pity's sake." He shook his head, as if in disbelief. "You're welcome to stay as long as you want. Make yourselves at home."

Kit nudged me with her elbow, and when I turned my face to hers, I saw her eyebrows raised in a look of mischief. "Let's have a look around and check things out," she whispered.

I grabbed the elbow she'd used to nudge me and guided her around the corner to the dining room.

"Wow, classy." Kit caressed the rich brocade fabric covering the chairs. They were elegant, and the mahogany table they surrounded could comfortably seat twenty people.

I lowered my voice, my lips close to Kit's right ear. "What on earth are you talking about? Check what things out? There's nothing wrong here, apart from the obvious."

"The house, of course. I'm wondering where the maid is. Looks like they'd need a whole army of them to keep this place afloat." As she said it, we both looked up in wonder at the chandelier. It sparkled like a giant cluster of diamonds as the light from the French doors at the far end of the room trickled in. "I just thought it'd be fun to see the whole place. I'd think the Realtor in you would also want to check it out."

"Too morbid." I headed back to the others, and Kit followed.

Now Virginia was also sipping wine from a cut-crystal glass. We got in earshot of them just as she was saying, "I can't believe this has happened. How could she be dead?" She set her glass down and wrung her hands. "I think there's something I should tell you . . ."

CHAPTER FIVE

Kit quickly joined Virginia on the couch, holding her wineglass carefully and sitting so close they were nearly touching. "What is it?" she asked.

Ruth Greenway's gargantuan glasses were focused in Virginia's direction, and my mother, seated across from the couch, leaned forward, as if she didn't want to miss a word.

"Uff da," Virginia said slowly, uncomfortable with all the attention placed on her. "It's just that—"

"Girls!" a voice burst from the entry into the living room. "Glad to see you here, finally. I brought over a casserole that I just took out of the oven."

We turned in unison to see Minnie Ebert, who had at least changed out of her shorts and was wearing a pair of Lululemon yoga pants.

I saw the look of relief in Kit's eyes as she took in Minnie's change of clothes. "Glass of wine?" my friend asked, assuming the role of hostess.

"Not for me," Minnie said. "I'm in the middle of a million things. Just wanted to be sure Stan was okay. Where is he, by the way?"

"He went back to the hospital to join William Stuckey and Margaret," my mom told her.

I noticed Kit quietly rise from her seat, and I followed her out to the large hallway, where I found her staring up at the infamous staircase.

"This would be one hell of a fall," she said.

I looked up, figuring it was close to a thirty-foot drop if Doris had started her descent at the top. I nodded. "Poor thing; what a way to go."

"Could be worse." Kit took the last sip of her wine.

By the time we rejoined the ladies in the living room, Minnie had taken the floor. She stood in front of the marble fireplace, giving an account of what had turned out to be Doris's last day on earth.

"She seemed anxious about her daughter's visit," Minnie said. "Margaret doesn't come here too often these days, but she was supposed to arrive later today. She must have set off early, as soon as she heard about her mother. Doris was planning for just the two of them to go out to dinner tonight. She said they had a lot to catch up on."

"Do the Dibbles have servants?" Kit asked. She was leaning on the back of the chair occupied by my mother.

I knew she was suppressing a smile at the name Dibble, like kids smirk when they come across a naughty word.

"Yes, of course," Virginia answered. "How could anyone keep this place up?"

"Live-in?" Kit went on.

"No. She has a housekeeper. Jacqueline Something. She doesn't live here, but she comes every day. Then for the heavy stuff, I think there are a couple of other women who come when they are needed. I'm not sure."

"So Jacqueline was here yesterday?" Kit asked.

Virginia frowned. "I assume so, but she usually leaves at the end of the day. Prepares an evening meal, I think, then goes home. Unless, of course, they are having a dinner party or something special. Then she stays."

"Hmm," Kit said, implying such great significance that we all looked at her, waiting for a brilliant revelation. "What?" she asked, catching our glances.

"Is that important?" Virginia asked.

"Ya know, everything is important in the end," Kit said.

I found myself wishing I had a Sherlock Holmes–type magnifying glass handy, if only to whack her on the head with it.

"Virginia, you were about to tell us something," Ruth said. "Before Minnie came in." As she spoke, she picked something from her bottom lip that I assumed was a cat hair.

"It was nothing. I've forgotten it already."

"So," Minnie concluded her oration, "I guess we should wait for Stan to let us know about the funeral arrangements."

"Yes." My mother rose. "Unless, of course, anyone wants another round?"

She didn't wait for an answer to her question, but instead gathered up her purse, and we all followed her to the front door.

***

We decided to head back to my mother's house, mainly at my suggestion so I could check on Emily. I tried her cell on the way to the car but got no reply.

My mother backed out of the long driveway in a maddeningly slow maneuver. "What in the world was Minnie Ebert thinking?" she asked. "Making a casserole, indeed! She wouldn't know a casserole dish if it flew in her kitchen window."

"That bad?" I took my cell from my purse and prepared to call Emily once more.

"Ha! She poisoned half of Door County at the last bunco game she had at her house. Good thing William Stuckey was there."

"Don't you think it's odd that Stan left the hospital?" Kit asked.

"Margaret probably pushed him out," my mom said, just as I heard the theme song from *Law & Order* that Emily had chosen for my phone's ringtone.

I was so certain that my daughter was the one calling me that I didn't even bother to put on my glasses to see who it was. Instead, I answered it. "Hey!" I said.

"Pankowski!" came the boom from way down south in Chicago.

"Tom?"

"Hey, Kiddo. It's your boss," he said, clearing up any possible misconception about where he stands in my affections.

"Hi, Boss," I said. "How're you?"

"I hear Doris Dibble died today."

It was incredible. Even though Tom Haskins rarely leaves his beloved Chicagoland, except for the occasional trip to Vegas for a poker tournament, he always seems to have a handle on everything going on in the world.

"How the heck did—"

"I know stuff, Val. Here's the thing. Is the family planning to sell the house? I hear it's a mausoleum. But hey, what better place for a mausoleum right now?" I could hear him chomping on his cigar and chuckling at his own macabre sense of humor.

"Your concern is overwhelming, Tom. Doris Dibble was a friend of my mother's."

"I'm sorry about that. Tell Jean she's still got the best-looking legs in the Midwest."

"That will mean *so* much to her." I didn't plan to pass his so-called compliment on to my mother. She'd act outraged, of course, but she has a big soft spot for Tom. He was my only brother's best friend when we were young, and she treats him as if he's her own long-lost son. "Just tell me this: how in the world did you know Doris Dibble?"

"I didn't know her, but I knew of her. She was big money, Val. Owned a lot of property all over the country. The company her dead husband started has beaucoup government contracts. She had a lot of fingers in a lot of pies."

"Not more than ten, I'm guessing."

"Do some poking around of your own. Find out if they are selling. I've got contacts up there I could steer the listing to. Good chance to return a favor. Or earn one. I hear her daughter lives in Minneapolis, so she might not want to keep the place."

"Er . . . Doris had a husband, in case you don't know everything."

"Stanley Dribble." Tom chomped and chuckled at the same time.

"Dibble."

"I prefer my way. Suits him better. He's a nobody. Talk to the daughter. Doris would have left everything to her."

"Tom." I switched the phone from my right ear to my left. "It may have slipped your mind, but I'm actually on a little vacation here. I wasn't planning on doing any Realtor work."

"When do you ever?" He hung up before I could get the last word in. As usual.

"Was that Tom?" My mother came to a halt at a stop sign.

"Great," Kit said. "Just what we need. Is he planning to charter a plane and fly up here?"

"Yes and no," I answered both their questions.

"What did he know about Doris?" Kit asked.

"I'll tell you later." My thoughts had already returned to Emily.

***

As we pulled into my mother's driveway, I felt a sudden panic when I saw my Lexus was not parked where I had left it.

"Where's your car?" My mother looked at me suspiciously, as if I'd arranged to have it stolen.

"Emily must have gone somewhere," I said. But I rushed out of the car and ran to my mother's front door, which I banged on loudly.

"For goodness' sake, Valerie." My mother appeared behind me and held up her keys. "Who do you think is going to open the door?"

"I don't know, Mother. I just thought maybe—"

"What?" Kit chimed in. "That Emily decided to move the car into the living room? Obviously, she's taken it somewhere."

I dialed her number again. Still no answer. Inside the house, I fell onto my mother's sofa and tried again.

"Where would she be?" I asked both of them. "She doesn't know anyone up here. And she has a headache."

"Oh no." My mother sat down beside me, her hand over her heart. "You don't think she drove herself to the hospital, do you?" (And my ex-husband wonders where I learned to leap from hangnail to cancer.) "We should call William Stuckey immediately."

"I think that's a little too dramatic, Mom."

Kit laughed. "Really? *You* think it's a little too dramatic?"

Emily probably feigned her headache because she didn't want to go to Doris's house, I told myself. And maybe the phone call I overheard was nothing serious. Still, I tried calling her one more time. And still got her voice mail.

***

We spent the rest of the afternoon relaxing. Well, at least my mother and Kit relaxed. They watched *The Way We Were* on TV, and I half watched while fully listening for the sound of my car returning to the safety of my mother's driveway.

William called to suggest we forego the art gallery visit, but he would most certainly like to take us all to dinner as planned. My mother agreed the gallery was out but told him we could get together at six for dinner.

As much as I loved *The Way We Were*, I couldn't concentrate on poor Barbra as she tried to hang on to Robert Redford. When the doorbell rang three-quarters of the way through the drama, I jumped up with relief.

Unfortunately, it wasn't Emily, as I assumed it would be, but rather Virginia Huntley.

"What's happened now?" was my mother's first question. She's always ready for bad news, which probably explains why she's quite good at receiving it.

"Nothing; I just wanted some company, if that's okay, without Minnie Ebert around." Virginia entered the living room and took a seat on the couch beside Kit.

"Would you like some coffee?" my mom asked.

"That would be great. Hey, where's the movie star?"

"Emily is running some errands for me," my mom said. I liked that she didn't go into detail with her friend, but the obvious wink she gave me as she said it might have been a giveaway.

"So what's going on?" Kit moved closer to Virginia. "Seems like you have something on your mind."

"Yes."

"Then you should share it," Kit said. I could almost hear her thoughts: *spit it out, lady*.

We waited for Virginia to continue.

"Go on," Kit said.

"Yes, for heaven's sake, spit it out," my mother said aloud.

Kit looked gratified.

"Apparently, Doris was giving money to someone, and she wasn't too happy about it. Uff da." Virginia gave her head a little shake.

"Blackmail?" Kit asked.

"Doris did not use that word," Virginia said quickly.

We were silent for a moment, until Kit spoke. "And *you* are the only one she told?"

"As far as I know, yes."

"Okay. Money to whom, and more important, why?" Kit asked.

"That, I don't know. What I do know is, about three weeks ago I stopped by her place to pick up a check. She was a big supporter of that women's shelter down in Green Bay. You know the one, Jean."

"I know *of* it," my mother answered. She isn't a big believer in shelters of any kind, particularly those designed especially for women. She thinks women should be able to take care of themselves. "Why do you think she was being blackmailed?"

"Not blackmail," Virginia insisted. "When I got to her house, the front door was unlocked. I rang the bell, of course, but there was no answer, so I let myself in and went to her study; she did all her bookwork and business stuff there. She didn't hear me come in; you know how big that house is. But when I got to the study doorway, I could see her sitting at her desk, and she was crying."

"Oh no." My mother's hand automatically went to her heart.

"Yes, I was alarmed. That was so unlike her; you know how strong she was. In fact, in all these years we've been friends, I don't think I ever saw her cry before. So I rushed over to her, as one does, and put my arm around her. She had her huge checkbook open, and I could see she had just written a check for five thousand dollars."

She stopped again, and Kit verbally kicked her in the rear. "Made out to whom? Who was it made out to?"

"That part I couldn't see. I was there to collect a check for five *hundred*, so you can imagine how surprised I was to see such a big amount. But as soon as she knew I saw the check, she slammed the checkbook shut and told me I wasn't to mention it. And of course I said I wouldn't, which would have been true if she was still . . . with us. You see, after a bit, she told me she was ashamed."

"Ashamed?" Kit and I said in unison.

"Did she say what she was ashamed of?" I asked.

"No. But she made me swear not to tell anyone. She assured me she had it under control."

CHAPTER SIX

Are you sure she never used the word *blackmail?*"
Kit asked Virginia again.

"She's quite sure," my mother answered for her
friend.

Kit shrugged. "It seems so—"

"So what?" My mother looked offended.

"Virginia, *were* you and Doris really close?" Kit asked.

"Absolutely." Virginia looked twice as offended as my
mother. "And I've always been so close to Margaret, her
daughter. She's always called me Aunt Virginia." A
bittersweet look washed over her face.

"It just seems extraordinary, that's all," Kit said.

"Good heavens, Katherine, what's extraordinary?" my
mom asked.

Virginia spoke before Kit had a chance to respond. "It
was like she was giving this money voluntarily, but it didn't
make her happy."

"That's not what I meant when I said *extraordinary*," Kit said.

"Then what the heck do you mean?" I asked. Suddenly I was captain of the Virginia/Jean team.

"Ya know," Kit said, looking at Virginia, "if Doris had gone to the trouble of hiding this money business from you and all her other friends—and let's face it, that wouldn't be difficult—why would she suddenly blurt it out?"

"She didn't *blurt* it," Virginia said. "She was upset, and I just happened to be there when she was probably at her wit's end. Maybe she wanted to share the burden."

"But why *then*?" Kit asked. "She could have easily explained away the check."

"What are you suggesting?" Virginia asked, and we all three stared hard at Kit. But I was probably the only one expecting some incredible insight.

"Nothing. I'm not suggesting anything."

I felt a little let down.

Then, as if to prove her acting talent, even if it was only for making remarkable entrances, the front door opened and Emily appeared.

"I'm sorry I just took your car without asking, Mom. I went to get some aspirin."

During our heated discussion, I had almost forgotten about her. I took a deep breath and sighed happily at the appearance of my daughter. All in one piece. Although her eyes were a little puffy . . . "No worries, honey." I faked a smile. What I really meant was, I was plenty worried enough for both of us.

"Emily, dear," my mom said, "there was no need to drive all over Door County. I have aspirin in the medicine chest in the bathroom. Right next to the ibuprofen and Tylenol."

Alongside the Preparation H, the Pepto Bismol, and the defibrillator, I thought. My mother is nothing else if not prepared.

"I didn't want to go snooping, Grandma."

46

"Emily! Have I not always told you my house is your house?" My mother sounded as affronted as if someone had accused her of not loving her granddaughter.

But it's true. If my mom has said that to Emily once, she's said it a million times. Emily learned at a young age that it meant she could help herself to anything in her grandparents' house, from food to jewelry.

I thought of the time Emily appeared at the Thanksgiving table when the adults were enjoying an after-meal cup of coffee. She wore at least ten of my mother's bangle bracelets on her arms as she wobbled on a pair of heels that were no doubt the highest she could find, and her entire face was covered with my mom's bright-red lipstick. My mother merely smiled and went for her camera. In her eyes, Emily can do no wrong. Ever.

But *I* wasn't so sure.

I watched as Emily turned and hung my car keys on the fish-shaped key holder by the front door. Then I watched as she excused herself and went into our bedroom.

Forcing myself to give her space (she'd tell me anything she wanted to tell me when she was good and ready), I went to the kitchen and busied myself peeling vegetables to go with the homemade ranch dip my mother had made for us.

I knew I should stay in the living room area with the others and let myself be distracted from my worry over Emily, but I perversely *wanted* to ponder what her problem could be, as much as it pained me. Surely she and Luke weren't having *marriage* problems. But could one of them be ill?

My thoughts were pulled away from Emily when I heard Kit ask Virginia, "Why didn't you want to tell us about Doris in front of Minnie?"

Virginia looked troubled. She opened her mouth twice to speak before finally answering. "Because I don't trust her," she said at last.

Before Kit could grill her further, Virginia was saved by the bell, the doorbell. *Now what?* I wondered.

"Margaret!" I heard my mother greet the intruder.

When I looked over the kitchen divider into the living room, I immediately remembered Doris Dibble.

Her daughter looked just like her: petite and pretty, with short dark hair and big green eyes. Margaret appeared to be about forty, with a deep tan and taut body that would have looked more at home in a tennis skirt and sleeveless top than it did in the frilly sundress she had on.

"Jean, I'm sorry to bother you," Margaret said, and then she fell into my mother's open arms and began sobbing.

My mom patted her back and then led her over to the couch, sandwiching Margaret in between herself and Virginia. "Margaret, honey, I'm so sorry."

I was suddenly overcome with the realization that there is just nothing good enough to say to someone in her moment of grief. But if anyone could make Margaret feel better, I had confidence it would be my mom.

Kit rose from the couch and moved down one person, forcing Virginia to switch places with her. Kit now sat next to Margaret and introduced herself. Ignoring my mom's pained look, she took the hand of this woman she'd just met. "We're all so sorry about your mother."

Margaret didn't acknowledge Kit. "I don't want to intrude, but I thought I might find you here, Aunt Virginia." She reached around Kit and grabbed Virginia's hand. "But I didn't realize you had company, Jean."

"No problem, dear. Girls, would you excuse us," my mother said in her best imperious-queen voice, looking at Kit and then at me.

"Kit," I said, "let's take some snacks out on the deck."

"I'm not hungry—"

"Kit!"

"I'm coming, I'm coming." Her look said she didn't want to leave, but she'd do it anyway.

I slid the door open, and Kit followed me out. As I was sliding the door shut, I realized I'd forgotten the veggies and dip. But no way was I going back into the house just yet. And I found myself hoping Emily would stay put in the bedroom until my mom and Virginia had had some time alone with Margaret. I knew how *I'd* feel if I'd just lost my mom, especially in such a sudden, shocking way.

"Let's go to Starbucks," Kit said, looking like an addict who was beyond needing a fix.

At the mention of our favorite coffee joint, I suddenly craved a cup of their java myself. "Sorry, Kit, there is no Starbucks in Door County. And by the way, what was up with all the questions you were asking Virginia?"

"There's no Starbucks? Why didn't you tell me? And as for your friend Virginia—"

"She's my mother's friend, not mine—"

"I find her story a little too convenient, don't you?"

"Not at all," I lied. Well, it wasn't so much a lie, but once Kit mentioned it, I *did* wonder if it rang true. Yet I didn't want to encourage whatever nonsense she was dreaming up.

"Think about it. Here's this woman with all these big financial things to do. Writing million-dollar checks every five minutes. And in comes Virginia Slim, and she suddenly breaks down and admits she's being blackmailed?"

"She never said blackmail."

"Okay. Not blackmail. But she was writing a big check that made her unhappy. How do we know Virginia's telling the truth? And if Doris *was* being blackmailed, how do we know Virginia wasn't the one doing the blackmailing?"

"Okay, stop right there, Kit. Why would Virginia tell us this story if *she* was the blackmailer? Not that Doris was being blackmailed. Virginia was clear on that point."

"Exactly. And she might have told us to throw us off. No doubt all of Doris's financial hoo-ha will come to light now that she's dead, and Virginny wanted to get in front of it. And by the way, I can't believe you'd bring me to this godforsaken island."

"It's not an island. It's a peninsula."

"A peninsula without a Starbucks. Next you'll be telling me there's no Walmart."

"Yes, as a matter of fact, there is. As if you would be caught dead in Wally World."

"But no Starbucks," Kit said sadly.

Was that *all I would have had to say to keep her from coming up here with us?* I almost smacked myself on the forehead for being so stupid. "Kit, do you really mean to tell me that you—"

"No, of course not; never mind. But how do you do it? How do you go a whole weekend without—"

"Well, it helps that I bring my own bag of Starbucks with me and slip it into my mom's coffee canister."

Kit chortled. "You're living on the edge, Valley Girl. Next you'll be slipping a little whiskey into her cocoa. I guess you haven't been hanging with me all these years for nothing."

"Darn tootin'."

But my levity was short-lived, as Emily slid open the door and stepped out, bringing with her not only the vegetables and dip, but renewed concern on my part.

"Who are Grandma and Virginia talking to?" she asked.

Actually, Emily looked good. Gone were the puffy eyes, and her voice sounded almost chipper.

"Doris's daughter." I took the tray from Emily and set it on the round wooden picnic table my mom had bought at a roadside sale when she'd first moved up to Door County. I'd never understood the purchase. It was big enough to seat ten people and took up three-fourths of the deck. "How are you feeling, Em?"

She sat down on one of the table's attached benches and helped herself to a carrot. After coating it with dip, she answered. "I feel better, thanks. I think it's allergies."

Well, *that* could explain the puffy eyes. I felt my concern begin to lift and my appetite suddenly appear. I grabbed a big piece of broccoli to dip. "C'mon, Kit, eat up. Who knows when we'll get out to dinner, if ever."

"Raw vegetables?" Kit took a piece of cauliflower and examined it carefully before dipping it lightly and taking a small bite.

We'd plowed through all of the carrots and much of the cauliflower, leaving mostly broccoli and green peppers on the tray, by the time my mother came to announce the all clear.

"Come back in, girls. Come sit down in the living room." We followed her back into the house and assembled in the living room once more, like a family about to hear the reading of a will.

"Her mother's death was ruled an accident, of course. The fall killed her."

"No shit," Kit mumbled, her head bent so low that only I could hear her. But I recalled my mother's uncanny hearing ability and worried that Kit might be grounded for the weekend.

"Unfortunately, Margaret feels guilty."

"Why? She didn't push her." Emily's voice was small and childlike.

"No, darling, of course not." My mother took several swift steps across the room and sat down next to Emily. She wrapped her arms around her granddaughter, cradling her as if she were ten years old. "She feels bad, that's all. She and Doris had a little argument over the phone, nothing big. Margaret is making some changes in her life that her mother didn't approve of. It happens all the time. When you have a daughter of your own, you'll understand."

Emily extricated herself from my mother's hug and sat up straight. "I understand *now*, but I don't see why she feels guilty. It was a horrible accident, but it wasn't her fault, no matter how much she and her mother had argued. Margaret wasn't even in Door County."

My mother touched a finger to Emily's chin. "It's just like the time *your* mother had a date with that juvenile delinquent who owned a motorbike, and she went tootling all over town without telling me."

My mother glanced at me for effect, giving me the same look she had when I was fifteen years old and had ridden less than half a mile on Bobby Streeter's new bike. It had been after school and, of course, Kit's idea. If Pastor Reegan from our church hadn't been driving his Oldsmobile on the same street and then blabbed to my mom, she never would have known.

But what that had to do with Doris and her daughter, I had no idea.

***

William changed the dinner plans to a cookout at his house, saying he was too exhausted to eat at a restaurant.

"That doesn't make sense," I said. "Wouldn't it be easier to be waited on than to *do* the waiting on?"

Kit the gourmet cook chimed in with my mother the cook (just as good, if not as gourmet) to assure me cooking was therapeutic. "He probably wants the distraction of planning and fixing a meal, ya know."

"Yes, maybe he just needs to do it to settle his nerves after the day he's had at the hospital," my mom said.

"Not to mention the night he had last night," I added, "coming upon the body . . . uh, the scene . . ."

"Valerie, where do you get this kind of language?" my mother asked, with a look I hadn't seen since I dented the door of her 1980 Chrysler LeBaron.

But I was too busy launching a plan to get her to tell me what she'd discussed with Virginia and Margaret to respond.

Kit grinned. "Your daughter watches too much *Law & Order*, Jean."

"*Can* a person watch too much *Law & Order*?" I shot back. "When do we leave?"

"As soon as Emily is ready." My mom picked up her purse and extracted her car keys, as if to prove *she* wasn't the holdup.

Within ten minutes we were on our way to William Stuckey's condo. It was only six o'clock, and he lived a short fifteen-minute drive away, but my mother drove so slowly I worried he would be asleep for the night by the time we got there.

But not only was he awake, he appeared so wound up I wondered if he was the head of a cartel smuggling Starbucks into the county.

CHAPTER SEVEN

William led us directly to his patio, with its round glass table that easily seated eight people. The maroon edging that encircled the table matched the plush, maroon-striped cushions on the chairs. Certainly a big step up from my mother's shabby-chic wooden picnic table, however big it might be.

He had a pitcher of martinis ready and immediately brought it outside and set it on the table. "Jean, are you in the mood for one of these?" he asked my mother.

"Certainly not."

William laughed and magically produced a glass of iced tea for her, complete with a sprig of mint. "Kit?" he asked next.

"I'd love a martini. How very James Bond of you."

"Ha!" He laughed again, and for a man who had practically witnessed the horrible death of a close friend the night before, he seemed a little too jovial.

When we were all seated with our drinks before us (I chose a martini, but Emily requested an iced tea like her grandmother), William proposed a toast.

"To Doris," he said. "A dear friend. A good woman. May she rest in peace."

We all raised our glasses to Doris and took a sip.

"Where is this cookout you promised, William Stuckey?" My mom placed her glass on the table.

"It will be here shortly. Don't fret. Ah, here it comes now."

We all turned toward the restaurant on the other side of the pool. Two young men wearing white jackets rolled a cart around the edge of the swimming pool, stopping at William's patio. The cart was covered with a white linen cloth and held several dishes, some of them concealed with silver bell-shaped covers.

"I like your style, William." Emily giggled.

"We do what we can, my dear. We're not nearly as glamorous as you Hollywood types, I'm sure, but we do our best."

Dishes were set before us: a platter containing five large steaks, a pan of rice pilaf, and a glass bowl filled with salad. My mother was silent as she sipped her tea and watched them set up. I could tell she didn't quite approve of William's showiness, but at the same time she was a little impressed.

"I hear Margaret came to see you," William said to her, after the waiters had left. He took the glass tongs and began dishing out salad onto small plates.

"How did you know that?" my mother asked.

"Ah, a little birdie. Ladies, please start eating, or all this will get cold."

We each speared a steak. I cut a small bite of mine, and it was tender and tasty.

"So did she have anything in particular to say?" William asked.

"She said a lot of things. She's very upset, of course."

55

"Naturally. I hope you don't mind, but I asked her to join us tonight. She has a few things to take care of, but she'll be along later. I thought she might prefer it to being home alone with Stan."

"You don't like Stan?" Kit asked.

"I like Stan. There's nothing wrong with him. He's not a big favorite among the ladies, but I enjoy his company. And Doris adored him. Did Margaret mention Stan to you at all, Jean?"

It looked as if William had launched his own plan to get information out of my mother, but to no avail. "No, we certainly did not discuss *him*," she said.

Our meal progressed nicely. When Emily's phone rang from the tiny leopard-skin shoulder bag she had placed on the empty seat beside her, she glanced at her grandmother for permission to take the call.

I watched in amusement as my mother nodded, smiled, and patted Emily's hand in approval. "That's probably Luke," my mom said. "Answer it."

My mother hates being in the company of people yakking away on cell phones; well, don't we all? So Emily rose, taking the phone out of her purse and swiping her finger across it.

I watched her walk slowly around the swimming pool, the phone to her ear.

While Emily was gone, the dinner conversation turned back to recent events. "What do you think Stan will do now?" Kit asked. "Do you think he will stay in that big house?"

"That rather depends on Margaret." William twirled the stem of his martini glass.

"How so?"

"There's been no reading of the will yet, of course, but I expect Doris left the house to her daughter. In fact, she probably left everything to Margaret. There was a prenup, you know, that Stan signed."

"Really? Now *that's* Hollywood," I said.

"No, that's reality. Doris was a very wealthy woman, and Stan came into the marriage basically penniless. She loved him, but she was also a shrewd woman."

"I wonder why she married him." Kit twirled her own glass.

"Love, my dear." William didn't bother to conceal the saucy wink he sent down the table to my mother. Even in the dim light, I could see her blush.

"And did Stan return the favor?" Kit asked.

"I think he loved Doris," William said. "In his way. She was a very attractive woman. And she was highly intelligent. She helped her first husband a lot. She was involved in the design of many of the products made by Edwards Industries. Did you know she had a master's degree? From MIT, I think. That was quite an accomplishment for a woman at that time."

I recalled how suspicious Kit was about Doris's conversation with Virginia. And it certainly was becoming apparent that Doris had been more than just a bunco-playing matron.

Emily returned to the table and sat down without saying a word.

"Luke okay?" I asked.

"Yes, he's fine. He was just checking in. Sends his love to everyone."

I wanted to question her, but this wasn't the time.

"Let me make some more martinis." Kit rose and took the empty pitcher.

"I can do that," William said.

"Let me," she insisted. "There's a little twist I know that you might like. Am I free to rummage around your kitchen?"

"I never stop a beautiful woman from rummaging around my kitchen."

Kit left the table, but before she slid the patio door open, she gave me the tiniest wave, indicating I was to follow her.

"I better keep an eye on her." I stood up. "She's kinda clumsy."

As Kit closed the patio door behind us, she put her hand on my elbow and steered me toward William's kitchen.

"What's going on with Emily?" she asked.

"What do you mean?"

"Didn't you see her phone? It wasn't Luke who called her. It was a woman's face that came up on the screen. Definitely not Lukey."

"Oh." I didn't know what to say. "Why would she lie?" I finally asked. Then I answered my own question. "Maybe he was calling from someone else's phone."

"Yeah, right. Some supermodel's phone."

"How did you see *that*?"

Kit was already opening cupboard doors, looking for her little twist. "Hmm. My farsightedness. It's a curse." She had moved on to the refrigerator and was busy perusing its contents. "Good; just what I need." She held up an unopened bottle of pink grapefruit juice.

I watched as she quickly prepared a new pitcher of drinks.

"This little baby is called The Blushing Lady." She scooped a handful of ice into the pitcher. "We really need some pomegranate juice, but this will work. When did you last speak to Luke?"

"I dunno. Maybe a week or so ago. And don't start getting all heavy. Everything's just fine with those two."

"Good to know." She vigorously shook the ingredients she had put into the martini shaker. As always, I was impressed with Kit's skills in the kitchen (and the bar, for that matter).

By the time we returned to the patio, Margaret Edwards had joined our little group. She looked tired, but she was gracious and seemed as intelligent as her mother had been.

The Blushing Lady was good. Even my mother had one, probably because of its name. She took a couple of sips and then asked Margaret, "Is there anything we can do to help you?"

Margaret patted my mother's hand. "That's so kind. I have to get working on the funeral arrangements, of course. Just having you and Aunt Virginia around will be help enough."

"What do you do in Minneapolis?" Kit asked.

"Just boring old computer stuff." She took a sip of her Blushing Lady and lightly licked her lips. "This is delicious."

"Emily's husband is in computers," I said. "I'm not sure exactly what he does, even though he's explained it a thousand times."

"He's a technician for one of the studios," Emily said quickly.

"That doesn't sound boring at all." Margaret smiled. "Do we know the studio?"

"It's a small one. He works mainly in special effects."

I wondered how I had never understood Luke's occupation. Emily made it sound simple yet exciting in just one sentence.

"Did he work on that *E.T.*?" my mother asked. I knew that was one of her favorite movies. "It was so clever how they made that puppet talk."

I stifled a grin.

Emily laughed. "No, Grandma, that's a little bit before his time. But it certainly would have been a good one to work on."

I wasn't sure what surprised me more, that *E.T.* was before Luke's time (it seemed like only yesterday) or the fact that Emily was laughing.

When our first batch of Blushing Ladies was done, William suddenly stood and walked over to my mother's chair. "How about a little walk, Jean?"

"Well, William Stuckey, that might be a good idea." She rose slowly, her eyes shining. She didn't seem to notice when Margaret excused herself and slipped into the condo to make a phone call.

"Emily, you should go with them," I said, immediately seeing a strange look of disappointment cloud William's face. But I didn't care. "This is such a pretty complex. Mom, give Emily the tour."

The three of them set off, arm in arm, with Emily in the middle.

"So are you going to check Emily's phone?" Kit eyed the purse strap draped over the back of the chair. "That's why you sent her with them, isn't it?"

"Yep." I took Emily's phone out of her purse. "Here, you do it." I handed it across the table.

"Why me?"

"You're not her mother. And I won't be lying if I tell her I wasn't checking up on her."

"But it's okay for me to do it?"

"She'd expect it from you. Just hurry, will you?"

Kit dug her reading glasses out of her own purse, but before she could switch on the phone, it started to vibrate in her hand.

I ran around the table to her side to see a beautiful blond woman's face appear on Emily's screen with the name NAOMI underneath. "You weren't kidding; she really *is* a knockout." I grabbed the phone and stuffed it quickly back into Emily's purse. "So why did she say it was Luke?"

Before we could discuss it further, the sliding glass doors opened. "Sorry I was so long." Margaret stepped onto the patio. "I needed to take care of a few things back home."

"Would you like me to make more drinks?" Kit asked.

"No, I've had my limit, thank you, but it was delicious." She took a seat at the table. "Whew—I am so tired. I think I will sleep really well tonight."

"Are you sure you are okay in your—at the house?" I asked.

"I hear you're not a big Stan fan," Kit said.

"I'm fine. And please, don't worry about Stan and me. I'm sure the rumors of the two of us not getting along are greatly exaggerated. I won't say he's my favorite guy in the world, but he made my mother very happy. And for that I'm thankful."

"I really am so very, very sorry about your mom," I felt compelled to say. "It's so tragic. What a terrible accident."

Suddenly she stood. "If you don't mind, I think I really should go back to the house. Would you give my thanks to William and tell Jean I'll probably call her tomorrow?"

She picked up her large leather handbag, put it on the table, and began digging through it, presumably for her car keys. I watched as she shifted stuff around, pulling out handfuls of papers, until she finally located the keys, obviously at the bottom of the bag.

"The bigger the purse, the more junk," she said with a little smile. "See you again soon, I'm sure."

CHAPTER EIGHT

I willed them to walk faster, when I saw William ushering my mom and Emily up the path toward us as they returned from their moonlight stroll. I wanted to ask what had taken them so long since it had still been light (albeit barely) when they'd set out.

But it was a moot point, and all I cared about was getting Emily alone back at my mom's and finding out what in the world was going on. I couldn't take the suspense anymore. I'd tell her Kit and I had sneaked a peek at her phone, if I had to.

"You're back," I called when they were in earshot.

"It's so lovely here," Emily said, squeezing my mother's arm but looking at William.

"Yes, we like it," he said. I assumed the *we* referred to him and his neighbors.

"Well, we should make a move to go home," my mother said. "It's been a long day."

"You don't have to go yet, do you, ladies?" William looked as disappointed as a kid who has to leave the circus before the fire-eating act.

"We're so tired," my mother answered for all of us. She took her purse from the chair she had placed it on and then looked around as if someone were missing. "Where's Margaret?"

"Well, it was *really* a long day for her," I said. "She was exhausted. She said to tell you and William thanks."

"Can't I get you girls a nightcap?" William asked. He was beginning to sound a little desperate.

"No, we should go," my mother insisted. "Come along, girls."

"Thank you for a lovely evening, William," I said.

"My pleasure, Valerie. And Kit, thank you for the delicious martinis."

"No problem."

I noticed she was the only one still sitting.

"Hey, William," she said. "A question for you."

"Yes, what is it, my dear?"

"I'm just curious who called Margaret and told her about her mother."

William half smiled. I wondered if he'd been waiting for the question or if he was simply humoring her. "Actually, it was me," he said.

"Really!" Kit sounded as surprised as if he'd said Doris herself had placed the call before being carted off to the hospital with a broken neck.

"Yes. I was there, as you know."

"Right. And Margaret of course was still in Minneapolis that night. She wasn't planning to leave there until later today."

"I assume so."

"You called her cell?"

"I called the number Stan gave me. He was very preoccupied with his wife. I'm not sure if it was her cell or her home."

"Right," Kit said again, in a tone that was beginning to annoy me.

"Let's *go*," my mother said, trumping Kit with a tone I found even more annoying.

But not everyone was tired or ready to call it a night.

When William opened his front door to walk us out, we all stopped for a moment of quiet surprise.

My mother, of course, spoke first. "Ruth Greenway! What are you doing here, at this time of night?" She glanced at her watch for emphasis, and I knew it confirmed that it was past her own normal bedtime of nine o'clock.

"Sorry to come by so late, William," Ruth said. Her enormous spectacles were illuminated by William's porch light. She wore a white sweatshirt that displayed a photograph of a banjo-playing cat. "I didn't realize you had company."

"No problem," William said. "My guests are just leaving. Unfortunately."

But by now my mother had her feet planted firmly on the doorstep. I took a position behind her, just so she knew I had her back should a rumble ensue.

"Um, I came about the donation, William. Remember, you said you had some items for the cat-shelter garage sale—"

"For heaven's sake." My mother took a step forward, dismissing Ruth and her unfortunate cats, as if they were of no immediate threat to her and there was little danger of her losing her man.

When we were safely strapped in, Kit and I in the backseat, my mother began her torturously slow drive home.

"Kit," I whispered. "What was all that stuff about who called Margaret?"

Kit whispered back. "When Margaret was looking for her car keys in that hideous bag of hers, didn't you notice the brochure for the Windsor Hotel?"

"No," I said in a normal tone. Then I whispered again. "*No.*"

"She had one. A hotel in Door County. She pulled it out, along with ten thousand other pieces of junk. I can't believe you didn't see it."

"So she had a brochure for a hotel in her purse. So what?" I thought guiltily of my own purse. It probably still contained the airline ticket for the Realtors' convention I'd attended in New York months earlier, whereas Kit's tiny clutch probably held only her Chanel lipstick and an American Express Gold Card.

"It seems odd, ya know. She was supposedly coming here only to visit her mother, so why would she need a hotel? I just wonder if she really was still in Minneapolis when William called her. What if she was already in Door County and didn't want anyone to know?"

Our conversation was cut short by my mother's orders from the front seat. "Girls, stop whispering. I can hardly hear myself think."

"Yes, mein Führer," I heard Kit mumble.

***

"I'm going to call it a night, Em," I said at eleven thirty. My mom had gone to bed with her book, and Kit appeared to be sound asleep on the pullout couch. Emily was sitting at the kitchen table, quietly turning the pages of a *People* magazine.

"By the way," I ventured, "you had a phone call while you were out walking with William and Grandma. I heard your phone ring in your purse."

She didn't look up but licked her index finger to turn the next page of the magazine. "I got it. It was Luke again, just checking in."

In a strange way, her little lie made me feel much better. Since she was lying to me about Naomi, I felt free to conceal the fact that Kit and I had read her phone screen. It seemed to me that Emily's misdemeanor was a lot worse than my transgression.

"Well, aren't you coming to bed?" I glanced over toward the couch, where Kit was as motionless as a mummy in a tomb.

"I'm not tired yet. I slept too much today, with my headache. You go to bed. I'll be there soon. I'll be quiet."

I opened my mouth to tell her we needed to talk. But instead, I turned and retreated to the bedroom to ponder the fine line between being helpful and being intrusive, the line I don't believe the mother of a grown woman should ever cross. Never mind that my own mother does it a hundred times a day.

But I sat on the edge of my bed for only a few minutes before I'd finished weighing the risk-reward and decided I'd rather risk her anger than pass up a chance to help her. I returned to the kitchen table.

"Emily!" I said in my loudest whisper. "We need to talk." I turned, and this time I crept back into the bedroom. Having committed, I really didn't want Kit to awaken and prevent my heart-to-heart with Emily.

I was relieved when she followed me.

I sat on one of the twin beds and patted the spot next to me, but Emily opted to sit across from me on her own. "What's up, Mom?"

"Well, that's what I want to ask you. What's the matter, Emily? You suddenly seem so . . . so morose."

"Morose? Don't you think that's a little dramatic, Mom?"

She looked and sounded exactly like her father, who'd asked me that question countless times in our two and a half decades of marriage. Shaking off feelings of bitterness, refusing to project onto Emily my contempt for her father, I finally answered her. "I hope I am, honey. But you just seem so—" I stopped before I said something she'd consider downright *melo*dramatic. "*Is* anything wrong, anything at all?"

"No."

"So you can honestly tell me there's nothing you're concerned about, nothing at all going on in your life that *I'd* be concerned about? You can look me in the eye and tell me that?"

She did not look me in the eye.

"Emily, I don't want to pry, really I don't."

Then she looked up at me, her eyes full of tears. "What in the world do you call what you're doing, if not prying?" A flash of anger on her face also reminded me of her father. Where was the Emily that everyone always says looks just like me? I didn't know, but the Emily I was speaking to now suddenly stood and turned her back on me, as if to leave the room.

Then, just as suddenly, she turned and sat back down. But this time she sat next to me, on my bed. "Okay, Mom, I'll tell you. I'll tell you what's bothering me." She reached up and removed the ponytail holder from her hair. In one swift motion that showed she'd done it thousands of times, she pulled her long blond hair between her hands and slipped the holder back around it. Then her arms fell to her sides, and her blue eyes looked forlornly into mine.

I reached over and grabbed her hand, and she let me hold it. I felt sick to my stomach. I suddenly wanted to discuss anything *but* what my daughter was about to divulge. That didn't last long, of course. "What, Em? You know you can tell me anything."

"Oh, Mom, I know, but you're going to be so disappointed in me. And Grandma . . . Grandma is going to freak."

I didn't say it, but that would be true of anything, from Emily breaking a nail to robbing a bank.

"Grandma will be just fine. We'll all be just fine." I decided *I* was the best actress in the family, as I squeezed her hand.

Emily squeezed back, and then her words rushed forth, tumbling out like popcorn from an air popper. " . . . thought this was taken care of . . . small part . . . weren't supposed to be able to see . . . talked me into it . . . Luke warned me . . . ruined my career . . ."

By now she was sobbing, and I was holding her in my arms, patting her back and reassuring her everything was going to be just fine.

And since I hadn't heard the word *dying*, I thought I was right.

Then all of a sudden I wasn't so sure everything was going to be okay. Because I heard the words *nude scene*.

For a fleeting moment I wondered if Emily was using a trick I've used since I was a preteen. When I've had something terrible to tell my mother, I've sometimes implied it was much worse than it really was, the hope being that the real and much lesser crime would seem like nothing to her. (This hardly ever works, by the way, but I've often given it my best shot.)

Mom, I broke one of your favorite things.

Oh no, Valerie, not my Royal Doulton serving dish.

No, Mom, the fruit bowl from JCPenney that Grandma gave us for Christmas six years ago.

Phew, that old thing; I was planning to give it to Goodwill. But you are a good girl for owning up.

"Okay." I let go of Emily's hand and gave her some tissues from the nightstand. "Blow your nose and tell me what's going on."

She blew, then sniffed deeply, and finally ran a tissue over her wet eyes. "Okay. Here goes. Remember I told you I got a part in a movie? *Blood Over Ice?*"

I nodded. "Go on," I said.

"Okay, so I got the script, and when I read it, I was so excited. It's only a small part, Mom, but I'm found dead in a hotel room. I mean—"

"Wait; didn't you tell me it was a speaking role?"

"Yes, it is. First, I'm the waitress in a hotel bar. I serve a man a drink. *What can I get you, sir?* That was one of my lines. And then later the police find me in a room in the hotel, still clinging to life, even though I've been stabbed in the chest. Two detectives try to revive me, and I point to the wall where I'd written the killer's name in blood."

"Clever of you." I nodded, even though the grisly scene made me queasy.

"I know, right? Only problem is, I'm lying on the bed, with my wrists tied to the bedposts, and—"

"Emily, wait; how can you point to the name in blood with your hands tied to the bedpost?"

I'd immediately spotted the noticeable flaw in the crappy plot.

"I do it with my eyes, Mom." She had stopped crying and actually rolled her eyes to show how easy it was to lead the detectives (who didn't seem too sharp) to the blood-drawn message.

"You wrote the message *before* your hands were tied?"

"Well, obviously." She was getting frustrated with me, almost defending the ludicrous story line.

"Okay, let's get to the nude part."

"Well, that's just it . . . I was naked." She started to cry again, softly now. "The director first told me I could wear a flesh-colored bikini, but then on the day of shooting he went all realistic and started talking about the integrity of the scene and told me I would have to be naked. But Mom, he promised me the camera would not pan down. That he would shoot only from the shoulders up—oh, I am so stupid. Why did I agree to do it? When I saw the rushes later that day, I nearly died. I mean, I was already dead, of course, but I nearly died for real."

I gave a big sigh. It was slightly worse than breaking my mom's fruit bowl.

"Is there any way you could have them edit it?" I sounded calm, but I felt frantic.

"No, no." She was a little wild-eyed. "I signed a contract. I already got paid twenty-six hundred dollars for two days' work. I called my SAG representative, and he basically told me to just get over it."

"Who's Naomi?"

"Naomi? She's my agent's assistant. She was trying to see if I had any legal recourse, but it turns out I don't."

I was impressed Emily had snagged an agent who had an assistant, or did they all? "Oh, Em, what a foolish thing to do."

"I know." She started to cry harder.

"Well, what's done is done. Is this movie going to be a hit?"

"*Blood Over Ice*? I doubt it. Turns out the man I served the drink to was actually a serial killer who'd murdered his own mother and now was after all the waitresses in the city 'cuz his mom was an alcoholic or something. Who'd wanna watch junk like that?"

"Hmm." I thought it sounded a lot like any of the hundreds of murder mysteries I'd seen on TV through the years. "Any big stars in this movie?"

"No. They're all hacks, like me."

"Oh, darling, you are not a hack. You made a mistake. No one is going to blame you. But one thing . . ."

"What, Mom?"

"Well, how much panning did this camera do? I mean, did it go all—"

"Down to my waist. Nothing below that."

"Well, that's good, at least." But I knew it wasn't good at all. Still, I wasn't sure what upset me most: the thought of her exposing her breasts or her being stabbed to death.

We both turned toward the door as we heard a tapping. "Girls," my mother whispered from the other side, "is everything okay? You should be tucked in bed by now. It's late."

"We are, Mom," I said. But if I hadn't been afraid she would hear me, I would have gone out and awakened Kit to share everything with her. She'd put the perfect spin on it.

Instead, I fell asleep wondering what kind of person would kill his own mother.

CHAPTER NINE

"V al, Val, wake up."

I did as commanded, mainly because of the flashlight shining a few inches from my face. Kit held it beneath her chin, turning her face into an eerie-looking mask. I noticed she was dressed—for church, no less—and her makeup was perfect. "What the—"

"It's nearly five. Everyone's asleep. Get up quickly; we gotta make a little trip."

I started to ask if she had gone insane, but there was no point in doing that. I wasn't even surprised; it wasn't the first time Kit had awakened me over the years of our friendship with a flashlight in my face. This was the twelve-year-old Kit sneaking into my bedroom on a Saturday night when all our parents were fast asleep. It was impossible to recall how many times she'd done it during our childhood, and the outcome of our midnight excursions usually ended with me being grounded and my mother insisting I never speak to *that* girl again.

I started to pull on some sweatpants, but Kit grabbed them away from me. "You can't wear those rags. Here, put this on." She handed me a denim skirt, and as I stepped into it, I watched her pull various items out of my overnight bag until she found a rumpled white T-shirt she must have considered suitable.

"Where on earth are we going?" I whispered, watching the sound-asleep Emily in the next bed.

"To the Windsor Hotel, where else? Come on; we gotta get there before the daytime staff does."

***

"Have you thought of what you're going to say?" Kit asked, as I backed my car down my mother's driveway without turning on the lights.

"Wait just a minute. *Me?* I'm along on this little joy ride only so you don't get arrested and embarrass my mother." But that wasn't totally true.

Once Kit told me about spotting the brochure for the Windsor Hotel, it did seem familiar. Margaret had taken out a bunch of legal-size envelopes and various papers from her purse, and maybe one of them *was* a hotel brochure.

Listening to Kit read directions from her phone, I turned on the headlights of my vehicle and sped up.

The Windsor Hotel was about six miles away. Its three stories were old but well preserved, by the looks of it. "Perfect spot to meet a lover," Kit said, as we pulled into the parking lot. "What are you looking for?" she added, watching me dig into my purse.

"Lipstick, makeup, anything."

"Here." She opened her clutch and took out a gold Chanel lipstick case and handed it to me. Before applying it to my lips, I turned it over to see the color. La Sensuelle, as if that mattered.

The lobby of the Windsor was warm and welcoming. It was also empty.

Kit strode right over to the small reception desk and punched the bell. Within a few seconds a young man appeared, wearing a suit and tie and looking as if he'd gotten dressed five minutes earlier. His name tag said he was Harold.

"Can I help you ladies?"

"Yes, you can, although it's a bit embarrassing, really," Kit said.

He raised his eyebrows, and his look said *I've seen it all, so hit me, lady.*

"It's like this," Kit began, and I was actually looking forward to whatever yarn she was about to hit him with. "My sister, Margaret Edwards, is supposed to be in town for the weekend. Mother's Day and all that. I think she reserved a room for Thursday or Friday, but the problem is, we haven't heard from her." As she said it, she turned toward me and pointed. "This is my maid, Gladys, and she's as worried as I am."

Harold glanced at me, and I could tell he had no problem believing I was a maid—one named Gladys, no less—even with La Sensuelle plastered over my mouth.

"So," Kit went on, "could you just confirm that she actually got here?"

"I'm not really supposed to give out guest information."

"No, no, of course not. But she's taking medication, and I want to be sure she didn't get into a problem driving here from Minneapolis."

"She doesn't have a *phone*?" Harold asked, as if she might not have a head, either.

"She does, she does." Kit nodded. "But to tell the truth, we are in a teensy bit of a family squabble. All to do with Gladys here." She leaned on the counter with her back to me, but I could see her balled-up fist and an extended thumb pointing over her shoulder in my direction. "Margaret thinks Gladys here stole the family silver," I heard her stage-whisper.

"Really?" Harold looked my way again, and I could tell he also had no problem believing I had the goods stashed away in a trailer somewhere.

"Yes, but that's another story," Kit continued. She was enjoying this way too much. "I just want to be sure my sister made it safely to your lovely hotel. I don't need to speak to her, you understand. I just want to know she's here."

As she spoke, I saw her unclasp her clutch and take out what looked like a small green square of paper, but was actually an indeterminable amount of money folded into four. She slid it discreetly across the counter.

Harold pretended not to notice, but instead turned to his computer and began tapping away on the keyboard. "Margaret Edwards, you say?"

"That's my sis." Kit looked so worried, I almost believed her.

"I see, Miss . . . Mrs. . . . ."

"James. Married name."

"I see, Mrs. James, that your sister did indeed check in on Friday night."

"Whew! That's okay then, huh, Gladys?"

I nodded. Evidently, Gladys was rendered mute from all the stealing.

"Yes." Harold sounded proud that his mission had been accomplished, as he palmed the money and it disappeared into his pocket. "Checked in Friday. And let me see . . . yes, stayed one night. Checked out yesterday sometime."

"Did she say where she was going?" Kit asked. From a paper holder on the desk she took the same brochure she'd seen in Margaret's purse and began fanning herself. It suggested the relief of knowing her sister was okay.

"Sorry, don't know that. I never actually saw her. I wasn't on duty then."

"That's okay. You are doing a fine job, Harold. Thank you. You've eased my mind a great deal. Gladys, we should go. You've got work waiting for you."

"Yes, ma'am," I said; apparently Gladys could speak. She even gave Kit a little curtsy. It was the very least a maid could do.

***

On the drive back to my mother's house, I shared Emily's story with Kit but made her promise not to breathe a word of it. My adrenaline was pumping after our little ruse at the Windsor Hotel, and my hands gripped the steering wheel tightly by the time I got to the naked-breasts part.

"So what do you think?" I asked, when I finished telling her everything.

She was silent for a moment. "Ya know, if it bothers Emily, then she was a very silly girl," she said finally.

"Well, obviously it bothers her. She's heartbroken about it." I realized I was waiting for Kit to tell me it was going to be all right, that it was no big deal, that we'd all get over it and laugh about it one day.

But she remained silent.

"Anything else? Just that she's a silly girl?"

Kit turned and gave me a sad smile. "I'm heartbroken too."

***

We got back to the house about six thirty. My mother was awake and in the bathroom with the door closed, and Emily was still asleep.

"You're amazing," I said to Kit. "Really. I don't know if this is any of our business or if we just committed a crime, but you're amazing."

"You're probably right about the crime part, ya know, but *we* didn't commit it."

"I bet my mom doesn't even know we were gone." I added a *hehe*; but it was premature, and I should have known better.

"Where in the dickens have you two been?" My mother stood in the doorway of the bathroom, her voice reaching into the living room, where we had thrown ourselves onto the couch.

She followed her voice into the room, and Kit jumped up and flung her arms around her. "Happy Mother's Day, Jean. I have a little something for you." She went to her luggage in the entryway closet to collect whatever it was.

"Me too," I said. "I have a little something too."

"And what else do you have for me, Valerie?"

"Oh." I stopped in the hallway on the way to my own luggage. "Happy Mother's Day, Mom." I returned and hugged her, struck by how tiny and delicate she felt. I shook my head almost imperceptibly, dismissing my morbid thoughts. I supposed they derived from Doris's death as well as my upsetting talk with Emily the night before, and I felt a little sadness mixed with anger creep over me.

"I meant an explanation of where you two were gallivanting all night. Hmm? Really, you never learn."

I left her to contemplate what exactly it was I never learned and tiptoed into the room where Emily was still asleep to retrieve my gift. It was a light-pink cashmere cardigan that had been marked down three times at Lord & Taylor. On the mannequin in the store, it had looked elegant. But now, as I stuffed it into a gift bag and crumpled some tissue on top, not so much. And because the bag was a tad too small, the sweater appeared more creased than the tissue paper when my mother took it out.

Kit, on the other hand, gave my mother a tiny blue box. It didn't need a gift bag. There was no mistaking the color: Tiffany Blue, which could probably be identified from space. Inside was a tiny gold cross. Simple, elegant, and classy. So like Kit to have the perfect gift.

My mother eyed it with total joy. "Katherine, this is way too much for me. It's exquisite. And Valerie, this cardigan is nice. Thank you, girls." She wrapped an arm around each of our waists. "You spoil me." She seemed to have forgotten our gallivanting, which I suspected had more to do with the cross than the wrinkled cardigan.

"So," she said, when she released us. "We probably should have some breakfast and then get ready."

"Ready for what?" I asked.

"Church, of course," she said with some surprise, as if I'd suggested we set off to Las Vegas.

I inwardly groaned. I couldn't believe that after all we'd been through the day before, my mother would still want to go to church.

"Today's more important than ever," she said, as if she'd read my thoughts.

Well, it *was* Mother's Day, after all. When Kit headed toward the bathroom, I followed my mom into the kitchen area.

"Happy Mother's Day to you, too, dear," she said. "I bet you are ready for some coffee. Should we take it out on the deck?"

"Sure."

I could see by the glass coffee decanter, which was about three-fourths full, that she was probably on her third cup. She opened the cupboard door, and after briefly studying the contents, she pulled out a mug for me that featured one of the Door County lighthouses. After pouring me a cup and topping off her own—a mug that appropriately declared itself belonging to MOM—she opened the sliding door and led the way to her picnic table, where I saw a plate of fresh cinnamon rolls waiting. They were still warm.

"When did you make these, Mom?"

"This morning. I couldn't sleep."

"Any reason, or just the usual?"

"More than the usual, I'm afraid. And the fact that you and Katherine were not in your beds didn't help any." She took a sip of coffee.

"You mean Doris?" I asked, hoping to deflect her thoughts from Kit's and my early-morning jaunt.

"Of course Doris. But also Ruth. What in the world was she doing, showing up at William Stuckey's last night, at that hour?"

"Well, Mom, not everyone thinks ten o'clock is all that late." I didn't believe that for a minute, but I felt sorry for her. I didn't care what she said. I felt certain she considered William *hers*, and I understood why she didn't like the idea of another woman—even her cat-crazy friend, Ruth—showing up at his place at any hour of the night. "And didn't she say something about a donation for her cats? It sounded rather innocent, if you want my opinion."

"What do you mean, *innocent*?" My mom sounded insulted. "I'm not accusing her of anything. The woman is a simpleton. I just don't know why she'd bother William Stuckey so late at night."

"Well, there you have it. A simpleton."

"What does *that* mean?"

"No boundaries."

"Oh, Valerie, don't start preaching all your European nonsense to me."

"Mom, it's not European; it's—"

"Is everything okay with Emily?" My mom's mind obviously hadn't aged yet. She still didn't miss a thing.

"Well, of course. Why do you ask?" I pulled my hand back from the plate of cinnamon rolls I'd just been reaching for, my hunger suddenly replaced by a sick feeling.

"She's so quiet; it's not like her at all. I didn't notice it at first—"

"I do think she's coming down with something," I said. "That headache and all. Maybe she does have allergies."

"Maybe she's pregnant? Are she and Luke in a position to start a family? What exactly does he do, anyway? He wears such thick glasses, I worry about his eyesight. Has he ever considered those contact lenses?"

Before she could go on a rant about Luke's vision, I had to stop her. "No, Mom, she's not pregnant. And Luke's eyes are just fine."

The bigger problem was that her precious granddaughter had been stabbed to death with her naked breasts exposed for all the world to see.

CHAPTER TEN

We made it to St. Luke Presbyterian Church ten minutes before the nine o'clock service began. We sat behind Minnie Ebert, her strong perfume wafting all around us.

William Stuckey arrived a few minutes after the service began, and we all squished together in the pew we occupied to make room for him.

When the service was over and we made our way down the aisle to the back of the church, I noticed Virginia Huntley and Ruth Greenway sitting in the last row.

Virginia looked stylish in a plum-colored business suit.

Ruth was also wearing a suit, but it was about twelve sizes too big and looked as though it had made one too many trips to the dry cleaners. On her head she had a red straw hat with a wide brim. The hat also looked too large, but I was confident it would never fall down and cover her face. The frames on those glasses of hers would keep a 747 at bay.

I was just beginning to think something was missing from her ensemble, when she reached down by her feet and sat back up holding a battered straw bag featuring a cat with two rhinestones for eyes and a tiara on its head.

Everyone gathered outside the church to wish Happy Mother's Day to those deserving the honor. I was listening to Virginia tell me she had stopped by Stan's that morning and he seemed to be bearing up, when out of the corner of my eye I saw Kit standing under an oak tree talking to a woman I'd never seen before.

I excused myself and hurried over to her and her new pal. In circumstances like these, I always feel a little nervous about Kit saying something inappropriate.

"Val, come meet Jacqueline Bakos. She was Doris's housekeeper. She's from Croatia."

"No kidding." I wasn't even sure where the heck Croatia was. I figured it was one of the countries that had moved around a little in recent times.

Jacqueline Bakos was a stunning woman trying to look dowdy. Her lustrous black hair was parted in the middle and caught in a ponytail at the nape of her neck. She wore no makeup that I could detect, but her green eyes were fringed with long, dark lashes, and there was no doubt her eyebrows had reaped the benefit of the threading method to gain their perfect shape. Something I would try myself, if I weren't so sure it would hurt like crazy.

"This is Valerie Pankowski," Kit told Jacqueline. "We're here for the weekend visiting Val's mother, Jean. She's over there." As she spoke, she pointed to my mom, who was busy conversing with Ruth Greenway and William. Even through the throng of people, I could see the rhinestone eyes on Ruth's cat purse glaring at me.

"Yes, I know Miss Jean. She's friend of Mrs. Doris."

"Nice to meet you, Ms. Bakos," I said.

"Please, you call me Jacqueline."

"Okay, Jacqueline." I took a quick glance at what she was wearing—a drab brown dress and clumpy black lace-up shoes (the kind nuns wear). But there was no mistaking that Jacqueline had a killer body underneath that sack, and what could be seen of her legs showed them to be slim and shapely.

"Jacqueline here was just telling me something interesting about Doris," Kit said.

"Really? What's that?"

"She said Doris had a big argument—"

"Not so nice at all," Jacqueline interrupted her. She obviously didn't want anyone speaking for her. "I cover my ears at some of the bad words I hear."

"Really?" I said again. "So you heard this over the phone?"

"No. I hear with my own ears in the person."

As she said it, she actually touched her earlobes, hidden behind her hair, and for a brief second I caught the flash of a diamond.

"Someone come to visit. Very day she die. They are in study. But Mrs. Doris never allow me to go into study. One room I am not allowed to clean. Mrs. Doris send me home early that day, but I was still in the house to finish chores. They didn't know I was there."

"Who came to visit, and what did you hear?" Kit asked. I was a little disappointed she wasn't taking notes.

"Not so much words. More just shouting. I don't know who person is, but words were nasty."

"A man or a woman?" I asked, wishing *I* were taking notes.

"Not so sure. Could be man; could be woman. All Americans sound same to me." She shrugged in a petulant way, and I could only imagine how stunning she would look if she actually smiled. "I know Mrs. Doris is angry, so I leave. Don't want her to be embarrassed if she see me there."

"You liked Mrs. Doris?" Kit asked.

"What's all this?" We turned to see William hurrying toward us. "Jacqueline, I didn't expect to see you here."

"Why not?" Jacqueline asked, raising her chin in a look of defiance.

"I thought you were a Catholic," William said, with his grin that I was beginning to find a little phony.

"Catholic, Methodist, Presby-whatever-you-call-this-place. All the same God. He don't mind if I choose a different house to come visit Him."

She walked away, and we were left with the grinning William Stuckey.

"Our Jacqueline is a little bit too dour for my taste," he said, putting an arm around each of us, and I wondered just how well he knew *our* Jacqueline. "But Doris seemed to like her, and by all accounts she did a good job." He led us away from the oak tree and back to the crowd outside the church. "I'll be seeing you ladies later. Valerie, I have a special treat for your mother."

***

When we arrived back at the house, the first thing we saw—as if anyone could miss it—was a huge bouquet of flowers sitting on my mother's front doorstep. It was at least three feet wide and filled with huge red, pink, and white roses. My mother slowly edged the car up the driveway, and I was afraid she would hit the garage door since she couldn't seem to take her eyes off the flower arrangement. I wondered if they were the treat from William.

"They must be from Buddy," my mother said. My only sibling lives in Washington, DC, and was long overdue for a visit to our mother.

After carefully putting the car in park and unbuckling her seat belt, my mother got out and approached the flowers slowly, with obvious delight. It was like watching a child's first glimpse of Santa Claus. She knelt down and removed a card from amidst the blooms. "Look, Valerie. If this isn't the sweetest thing I've ever read." She waved the card at me, one hand over her heart.

I felt happy for her. I dug my reading glasses out of my purse and took the card from her.

"Good grief," I said, shaking my head, after I skimmed the words.

Dear Jean,

It's been a privilege to know you all these years. Since the day we met, you've treated me like a son. On your special day, I want you to know how much you are thought of and loved.

Tom

"Crap," I said, as my mother disappeared into the house with her flowers. "Tom Haskins did *not* write this. Who's he kidding?"

"No shit," Kit said from behind me. "And so many roses; a little gauche, don't you think? Even for him."

I hurried into the house, where Emily was helping her grandmother find the perfect spot for the bouquet. I didn't want to leave them alone, for fear her grandma would wrest Emily's secret out of her. She could probably do it with little effort, in spite of the fact that Emily worried her grandma would "freak." They had a special relationship that only a grandma and her granddaughter can have, a relationship that doesn't judge and doesn't try to control—in other words, the perfect antidote to a parent/child relationship.

I joined Kit on the couch and watched as Emily and her grandma admired the bouquet they'd placed in the middle of the kitchen table. Then my mom put her arm around Emily's waist, and I heard her say, "Why don't we go sit out on the deck, Emily?" *And then you can spill your guts, Emily.*

Kit jolted me out of my disturbing thoughts. "Ya know, Val, has anyone confirmed where Stan really was before he returned home Friday night? I mean, who goes running that late?"

"For Pete's sake, Kit, millions of people go running at night," I said, even though I wasn't at all sure that was true. "David used to run late at night, remember?"

"Hmm. Exactly my point."

My ex-husband had made a lot of excuses to leave the house at odd hours, running being one of them. I suspected he was meeting, or at least on the phone with, his latest squeeze.

"But Stan looks like a runner, don't you think?" I asked, trying to distance myself from thoughts of my errant husband.

"I'm just saying Stan was running awfully late." Kit sat up straighter and placed the church program she'd been holding onto the coffee table.

"Why don't we go out on the deck?" I changed the subject abruptly. "I don't want my mother grilling Emily."

"Yeah. Ya know, that girl is likely to crack."

My mom looked up as Kit and I stepped onto the deck. I saw the frustration in her eyes when they met mine. The kind of frustration I remember feeling whenever David interrupted a conversation Emily and I were having just as she was about to really open up.

Good. Mission accomplished. I smiled at my mother.

Kit sat on the bench on the other side of Emily, but I stood in front of my mom, as if I could keep her from having even a second of private conversation with her granddaughter.

"I was just saying to Emily how much I'd love it if she could stay a few days longer." My mother put an arm around Emily's shoulders and pulled her closer. I saw her hand pat Emily's upper arm.

"It'd be nice to hang out here a little longer, Grandma." Emily smiled, and once again I felt both mad and sorry for her at the same time. How *could* she have been so stupid?

"I'd love to stay longer!" Kit said, which elicited a frown from my mother.

"Don't you have a husband to get home to, Katherine?"

Before Kit could answer, I chimed in. "What are you people talking about? *I* have a job I have to get back to. We have to leave in the morning."

85

I thought I had closed the subject, but of course Kit reopened it.

"I could rent a car," she said, "if we wanted to stay longer." She looked at Emily, who sat up straighter and turned her head toward my friend.

I looked at my watch and then at my mom. "Are we going to William's or what? I thought he was going to cook for us today."

For once, my mom said the perfect thing. "Valerie's right. Let's freshen up and get going." She stood and smoothed her church dress. "We'll talk about this later, Emily."

Kit, I noticed, pulled her phone from her pocket and was no doubt looking for a car-rental place. The three of them walked back into the house, and I stood on the deck alone for a moment, wondering what the heck just happened.

***

As we grabbed our handbags to head out for William's, he called.

"What are you saying, William Stuckey?" I heard my mom ask, after she'd answered the phone and then remained quiet long enough for me to begin paying attention. "Are you sure that's what we should do? Yes, yes, I know it's Mother's Day, for goodness' sake."

I watched her nod more, and then finally she returned the phone to its cradle on the wall.

"Well, seems like we have a change of plan," she said. "Margaret called William Stuckey, and she and Stan invited us all over to her mother's house to eat. They say there's a lot of food from neighbors and friends, and she claims they will never eat it all."

"Sounds good," Kit said, emerging from the bathroom. She was wearing a pantsuit made of a silky fabric in a turquoise color that highlighted her auburn hair.

"I think it'd be nice for Margaret to have some people around, don't you?" Emily asked, looking at each of us in turn for confirmation.

I had to shake my head a little to eliminate the image of her tied to a bedpost with a knife in her chest. "Yes, I think so too," I said at last.

"Well, I'm going to make a quick trip to the store to get something to take," my mother announced.

"Why on earth would you do that?" Kit asked. "Aren't they asking us over to help them eat what they already have? Surely we don't want to add to—"

"Katherine, you don't go to someone's house empty-handed." My mother's look and tone both softened midsentence, as if she suddenly remembered the gold cross Kit had given her. "You can be sure Minnie will be honoring us with one of her so-called *homemade* casseroles."

***

The rest of us were getting antsy by the time my mother returned. She was gone far longer than necessary, it seemed to me, to purchase a cherry pie.

But none of us questioned her as she came in the house and made her way to the kitchen area. I watched as she dug out a pie carrier from the cupboard and then removed the plastic wrap from the pie. Voilà! We soon left with a pie that no one would doubt for a minute was homemade. At least as homemade as Minnie's casserole.

CHAPTER ELEVEN

My mother was at a four-way stop, busy looking left and right and then left again at the empty street.

She waited several seconds before deeming it safe to move on.

I was glad to be distracted by my cell phone's rendition of the *Law & Order* theme song. I quickly answered it.

"How are ya, Val? What're you doing?" I heard my boss ask.

"Hi, Tom. Actually, we're on our way to the Dibble house. Margaret and Stan invited us to eat."

"Lucky you. Wish I were there, Kiddo."

"Really?"

"No. Of course not *really*. But this is good. Get a look around that house, square footage, all that stuff. I've got a pal that's interested in getting the listing. Try to take some pictures."

"Tom, isn't that a bit premature? We don't even know if Margaret and Stan want to sell. We don't even know who *owns* the house now."

"Yet; we don't know *yet*. Find out and call me as soon as you do."

"Er, it might take a few days. Do you mind if I stay up here a bit longer?"

"You got anything hot working down here?"

"Not really."

"Okay. Take a couple of days. Knock yourself out, Pankowski."

"I'll try to. Thanks, Boss."

I hung up and turned to Kit. "That was—"

"Tom. Yes, but I think there were a couple of hard-of-hearing folks in Green Bay who didn't quite catch what he said."

When we finally made it to the Dibble driveway, it seemed as though every light in the mansion was lit. The front door was unlocked, and a lot of chatter was coming from inside, so we let ourselves in.

It looked like everyone in Door County was there. Most of them, of course, I didn't know. But I did spy Ruth Greenway sitting on one of the couches in between two women I had never seen before.

She was wearing a red hat with some kind of netting perched on top that was covered with sequins the size of pennies. The rest of her ensemble consisted of a black oversize sweater and baggy black pants. I was shocked to find no feline decoration, until I noticed her black velvet slippers adorned with a cat's face on each one.

"Hi, Valerie." She waved. "Come meet—"

"I will." I smiled. "But first let me say hello to Margaret and Stan."

I took Kit's elbow and steered her down the hall toward the back of the house and the vast kitchen. "Seems odd to say *Margaret and Stan*," I whispered to her. "They sound like a married couple."

"They're a couple of something, all right. And it looks like we're having a party here."

When we found the kitchen door, I peered through the round circle of glass in its center. I could see Stan and Margaret at the Bosch double range, their backs to me, clearly enjoying a laugh together over something.

"Should we go in?" I turned to Kit, who was on my heels.

Before I could answer, we were pushed a little to the side, and turning, I saw Jacqueline Bakos. She stood next to us, holding a silver tray covered with hors d'oeuvres. "Go. Don't go. But move out of my way."

"Are you working today?" Kit eyed the tray.

"What? You think because there has been a death in the house, it no longer need cleaning? You think Mr. Stan can boil an egg and feed himself? You think the dust on the furniture blows itself away because the mistress fell down the stairs?"

"So that would be a yes?" Kit asked.

She gave us a long sniff, eyeing Kit's gorgeous outfit. Jacqueline was dressed in a homely sack similar to the one she'd worn to church. This one was gray, with a white stripe running through it. She wore a cheap black belt, which emphasized her tiny waist, and her hair was pulled into a chic bun at the nape of her neck. Once again, she managed to look stunning behind all that drab attire.

She pushed past us into the kitchen, and we followed. Margaret and Stan turned to see us and stopped laughing immediately.

"Kit. Valerie." Margaret came over and wrapped her arms around our shoulders, as if we were old friends she hadn't seen for a long time. "Thank you for coming. I couldn't bear to be alone, not on Mother's Day."

"No, of course not," I said. "We're happy to be here."

"And she invited the whole county." Stan smiled and reached out to shake our hands. The atmosphere definitely was not one suggesting a very recent death in the family.

More like a Super Bowl party with the Packers sure to win. Hosted by the happiest married couple in America.

But then, as Margaret directed us away from the kitchen and back down the long hall toward the living room, her demeanor changed.

Kit noticed it too. "Are you all right, Margaret?" she asked.

"Yes. No. Oh, I need to share this with someone."

"What?" I asked. We had all stopped, and Kit and I stood facing her.

She looked up at us, and her green eyes filled with tears. "I'm just not so sure my mom *fell*. I can't help but wonder if someone *pushed* her."

Kit looked at me knowingly—but I wasn't sure what she knew.

And then just as suddenly as Margaret had broached the subject, she closed it. "Just forget it, please. I don't want to burden you guys. Really, please forget I said anything. Now, where are Jean and the lovely Emily?" She practically shoved us the rest of the way into the living room. "There they are," she said.

I saw them standing in front of the fireplace, Emily's arm linked through her grandmother's.

"What would you ladies like to drink?" Margaret gave them two kisses apiece, one on each cheek. It was a form of greeting I knew my mother found pretentious and entirely too European for her taste. One cheek, one kiss, was good enough for her.

"William Stuckey isn't here," she said, as soon as we reached her. "He said he'd be here."

"Guilty." Stan raised his hand as he walked into the room. "He's running a little errand for me." He looked as though he were dressed to play tennis, with white shorts cut to his knees and a white shirt open at the neck.

"Valawee." We all turned to see Minnie Ebert approach, holding a glass with some pink liquid inside. "Isn't this just so festive?" she asked. At least she had her legs covered in a long pleated skirt. It was the type you could twist into a rope and strangle someone with and then wear it immediately afterward without any unwanted creases. Her makeup shimmered, and her lips—drawn larger with a lip pencil—were a deep, glossy crimson.

"Stan was just telling us William Stuckey is running an errand," my mom said.

Minnie snickered. "A little too old to be an errand boy, don't you think, Jean?" She took a sip from the pink drink.

"Where's Virginia?" Kit asked. I watched her eyes pan the room for the people we knew.

"She'll be here." Ruth Greenway joined our little group. "I spoke to her after church. She wanted to change clothes. I didn't think I'd be here so soon myself. One of my cats—"

"What kind of an errand?" My mother looked at Stan for an answer.

"Actually, he went to Virginia's. She's been having some car trouble."

"I could have picked her up myself," Ruth piped in, "but Caesar, he's my short-haired domestic—"

"What a kind man William is," Minnie said menacingly, her eyes trained on my mother above the rim of her glass. "Soooo accommodating. He gave me a lift to the grocery store a couple of days ago when my knee was acting up." She raised her leg beneath her long skirt as proof that she was fully recovered.

"Oh, he's a treasure," my mother said.

Stan left us to prepare drinks, and my mother and Emily took seats on an empty spot on the couch.

Kit grabbed my arm. "Let's take a look around," she whispered. "I'm really bothered by what Margaret said about her mother maybe being pushed."

"Well, okay, but let's don't be obvious about it."

We headed out into the hallway and made our way to the back of the house to the study.

"This would be a good place to start," Kit said, her hands already placed on the brass handles of the double mahogany doors. "Get out your Realtor badge or something."

"I don't have a badge; I'm not a policewoman."

"You are needing something?" We turned to find Jacqueline standing behind us; her tray had obviously been delivered. I was learning that she had the silent creeping ability of one of Ruth Greenway's cats.

"Just looking around," Kit said.

"In my country we don't go into rooms unless we are invited."

"Welcome to America." Kit swung the doors open. A massive desk took up one corner of the study. Two of the walls were lined from ceiling to floor with book-filled shelves.

"Is this where Mrs. Dibble did her work?" I asked the huffy Jacqueline, who had followed us in.

"What you think she do in here? Practice the salsa dancing?"

"Funny," Kit said, walking around and studying the books on the shelves. "I thought you told us you never came into this room."

"Is not a lie. I never do. And neither should you. Mrs. Doris keep her private things in here. Not for you to look around like thieves." She had returned to the study doors and stood like an usher, urging us to leave.

"No problem." I grabbed Kit's arm and escorted her out. "It's such a lovely house, we just wanted to see as much of it as we could."

"Val is a Realtor," Kit said, as if that gave me carte blanche to go anywhere I liked.

Jacqueline gave us a *so what* look, and once we were back out in the hallway, she firmly closed the doors behind us and then disappeared toward the kitchen.

"We need to get back in there," Kit said, as soon as Jacqueline was gone. "Did you notice that desk was covered in papers?"

"Not really."

"I have a feeling Margaret might be onto something, about her mom's death. So first chance we get, when good old Jacqueline is out plowing the lower forty or feeding the chickens, we need to check out that study."

Back in the throng of guests in the living room, we listened as Stan and Margaret told affectionate stories about Doris, and a few people were laughing as they reminisced.

"I'm concerned about Virginia," Ruth Greenway whispered, suddenly appearing out of nowhere beside me. "She should be here by now. I phoned her, and she isn't answering."

"Mom," I called across the room to where she was still sitting with Emily, "why don't you call William and see if they're on their way?"

"Where's the telephone?" she asked.

I remembered my mother is the only woman in the world who doesn't carry her phone with her, but I saw Emily whip her own phone out of her pocket.

"What's the number, Grandma?"

"Good heavens, I don't know. I have it in my speed-up dial at home."

I took out my own phone to call William. Luckily, I did have his number stored, for emergencies.

He answered on the first ring. "Valerie, I'm just pulling into the driveway."

"Good." I distanced myself from the group and went out to the hall. "Is Virginia with you?"

"Actually, no," he said.

As I listened, I became aware that Jacqueline had silently followed me into the hall.

"I stopped by her house to pick her up because she had car trouble earlier today," William told me what I already knew. "But she wasn't home. Isn't she there with you? I assumed Ruth or someone else had beaten me to it and already driven her to Stan's."

"No, she's not here."

"That's strange."

I heard the sound of his Mercedes in the circular driveway, and I went to the front door, my phone still to my ear.

"Ah, there you are," William said, getting out of his car. "Looking lovely as ever."

I smiled at his compliment.

"And where is your equally lovely mother?" He shut off his phone and put it into his jacket pocket.

"Follow me." I led him into the living room, where he made a beeline for my mother. I watched him carefully place a kiss on her cheek and saw her eyes light up.

***

"I'm really worried about Virginia now," Ruth said.

I glanced at my watch. At least an hour had passed since William arrived.

"Did you try to call her again?" I asked.

"Yes. Three times. It's unlike her not to pick up. Where can she be if she doesn't have a vehicle?"

I put an arm around Ruth's shoulders. Beneath her fancy red hat, her cheeks were almost the same color. She looked scared.

"Would you like me to go to her house and check?" I asked.

"Would you, please? You see those ads on television of people who have fallen down and can't get up. I've almost done it myself. Just this morning I nearly tripped over Gwendoline; she's my American shorthair and a real terror. I didn't see her and—"

"Look," I said, realizing I had become one of those people who cut poor Ruth off every time she mentioned a cat. "Kit and I will drive over and see if she's okay. Does she live far?"

"No, it's only about a mile down the road. She has the house with the blue shutters. It's very pretty. I can go with you."

"No, no, you stay here. Maybe she'll show up. Kit and I will go."

I asked my mother for her keys and was subjected to the briefest of lectures on the dangers of speeding. Once it was over, I grabbed Kit's arm. She was deep in conversation, perched on one of the couches beside Minnie Ebert.

"Excuse me, Minnie. Kit, come with me. We need to check on Virginia. William said she wasn't home, but Ruth is worried."

"Now?" Kit jumped up. She grabbed her purse from the hall table and then followed me out to the Escalade. "Thanks for saving me. I was in the middle of a discussion with Minnie Pearl on how to apply makeup that lasts all day."

"Use a shovel?" I climbed into the driver's seat of my mom's car and shifted it back a good six inches.

"Or a blow torch." Kit fastened her seat belt on the passenger side. "Do you know where we're going?"

"Yes. Turn left at the stop sign at the end of the road, and go for about a mile. We are looking for the pretty house with blue shutters."

We found the house easily. It was indeed pretty. A warm glow emanated from behind one of the shutters, and the light filtered onto a window box full of colorful blooms.

We knocked several times, with no response. Then I located the doorbell and listened to the chimes of Big Ben echo through the inside of the house. "She's definitely not home," I said.

"Really?" Kit was already walking to the side of the house.

"Kit, come back. She's not home," I said again.

"Then she won't know if we have a look-see."

I followed Kit around the one-car garage to the backyard. It was as lovely as the front. Well cared for and tastefully landscaped. The back of the house was constructed much like the front. A French door covered on the inside with a vertical blind, and generous windows on either side.

The light from inside the house cascaded onto the small lawn.

"See? There's a light on." Kit knocked on the door and then one of the windows.

"Satisfied? She's not home. Let's go."

"Wait." Kit had her face pressed close to the window to the right of the door. She had her hand cupped over her eyes, peering into the room.

"Kit, let's *go*. We don't want anyone to think we're snooping."

"I think someone should snoop." Kit turned to face me. "Take a look."

She moved away from the window, and I took her spot. I looked in for several seconds and then shook my head, as if it would clear the vision.

Virginia Huntley's body lay peacefully on the kitchen floor, as if she had decided to take a nap there. She was wearing the same plum-colored suit I'd seen in church that morning, her hair was in place, and she looked very serene. Except she also looked dead.

CHAPTER TWELVE

Hey," I said, "did you know Doris was sending a thou a month to a school in Senegal to help teach kids to read?"

"How would I know that?" Kit responded vaguely. She was seated across from me at Doris's wide desk, her reading glasses balanced on the end of her nose and a sheet of paper in each hand.

We were the only ones awake at Doris's—or whosever house it was about to be—taking the huge risk of rifling through the papers on her desk. Everyone else had either left or gone to bed.

After our painful discovery at Virginia Huntley's house, we had called 9-1-1. We were advised that an ambulance was on the way, and the operator suggested we break in if necessary to see if we could assist.

But it wasn't necessary.

Kit was way ahead of them. She'd already tried the doorknob, found it unlocked, and walked in. While she knelt beside Virginia, I stayed by the door, still thinking how peaceful Virginia looked.

I watched Kit place two fingers on Virginia's neck, and then she looked up at me. Her expression was sad.

"Is she . . . ?" I asked.

"Dead? Yes. I think so. I can't feel a pulse."

"Are you serious?"

"Dead serious." Kit quickly placed two hands on Virginia's chest and began pumping. "One, two, three," she said. "Val, look around the house. See if anyone else is here."

"Right," I said, not moving.

Kit counted to three again and then stopped briefly before repeating her attempts to revive Virginia's heart. Once again, I was impressed with her for knowing what to do.

While I stood there motionless, I heard the faint sounds of a siren. As it got closer, it became deafening. Turning, I saw an ambulance pull into the driveway. Two men hopped out and ran into the house past me. Within seconds they had knelt beside Virginia, and Kit got out of their way.

Looking defeated, she stood and watched them take over. "We're too late, aren't we?" she asked. "Who knows how long she's been lying here. She didn't even change out of her church clothes from this morning."

One of the men disappeared out the door and returned with a stretcher on wheels. His companion had taken a stethoscope and was listening to Virginia's chest. I watched him shake his head. Then he looked at his watch. "Are you relatives?" he asked us.

I didn't like his tone of voice. It had such a note of finality, when I was still hoping Virginia would sit up and give us one of her famous *uff das*.

"She's a friend," Kit said. "We were just here to give her a ride. There's a gathering at the Dibble house. Virginia was supposed to be a guest."

"Virginia? That's her name?"

"Yes. Virginia Huntley."

"I'm sorry." The man removed the stethoscope from his ears, and then the two of them lifted Virginia onto the gurney. From somewhere they produced a white blanket that they put over her.

I watched in silence as one hand fell out from under the cover, and I marveled at her perfect manicure and the silver charm bracelet that slid down her wrist. As they wheeled her body out to the ambulance, the hand moved back and forth in a gentle swinging motion. It seemed like a weak attempt to wave good-bye.

I remained standing in my corner, while Kit disappeared into the rest of the house.

"Nothing looks disturbed," she said, when she joined me back in the kitchen.

I should have asked her how she knew that, since she'd never been in Virginia's house, but I was thinking of that waving hand and listening to the ambulance guys slam the door shut in the back of their vehicle. Then one of the guys returned to the kitchen, with a clipboard in his hand.

"Heart attack?" Kit asked, opening the cupboards and inspecting the contents.

"Could be," he said. "Won't know till the M.E. examines the body. Could I take down your information— names, telephone numbers, et cetera? And do you know her next of kin?"

"No," Kit said. "We really didn't know Virginia well." She took the man's clipboard, and I watched her write something on the form.

"Someone will be in touch." He smiled weakly. Then, looking at Kit, he said, "You might want to look after your friend. She seems very upset."

"I will." Kit nodded. "I always do."

By the time they told us we could leave, it had long since grown dark. We drove slowly back to Doris's house to break the news.

Ruth Greenway met us at the door. Her face was flushed, and she put her tiny fist in her mouth as she looked over my shoulder, as if expecting Virginia to be with us. I put my arm around her and led her back into the living room.

"Take a seat, Ruth," I said. "We have some bad news."

The crowd had thinned considerably. Everyone was silent and seated, and Kit and I stood with our backs to the fireplace and faced them.

I cleared my throat. "Well, guys," I said, "I'm so sorry to tell you this, but, um . . . well, it's . . . um, about Virginia. I have some really bad news. It's . . . well . . . she's—"

"For heaven's sake," my mother said from her place on the couch. "Spit it out, Valerie. While we're all still alive."

"She's dead," Kit spoke up. "Sorry to be so blunt, but ya know . . ." She paused long enough to look at me. "Sometimes it's easier if you just say it like it is."

I glanced over at Ruth, who was softly crying. "It can't be," she said. "What happened, Valerie? Was it her heart?"

I looked at Kit again, silently urging her to continue with the details.

"Possibly," she said, taking my cue. "We found her lying on her kitchen floor. She was still wearing her church clothes."

"My goodness," Minnie shrieked. "She bought that suit in Green Bay. And she *always* takes her church clothes off as soon as she gets home. She's such a saver—"

"I'll call the medical examiner," William said, looking very concerned. "He's an old friend of mine. We play golf together. And I'll make sure someone's notifying Virginia's family."

"We're not sure when she . . . when she died," Kit was saying. She had to raise her voice to be heard over Ruth's sobbing.

Everyone had a lot of questions, none of which we could answer. So instead, Kit said, "I think the best thing to do is for everyone to go home and get some rest."

"Good plan," William said. "Jean?" He extended his hand in a gallant gesture.

"William," Kit said, "why don't you take Jean and Emily home. Stan, could you see that Ruth and Minnie get home okay? Val and I will stay and help clean up a bit."

"Ha!" I heard from the living room entrance. Jacqueline had appeared, as she always seemed to, from out of nowhere. "You two will clean up? This is one I have got to see with my own eye."

"Jacqueline." Kit smiled sweetly. "Why don't you go home too, dear? You must be exhausted."

"I take my orders from Mr. Stan, not you." The closest to a smile I had ever seen from her formed on her lips.

"Kit is quite right," Stan said. "You go home. We'll manage here." He walked Minnie and Ruth to the front door, after they insisted they were perfectly able to get themselves home.

I followed my mom and Emily to William's car and gave them each a hug. I quickly weighed the risk of Emily blabbing to my mom about her nudity against the risk of Kit killing me if I left before we had a chance to check out Doris's study.

No contest.

"We won't be long here; we'll be home soon," I said.

"Make sure all the food is carefully wrapped in foil and put in the refrigerator," my mom whispered to me, as she extended her cheek for me to kiss her. "And for goodness' sake, don't let Katherine go digging around in Doris's stuff."

"Of course not. I'll keep an eye on her."

When I returned to the house, Stan thanked us for our help. Even in his crisp white tennis outfit he looked stunned and tired. "What a terrible thing about Virginia," he said. He drained the remains of some whiskey from the heavy crystal tumbler he was clutching. "I always thought she was in good health. I never heard of any heart problems."

"The medical examiner has to confirm it, ya know." Kit straightened a cushion on the couch.

"I'll phone the authorities in the morning," Stan said. "If you don't mind, I'm gonna call it a night. You two should just leave; it really can wait for Jacqueline to clean it all up tomorrow."

"No, we'll just put the food away. Won't be two seconds. You go up to bed," Kit said.

"Okay. I owe you one." Stan handed me his glass.

"If you're sure you don't mind, I'm going to call it a night too," Margaret said from the window seat, where she had been sitting. They were the first words I'd heard her say since we returned with the news.

She gave me a hug, and I watched her retreat up the same long stairway that Stan had just ascended. The one Doris had descended to her death.

"We should have asked her what she meant, who she thinks might have pushed her mom," I whispered.

"We can do that anytime. We gotta check the study while we have a chance, so let's get busy." Kit started gathering up plates and empty glasses.

"Aren't you sad?" I asked, picking up a plate of leftover miniquiches from the coffee table.

"Of course. She seemed like an okay gal. But it's odd, don't you think?"

"What? What's odd?"

"When she was over at your mom's, ya know, there was definitely something on her mind. I think she wanted to tell us something."

"Something *else*, you mean. Besides the fact that Doris wrote a check—"

"The blackmailer."

"Virginia made it very clear it wasn't blackmail."

"Unless, of course, Virginia was the one doing the blackmailing."

I sighed deeply. "It wasn't blackmail. And I already told you Virginia wouldn't bring it up if she was the one getting money. It wouldn't make sense."

"Who says it has to make sense?"

We got back to work, and in record time, Kit and I cleaned up the living room and the kitchen, hoping we'd taken just long enough for Margaret and Stan to fall sound asleep.

And now the study was all ours, as we sat rifling through Doris's piles of papers.

But I was keeping an eye open for Jacqueline while I continued shuffling through a stack of mail before me. Even though I had watched her get into her pale-green Volkswagen Bug and drive away, I figured she could be lurking somewhere back in the house. I didn't trust anyone who moved as quietly as she did.

Each envelope I came across had been expertly slit open with what must have been a sharp letter opener, but the contents were intact. They mainly consisted of bills to be paid and requests for money from various foundations and charities around the world.

"Kit, should we be doing this? It seems like such an invasion of privacy." A fleeting thought ran through my head of two strangers going through my personal mail back in my Downers Grove apartment.

"Keep digging."

"Look, the SPCA sent her a stack of return address labels with lighthouses next to her name," I said. "Those people are so good. They once sent me a pair of gloves that are perfect for gardening."

"That's *such* great news, Val. But do ya think you could move a little quicker over there? I don't trust Miss Croatia; she could return any minute with a tray of poisoned deviled eggs."

"No kidding. I was just thinking the same thing. Did she ever mention where she lives—"

"What the hell is this?" Kit interrupted me, but then she quickly added, "Oh, never mind. I was wrong. It's nothing."

"What?" I looked across at her.

"Nothing. It's nothing."

"Nice try, Kitty Kat. You found something. Show me."
I stood and walked to her side of the desk, peering over her
shoulder.

She didn't bother to put down the paper she was
holding. "Okay. But don't freak out. This could mean
anything."

CHAPTER THIRTEEN

Imight have slept a total of one hour. Max. It was three in the morning by the time Kit and I finished snooping, er, sleuthing and had crept back into my mom's house. I was not surprised to see she had opened Kit's sofa bed and turned down the covers. I looked at the pillow, expecting to see a fancily wrapped piece of chocolate.

I hugged Kit good-night and crept into the spare bedroom, where Emily lay sound asleep in her bed. Youth! They can sleep no matter what, whether their breasts are about to be exposed to the world or not.

And the next morning I lay in the opposite twin bed, not sleeping. I heard my mom running water for coffee, but she was the last person I wanted to see right now. I had to formulate the questions I needed to ask her first.

I brought the covers up to my chin and resumed the thoughts that had kept me awake during the few hours I'd spent in bed, thoughts of what Kit and I had found in Doris's study.

The first piece of damning evidence, the paper Kit hadn't wanted me to see, was a note signed *Wm.* Presumably one William Stuckey.

Doris,

Remember, above all, that Jean cannot know about this. She'd kill you—and maybe me. And we don't want that, do we?

I hate matters of money, don't you? So vulgar. But a necessary evil.

Wm.

That note alone would have been good for a few sleepless hours, making me wonder if maybe someone *had* been blackmailing Doris, and the someone was William. And what could possibly be my mother's involvement? *What* should she not know? Hopefully, nothing that would make her want to push Doris down the stairs.

And then there was another problem to keep me from sleeping. I needed to be thinking how to get Emily out of her predicament, not spending time worrying about a bunch of old people whose troubles would be dying along with them before Emily was even old enough to worry what her kids would think about her topless scene.

But one of those old people was my mother, and she posed my biggest problem of all. My worries about her now surpassed my worries about Emily. Kit and I had seen *her* name in Doris's check register on the first of every month for as far back as the register went. I had to find out why Doris was giving my mom five thousand dollars every month. The car phone, iPad, and other gifts from Doris to my mom were beginning to make a kind of scary sense.

I decided to buck up and go out to the kitchen and face my mother. I had to ask just what in the world she'd gotten herself involved in.

As I approached the kitchen area, tiptoeing so as not to awaken Kit, I realized my mom was on the phone, talking barely above a whisper—no doubt also so as not to awaken Kit. A flood of annoyance washed over me. Why the hell didn't she use the cell phone I gave her?

I retreated to the bedroom and plucked my own cell from my purse. Creeping out the front door to protect my privacy and Kit's sleep, I found Tom in my contacts and pressed *call*.

"Hey, Boss," I spoke to his voice mail, which I knew was the only way I could connect with him that early in the day. "I wanna thank you for the days off. Turns out my mother . . . well, she still needs me up here. Um . . . this thing with her friends . . . well, she's lost another one." *They're dropping like flies*, I thought.

As soon as I ended the call, my phone rang. "Tom?" I said. "I can't believe you're awake." I sat down on the front steps.

"You and me both. What the hell are you doing calling me at this hour? And what the hell time is it, anyway?"

"I dunno. It's early; let's leave it at that."

"You sound upset. What's going on, Kiddo?"

"Tom, you wouldn't even believe it."

"I'll believe it. Start from the beginning and talk slowly."

I started with our discovery of Virginia, trying not to make it sound like such a big deal. Like finding an eightysomething woman lying dead on her kitchen floor was as common as discovering a favorite rosebush has died. I tried to keep Kit's involvement out of it since, on a good day, Tom finds Kit to be nothing short of a lunatic.

He listened without saying a word, which in itself was unnerving.

"So," I said, when I'd finished telling him about Virginia's death, "you can see things are a mess up here right now."

"What else?"

"That's about it."

"Nah, something else is going on in that overactive mind of yours. Out with it, Pankowski."

I debated which other devastating concern I should share. I could go with my mother possibly being a blackmailer or worse. Or I could let him in on Emily's entry into the porn world.

"How's Emily?" he said, making the choice for me.

I took a deep breath. "Okay, well, there is something else you should know."

I described my daughter's predicament. He was silent again, while I spelled out the details. When I finished, I realized the only sound between us was my own sobs. When had I started crying?

"Okay," Tom said. "Get me the name of the film studio that's distributing this hack job."

"Tom, I'll try, but you know it's difficult to talk to—"

"Who got her into this piece of shit?"

"I don't know her agent's name. Wait. Naomi. 310-555-1812. That's her agent's assistant."

I had stopped sobbing, and if it would have been possible, I would have patted myself on the back for remembering the telephone number from when it had flashed onto Emily's phone screen. The area code and first three digits were the same as Emily's. But the credit really went to Mr. Tchaikovsky for composing his fabulous *1812 Overture*.

"Leave it to me," Tom said, and I nearly fell over with relief.

"Tom, I just can't thank you—"

"I haven't done anything yet."

But you will, I thought.

***

"How did Margaret seem to you yesterday?" I heard my mother ask when I entered the kitchen area, putting my phone into the pocket of my pajamas. She and Kit were sitting at the table, a steaming cup of coffee in front of each of them.

"Quiet," Kit said. I was glad she didn't share what Margaret had said about her mother being pushed.

109

My mom took her cup with both hands and held it halfway to her mouth. "She has a heavy heart right now."

"At least she has you to talk to," Kit said.

"What do you mean by that?" my mom asked.

"Her little talk with you and Virginia on Saturday—ya know, you'll be a big comfort to her now."

"Hmm." My mom's forehead furrowed in thought beneath the pink bonnet thing on her head.

I poured myself a cup of coffee, eager to see if she would share the details of her talk with Margaret.

"It must be nice to have a confidante like you," Kit continued pushing, sounding as eager as I was.

"Hmm," my mother said again. "She's walking around with a pile of guilt these days."

Kit was silent. And I was too, as I took a seat at the table.

"You don't think she had something to do with her mother's death, do you?" Kit finally asked.

"Of course not." My mother sounded incredulous. "Not directly, anyway. But I'm a little annoyed with her. Their last exchange was not pleasant."

Just tell us, I thought. And then she did.

"Margaret had called her mother and asked her for money," my mom said.

"Really?" Kit took a sip of her coffee. "How did that go?"

"Not so well. Doris turned her down flat."

"No kidding," Kit said.

"Margaret has gotten herself into a little financial difficulty. Valerie, you know I've always told you to have at least six months' living expenses in the bank at all times." She looked at me for confirmation that I was following her financial plan.

I nodded, but thought grimly of my own bank account. I'd be lucky to survive six days, let alone six months.

"Well, Margaret was not so smart. She told me she was about to lose her home. She has some kind of condominium in Minneapolis, and the bank is threatening to take it over. I guess she's made some bad investments. So she asked her mother for a loan. Not a large one, she assured me, but Doris turned her down."

"Wow," I said. With all I'd heard in the last few days about Doris's generosity, that surprised me.

"It wasn't really like Doris," my mother echoed my thoughts. "She was so bighearted."

The image of Doris's check register, with my mother's name beside the monthly five grand, flashed into my head. Talk about understatement.

"I'm guessing Margaret didn't take the rejection very well," Kit said.

"No. She told me she said some ugly things to her mother. They ended their phone call on a very nasty note. Margaret wasn't even sure she wanted to come visit this weekend."

"And now she feels guilty," Kit said.

"Exactly. I tried to comfort her, of course, but the truth is, I'm still a little irritated with her. This should be a lesson to you girls. Some bells you can't unring."

My thoughts immediately turned to Emily and her naked breasts. How the heck were we going to unring *that* bell?

***

"Look at these adorable golf-club covers. I think I'll get one for Larry," Kit held up a head cover in each hand. "Should I get the Bernese mountain dog or the pink flamingo?"

We were in Jane's Closet, a clothing and gift shop in Sturgeon Bay. We'd come down to Walmart to get some things my mom needed, now that her guests were staying longer.

I'd always wondered why she kept only enough in her refrigerator and cupboards to get her through the next few days—until I moved to my own small place. Then I understood. *It's certainly not because she can't* afford *to stock up*, I thought, *not with the five thousand dollars she got from Doris every month*. My stomach felt sick, as I knew it would until I had the chance to confront her about it.

Emily had joined us all in the kitchen that morning before I could bring it up, and the next thing I knew, my mom was sending Kit and me off for "supplies," as she called the items on her list: coffee, toilet paper, eggs, and—the reason she wanted us to go all the way to Walmart—a toilet plunger. I wasn't sure if she thought Walmart was the only place in Door County that carried them or if she didn't want anyone she knew in Egg Harbor to think her toilet could clog.

When we finished at Walmart, Kit had insisted we drive through downtown Sturgeon Bay, one of her favorite places in Door County. And so we found ourselves in Jane's Closet, the sort of shop frequented by people with way too much disposable income. Which certainly didn't describe me, and apparently not Margaret Edwards, either.

"Do you honestly think Larry would like either one of those covers?" I asked, spinning a carousel of Door County postcards.

"Of course not. Who would? But it will be fun to see him *pretend* he does. And payback for the Statue of Liberty letter opener he brought me from New York last year. I mean, really? Who goes to New York and bypasses Tiffany's when looking for a gift for the wife?"

"I thought the letter opener was nice." I pulled out a card with a map of the peninsula that highlighted the wineries.

"Ugh. I thought it was so tacky I nearly stabbed him with it. Hey, Val, two o'clock. *Look*. No, don't look now." She tossed the club covers back on the shelf and came up behind me, grabbing my arm. "Turn slowly, and don't stare."

"What the—"

"Behind you, two o'clock."

I wasn't quick enough to figure out if two o'clock was hers or mine, but I glanced around and then whipped my head back to the cards. "*Jacqueline*," I whispered. I turned the carousel, and we both followed it around so that it was in front of us and we could see through it.

There, indeed, was Jacqueline, looking like a movie star who should have a gang of paparazzi following her. She had discarded her box-shaped hausfrau dress for skinny jeans that hugged her long, shapely legs and were tucked into cowboy boots. Her luxuriant black hair fell loose below her shoulders, and her cream-colored leather jacket looked as if it cost a month's wages.

"Wow," I said.

"Yeah, she cleans up good. Let's go talk to her."

"No, no; what would we say?"

But it was, of course, too late. Kit had already made her way past the tables stacked with useless but costly knickknacks, and I watched her tap Jacqueline on the shoulder. "Fancy seeing you here," she said.

Jacqueline turned and then took a step back. "Fancy? Why fancy? You think a housekeeper can't shop in a place like this?"

"Calm down, Molly Maid. It's just an expression we have here in America."

I decided Jacqueline was the most defensive person I'd ever met. I watched her as she hoisted the strap of a soft leather purse (emblazoned with a Coach emblem that looked real) over her shoulder. Five hundred bucks, easy.

"How are you this morning?" I asked quickly, jumping in like a superhero to save the day.

"Pretty much the same as I was yesterday. Everything hunky-dory. Is another expression you have in America, no?"

"So sad about Virginia Huntley," Kit said, trying hard to *look* sad.

"She was an old woman. Heart give out."

"Did you know her well?"

"I know she one of the busybodies." She carefully enunciated the four syllables, *biz-ee-bod-ees*, spitting them out of her mouth as if she'd just eaten a bug and had to get rid of it.

"So you didn't like her?" I asked. *Did I really say that?*

Jacqueline gave one of her shrugs, as if she suddenly had no opinion on the subject. "Why I like any of those women? I just do my job."

"But you were very fond of Doris Dibble?" Kit asked, making me instantly wish I'd taken that kinder approach.

"Ha. I do my work. She pay me. Business arrangement. That is all. You will excuse me now; I have to go clean toilet and shower stall. You understand a poor working girl cannot stand around all day chatting."

"One thing, before you go." Kit placed a hand tentatively on her arm. "About Croatia."

"What about it?" Jacqueline shrugged off Kit's hand.

"That used to be in Russia, right?"

"Was never in Russia. We declared independence from Yugoslavia in 1991." I watched as Jacqueline literally looked down her perfect nose at us. She didn't exactly say it, but her expression implied we were stupid Americans who knew nothing.

"My husband and I are planning a European vacation, and I was just wondering if we should include Croatia in our plans. Do you think we would like it?"

Jacqueline took a deep breath before answering. Her voice rose a little. "How I should know what you like? Croatia has many villages that are as perfect as your Sturgeon Bay and your Egg Harbor. You think only America has such places?"

"No, no, not at all. That's not what she means," I said.

"My advice?" Jacqueline swung her purse strap firmly onto her shoulder again. "Stay home in America. Don't go trampling over other countries where you have no business. Enjoy your Subway sandwich and your Big Mac in your own country. Now I must go."

We watched her stylish figure as she left the shop. Her Volkswagen Bug was parked across the street, and we watched her climb into it. It really was a shame there were no paparazzi parked outside Jane's Closet to capture her image. She exuded glamour far beyond a woman who cleaned houses for a living.

"Wow." Kit took out her phone and tapped the screen with her thumbs. "Some attitude on that girl. I guess everything isn't quite as hunky-dory as we think with little Miss Croatia."

"What are you doing?" I asked her.

"Checking out Croatia. I'm just wondering if there's a reason for Jacqueline's sunny disposition."

CHAPTER FOURTEEN

Whole if Virginia didn't have a heart attack?" Kit asked. We were settled back in my car now, halfway to my mom's, and Kit was tapping away on her phone again.

I pulled my thoughts away from the infusion of money my mom's bank account had been receiving on the first of every month and answered my friend with a question. "What do you mean?"

"I mean, what if a heart attack wasn't the cause of death?"

"Well, then I suppose it was a stroke. It certainly wasn't cancer, for Pete's sake. Or a car accident."

"Seriously, I mean, what if it wasn't really a heart attack?"

I slowed down as we entered Egg Harbor. "What are you trying to say, Kit? No, not her too. You're not going to try to tell me you think she might have been . . ."

"Having trouble saying the *M* word? I'll say it for you. Yes, I think it's possible Virginia might have been murdered too, and I think you and I might be the only ones smart enough to pursue it. For one thing, we're the only ones who think Doris might have been—"

"Speak for yourself," I said.

"If Doris *was* murdered, then isn't it just a bit of a coincidence that one of her good friends would die so soon after her? The one friend who knew she was being blackmailed, by the way?"

I heaved a sigh. "First of all, Kit, we *don't* know that Doris was murdered. The only one besides you who seems to have even entertained the thought is Margaret. And she was probably speaking out of grief. And second of all, Virginia said it was *not* blackmail. The only thing I care to get to the bottom of, quite frankly, is what my mother has been up to, why Doris was giving her money. And if it turns out—"

"I know, honey, I know." My best friend reached across the front seat and patted my arm, giving me the comfort I couldn't get from anyone else. "Val, honey, I know your mom didn't have anything to do with any . . ."

"Suddenly having trouble saying the *M* word?"

"No. I know your mother would never *murder* anyone. Not on purpose, anyway."

"Huh?"

"But ya know, Virginia really might have been murdered, by the same person who felt the need to get rid of Doris, for the same reason. Virginia knew *something* about Doris."

"Virginia had a heart attack, Kit." I hoped the firmness in my voice would stifle her imagination.

"I'm not so sure. I was just googling—"

"Great. And what have you found this time? And don't forget to cite your source."

Kit is a veritable fount of Google-based wisdom and "facts," but often, when pressed, she admits her sources and *their* sources are bloggers who lack credentials at best and sound like snake-oil salesmen at worst.

"Forget it," she said. "We'll talk about it later. When you're not in a mood."

She was right. I was enveloped by worries about my mom *and* daughter that left me caring, quite frankly, about nothing—and no one—else.

But before I could apologize, my irrepressible friend continued. "There really are drugs, Val, that can make it look like a heart attack. I found 'em." She held her phone up as if for proof. "I just want you to be aware of that and keep your eyes open. And your mind too."

"Open for what?"

"Who do you think could most likely get his hands on such a drug? Who wrote Doris that note?" When I didn't respond, she answered her own questions. "Dr. William Stuckey, that's who. We need to be keeping an eye on Dr. William Stuckey."

"Kit, please." But I wondered . . . *was* my mother *somehow in cahoots with her William Stuckey, her Doctor William Stuckey?*

"I have just one word to say to you, Valley Girl."

She paused long enough for me to grow impatient. "Then for heaven's sake, say it."

"Succa, uh, sucksa . . . hmm . . . suck sa nell koe lean. Yeah, succinylcholine."

In spite of myself, I had to giggle at the sight of her, the phone held only inches away from her face as she struggled to pronounce the unfamiliar word. "Easy for you to say, Kitty Kat."

"Actually, there are a lot of ways to kill someone with a poison and make it look like death by natural causes—and those are ways I *can* pronounce, smarty-pants. Mushrooms, cyanide—why, even rhododendrons. But ya know, this succa . . . suck . . . sucks—"

"I know what you're trying to say, for Pete's sake. What about it?"

"It's a strong muscle relaxant that paralyzes the respiratory muscles," Kit read from her phone. "It's meant for use in a hospital, for when they put in breathing tubes. Blah, blah, blah. It would be fast acting, and an autopsy would show a heart attack. Okay. We need to get the M.E. to look for needle marks. And we need to think about who could get ahold of it and who would know how to give her an injection."

We were in my mom's driveway by now, and I felt glad that our insane conversation had to come to an end.

But all too soon, I found myself thinking it didn't sound so crazy after all.

***

Flimsy Walmart sacks in hand, the holes in the bottom of them growing bigger as we walked, Kit and I made our way from my car to my mom's front door.

"Watch it, Val. The egg carton is poking out of the bottom of that bag. You're going to have scrambled eggs before we even get to the kitchen."

"Ha ha. What's up with these useless bags, anyway? They need to switch back to the only slightly flimsy ones. I think it's double savings for them: cheaper bags and then customers have to repurchase the items that get ruined when they fall out."

"That's why I shop only at Whole Foods. Now *there's* a place that knows a sack when it sees one."

"Not to mention an idiot when it sees one." I had been forced to kneel down and rescue the carton of twelve eggs. "Don't you pay fifteen percent more at that place?"

"Possibly; I don't check prices. And I've never bought a toilet plunger in my life," she added.

It had amused me how clueless Kit was in the hardware section of Walmart. "Forgive me," I said, "I forgot you had your plumbing installed by NASA. But I know you do buy an egg occasionally."

"Yes, but the chickens from Whole Foods spend the weekend at Four Seasons before they drop an egg."

"Good for them. But I'll stick with my Motel 6 birds and these useless bags."

I hadn't seen any car in the driveway but my mother's, so I was shocked when Kit and I entered the house to see William sitting cozily next to my mom on the sofa. I almost dropped the eggs.

"William!" Kit said, and I felt nervous she was going to accuse him on the spot. But she actually waited a few minutes.

"William Stuckey just dropped by." My mother smiled up at us and then rose to help with the groceries.

William barely said hello, and he didn't look nearly as happy to see us as he had upon our arrival in Door County.

"Would you like more coffee?" my mom asked him, as she walked to the refrigerator with the eggs. "Girls, do you want a cup?"

"Where's Emily?" I followed my mom to the refrigerator and held the plunger up for her to see when she turned back from putting the eggs away.

"For Pete's sake, Val," she whispered, just loud enough for me to hear. "You don't need to announce to the whole world—"

"Settle down, Mom. Everyone has to unplug the toilet at some point."

"Yes, well, we don't need to send out invitations. And why on earth did you buy red?"

"It was all they had and—"

"Valerie, just put that thing away." She waved a hand in front of her face, which was scrunched up in disgust, as if I'd already used the plunger on the toilets at Lambeau Field. "Under the sink in the bathroom," she added.

"*Really*, Mom? I was thinking it might look nice on the kitchen table."

She pushed me in the direction of the bathroom. "I don't like that kind of talk, Valerie. We are not in Europe."

"No kidding," I answered, but my lighthearted moment was over. "Where's Emily?" I asked again.

"She took William Stuckey's car to run an errand. He thought she might enjoy driving it. I told them you guys wouldn't be back for a few hours."

"A few hours?" I felt irritated at my mom's exaggeration. But what I was really frustrated about was not knowing Emily's whereabouts.

"Well, I assumed Katherine would want a lot of time in the shops."

"Mom, this has hardly turned out to be the kind of visit where anyone is going to souvenir shop." I headed to the bathroom, hoping Kit wouldn't produce the Bernese mountain dog golf-club cover.

After stashing the plunger behind the pipes underneath the bathroom sink, I returned to the living room area to see my friend seated beside William on the couch. I heard my mom rattling dishes and pans in the kitchen.

And I heard Kit ask William a question that made me want to scream.

It must have made William want to scream, too, because he practically did. "*What?*" he asked. "What are you talking about?"

"I just thought you could mention it to him, ya know?"

"Mention what to whom, Kit?" Instinctively, I knew I had some damage control to do.

William looked irritated, shaking his head in disbelief.

"I told him I thought he should suggest to the medical examiner that he check for evidence of needle marks on Virginia; ya know, in case she was injected with something like succinylcholine."

I was pretty sure she hadn't pronounced it right, and was certain of that when William spoke.

"I don't know why in the world I would suggest the M.E. look for needle marks *or* succinylcholine." The word rolled off his tongue as if it were something he put in his coffee every morning.

My mom had returned and sat down on the other side of William, glaring at Kit. She obviously assumed the distress she noted in William's voice was attributable to Kit, that same troublemaker who used to be so good at annoying my brother when we were kids.

More than once my mother had declared it was time for Kit to go home because she was sick of hearing the bickering between Buddy and my best friend. I knew she wished she could tell her to go home now. Instead, she asked, "What are you guys talking about?"

"Your friend here wants me to ask the M.E. to check Virginia's body for needle marks and a drug that is normally not tested for in a toxicology screen."

"What kind of drug? Virginia would never take anything stronger than sleeping pills."

"Succinylcholine." William briefly explained the drug's use in a hospital setting.

"Well, why on earth would Virginia take something like that?"

"She wouldn't *take* it, Jean," Kit said. "My fear is that someone *injected* her with it."

"Well, why on earth—"

Much to my relief, Kit interrupted my mother, who seemed to have only one response to everything she was hearing. William, however, looked more furious than relieved.

"In higher doses," Kit said, as if she'd memorized the information she'd read online, "it can paralyze the entire breathing apparatus so the victim slowly suffocates to death, and an autopsy would likely rule death by a heart attack. Worst of all, its effects can make it impossible for the person to communicate. Can you imagine the horror Virginia—"

"Well, why on earth would Virginia be injected with suc . . . suc . . ."

William came to her rescue. "Sux," he said. "Just call it sux." He rose, and I expected him to head to the front door, even though Emily had his car. "Don't call it anything," he said. "I cannot believe we are having this conversation, when I thought . . ."

"You thought what, William?" Kit asked, when he didn't finish his sentence. I knew that look on her face. It was her *I gotcha* look.

He turned around and looked at Kit. I felt sure he was about to say it was none of her business. But instead, he took a deep breath and smiled. "I'll mention it to the M.E., Kit. Now, how about we all go out to lunch?"

"That sounds delightful," my mother said, as if he'd just asked her to prom.

"I thought we might include Ruth," he said. "She's very down about this Virginia business."

"Hmm," my mother responded. "If you think that's the right thing to do," she added, making it clear it was the worst idea she'd heard since Germany invaded Poland.

William turned to me. "Valerie, would you and Kit mind driving Ruth? She's a bit unsteady right now."

"No problem," Kit said.

I felt as if I were watching a movie, wondering what was going to happen next. And then the director cut to a completely different scene.

Coming through the front door, Emily once again made an actress-worthy entrance.

CHAPTER FIFTEEN

I followed Emily into the bedroom. She looked flushed, her cheeks rosy. I watched as she flopped down on the bed and looked up into my eyes; and heaven help me, even though she was wearing a black T-shirt with the famous Hollywood sign printed across her chest, an image of the same girl without the accompanying shirt flashed into my head.

"Mom, stop looking so worried."

"Was I? Sorry; I'm not worried at all." A lie, of course, although since I had shared her dilemma with Tom, I was trying to convince myself it would all work out. Still, there was one big thing Tom couldn't help me with. "Emily," I said, "I need to ask you a huge favor."

"Sure. What?"

"Will you please never say anything to your grandmother about your movie?"

"I want to keep it from her as much as you do. But she is the last one who would change her opinion of me—"

"Emily, please."

"Settle down, Mom. I won't tell her." She sounded convincing, but then she *was* an actress.

She also sounded just like me, talking to my own mother. *Settle down, Mom.* Well, like mother, like daughter—three generations' worth.

"I guess I'll change for lunch," I said, removing a plaid shirt from its hanger in the closet. "William's taking us somewhere. By the way, where were you in William's car?"

"Nowhere, really. I kinda felt he and Grandma wanted to be alone, so when he asked if I'd like to take his Mercedes for a spin, maybe run some errands, I jumped on it. That's a great car."

"Yep, it sure is. So you didn't go anywhere in particular?"

She sat up and ran her fingers through her long hair. "Well, I did run down to Sturgeon Bay to see if they had any pole-dancing vacancies in the clubs there."

"Very funny." I buttoned my shirt.

"Mom, you gotta let this go. There's nothing we can do about it except hope and pray the stupid film never gets released."

"Right," I muttered, looking at myself in the mirror and turning down my collar. But I hoped and prayed she was wrong and that there *was* something we could do, or rather *Tom* could do.

Emily and my mother were going to ride with William, so Kit and I set off to pick up Ruth. I watched Kit sitting beside me, her hands in her lap, studying the scenery like a twelve-year-old on a special outing.

"This is gonna be gooooood," she said, finally turning toward me.

I waited for her to explain.

"We'll have Cat Woman alone. We can ask her a few questions."

"Now, wait." I deliberately slowed down before the turn onto Ruth's street. "She just lost her best friend. No, make that two best friends. She doesn't need to have us interrogating her. To lose two close friends must be devastating."

As I said it, it occurred to me how I would feel if something happened to Kit. Not just my best friend, but really my only true friend. The one who always has my back and knows me better than I know myself. As we stopped in front of Ruth's house, I put a hand on her forearm. "Kit . . . ," I said, suddenly awash in sentimentality.

"What?" She was already unbuckled and opening the car door. "What?" she asked again, looking back at me.

"Nothing. Just go easy, please."

"I will; I promise," she said, in one of those weird moments when we seem to read each other's mind. "Nothing is going to happen."

When Ruth Greenway greeted us at the door, it was clear she had been crying. Her large specs didn't hide her red-rimmed, watery eyes; on the contrary, her glasses spotlighted them. She wore a black-and-white-houndstooth cap and a blue sweatshirt that pictured two cherubic white kittens, complete with wings, indicating they were on their way to heaven. I wondered if the kittens were a tribute to her two lost friends. It seemed appropriate.

"I understand we are being treated to lunch by William," Ruth said, patting each of us on the arm. "You are so kind to offer to chauffeur me. Another treat."

"It's *our* treat," I heard Kit say.

"Okay, ladies, I'm ready to go." She took a step outside the front door and pulled a key from her pocket.

"Ruth, would you mind if I used your bathroom first?" Kit asked her. "Way too much coffee this morning."

I thought Ruth looked a little uncomfortable, but she graciously turned and opened her front door, leading us into a small, dark house. The layout was similar to my mother's. At least what I could see.

"The bathroom is that way." Ruth pointed toward the back of the house. "We'll wait here for you." She had wrapped her arm around mine in a girly gesture, making sure I didn't step a foot farther into the room.

"What a sweet house," I said. We could have been standing at the gates of hell, for all I knew. Heavy, dark curtains covered the windows, and although I could make out the shape of a lamp on an end table, it was too dark to really see it. Suddenly I felt something soft and furry rub against my shin, and I looked down to see a large black cat investigating my shoe.

"That's Barnabas," Ruth said, still grasping my arm. "He's so inquisitive. They all are, of course, but Barnabas is the leader. He's my little Sherlock Holmes."

"How many cats do you have?" I asked. I was eager to bend and scratch my shin but unable to move while locked in her grip. She put her index finger up to her lips and shook her head. But just then the room lit up, as Kit flicked on a light switch.

As I expected, there seemed to be cats everywhere. At least four on the couch, one on the coffee table, one asleep on a rug in front of the fireplace, and another on the kitchen counter.

"Ready?" Kit switched the light back off and headed toward the door.

I watched Ruth turn to lock it behind us, her hand shaking a little. "Are you okay?" I asked.

She took a tissue from her pocket and wiped under her eyes. "You won't say anything, will you?"

"About what?"

"The cats. I don't know how many cats a person can legally own, and believe me, I don't want to break any laws. But they have nowhere else to go."

Kit stopped her march toward the car and came back to put an arm around Ruth's shoulders. "Did you say you have a cat? I don't think I even noticed. Did you see any kitties, Val?"

"Not one." I took Ruth's hand and led her to the backseat of my car. "Now, shall we go and spend some of

William's money?" I buckled Ruth in and then stood up and closed the door, while Kit remained standing on the passenger side.

"Anything in the bathroom?" I whispered to her over the car roof.

"A lifetime supply of Tape Worm Tabs for cats. She must have PetMeds on speed dial."

"So that's all, huh?"

"I didn't find a syringe marked *Administer to Virginia Huntley to induce fake heart attack*, if that's what you're hoping to hear."

"Too bad."

"But I did find this."

From her pocket she produced a small, unmarked glass bottle. It was the kind I'd seen hundreds of times on television shows, not to mention at real hospitals, where a nurse plunged a needle into the top and withdrew the contents.

"What is it?" I kept my voice low. "Oh, it's probably something for her cats."

"Maybe. Or maybe it's that sux stuff. I bet we can find out." She turned the bottle slowly in her hand. "By the way, did you know that Ruth Greenway used to be a registered nurse?"

"*Get out.*" I bent over and glanced in the car window, relieved to see Ruth busy reading a *People* magazine Emily had left there. I stood back up. "How'd you come up with that little gem?" I asked.

"There was a picture of her in a nurse's uniform on her bedroom dresser. I could see a name badge. Ruth Greenway, RN. Looks like it was taken a million years ago. She was standing next to a young doctor. And guess who the doctor was?"

"William Stuckey," we both whispered at the same time.

I wasn't sure what surprised me most. That Kit had had enough time to check out Ruth's bedroom, or that she'd swiped a glass bottle of something or other. "Good work." I opened my car door, but before I could climb into the car, Kit whispered one more thing.

"You bet your ass it's good work. I just wonder what the hell we've got here." She dropped the bottle into her purse.

***

As we drove to Mel's Place, a homey restaurant in Sturgeon Bay, Ruth told us how much she had loved and would miss both Doris and Virginia.

"We three were the greatest friends," she said. "A day didn't pass when we didn't see each other or at least call to check in. I'll miss that the most. The check-in calls." From my rearview mirror I could see Ruth wipe away tears that rolled from under her glasses and down her cheeks. And then her mood did a one-eighty. "Here it is. We're here— Mel's Place."

William had secured a table, where he sat at the head with my mother and Emily on either side.

Alone at the other end of the table sat Minnie Ebert. She rose as soon as we entered the restaurant, waving her napkin. "Valawee, come sit here, next to me. I'm so glad to see you." I took my seat beside her. She was wearing cropped pants—*so* much better than her shorts.

"Good to see you too. I didn't know you'd be here."

"I nearly wasn't. I just stopped in to see Jean, and they were on their way out. Only polite thing to do was invite me along." She winked at me, and I was afraid one of her false eyelashes might drop into her iced tea. But they stayed put.

When the rest of us had our own iced tea placed in front of us, William proposed a toast to Doris and Virginia. At the other end of the table I could see Ruth's sad face as she took a sip.

"So you went to pick up Ruth?" Minnie whispered to me. "Did she let you inside the cat sanctuary?"

"She invited us into her home."

"So you saw all the cats?"

"I saw one or two; I didn't really count."

"One or two." Minnie threw her head back in a hearty laugh. "Valawee, you need to get your eyes checked. And maybe your nose."

"What's wrong with Ruth having cats? She's not hurting anyone, and she sure is helping the cats."

Before answering, Minnie moved in closer to me, her heavily rouged cheek almost touching mine. She smelled strongly of lavender. "It's a scam. A great big scam. Do you know she had Doris giving money every month to some stupid cat-rescue thingy? She even managed to talk Doris into setting up a trust in her will, leaving money to those critters. Wait until the family finds out about that."

I thought of Margaret being turned down by her mother when she needed a loan. "Well, I guess that was Doris's business. As I understand it, she was financially very savvy."

"She was savvy, all right."

"Ruth is going to miss her."

"Hmm, not so sure about that. Not after the argument. They weren't even speaking when Doris took a dive. But she will miss the money, all right."

"What do you mean?" I didn't really want to have this conversation, but I was afraid not to. "I thought they were great friends."

"They were, for many years, but a week or so ago, there were fireworks. Doris stopped the monthly cat payment and told Ruth she was changing her will. I doubt she had time to, though."

"Why did she want to cut the cats, er, Ruth off?"

"Because it was all a scam, as I just told you." I was pretty sure she was about to tell me to get my hearing checked along with my eyesight.

"Minnie, how do you know this stuff?"

"Valawee, this is a small town. And people confide in me."

Before she could tell me just who those people were, a chicken salad was delivered to my place mat.

***

On our way back to my mother's, after dropping Ruth off at her front door (and not being invited in), I gave Kit a recap of everything Minnie had said.

"On the first day we met, right after Doris's fall, Ruth seemed as upset about it as everyone else, right?" she asked. I could feel her peering at me, as if wanting to see as well as hear my reassurance.

I kept my eyes on the road. "Right."

"So she was either faking it, or Minnie is telling lies."

"Who's your money on?" I asked.

"Normally, ya know, I'd think the least stable of the two was lying. So let's see. We have Ruth living in the dark with ten million cats for company and dressing like a three-year-old. On the other hand, we have Minnie, who as far as I can tell is never invited anywhere but shows up just the same. No one seems to like her, but she's privy to everyone's private life. Plus, she wears false eyelashes and can't say her r's."

"You forgot her shorts."

"Do I really have to mention those?"

"So you think Minnie is lying?" I asked.

"Not necessarily."

"Okay, so you think Minnie might be telling the truth?"

"Not sure about that, either."

We pulled into my mom's driveway, next to William's car. "I wish he'd go home once in a while," I said.

"He doesn't want to leave his *girlfriend*."

"No kidding. You'd think he'd be a bit more sensitive and leave her some time alone with her family."

"You want *more* time with your mother?"

"Of course. How else am I gonna find out about those checks Doris was giving her every month?"

"Right. I could distract William—"

Before Kit could expand on her plan to sidetrack the good doctor, my phone rang. I pulled it out of my purse and saw Luke's face appear on the screen. My adorable son-in-law. His black hair was a little too long, and behind his glasses his eyes twinkled in a cheeky manner, as if he'd just heard a joke.

"It's Luke," I said. "You go on in. I want to take this."

"Give him hell," Kit said, leaving the car.

"Hi, Luke." I tried not to sound too heavyhearted, although I wanted to wring his neck for allowing Emily's foray into R-rated movies.

"How's my favorite mother-in-law?" he asked. "Just wanted to wish you a belated Happy Mother's Day." I had forgotten that he hadn't contacted me the day before, which was very unlike him.

Luke is an only child whose parents are both deceased. From the day Emily first brought him home to meet her father and me, we had become surrogate parents to him. He'd been more than a welcome addition to our little family. Until now.

I took a deep breath. I had to remember this was my daughter's deal. Luke wasn't to blame for Emily's indiscretion.

"Luke, how could you let it happen?" So much for Luke being blameless.

"Val, before you say another word, let me say this. I had no idea what Emily was getting herself into, at least not until after the damn thing was shot. All I knew was that she had a role in a creepy movie. She was so excited to get a speaking role—"

"Who's gonna be *listening*?" I countered. "Luke, I am so disappointed—"

"Me too." His voice had risen, and I could hear that he was upset.

I softened a little, remembering what a good husband he is. How he gave up a lucrative career in computers in Chicago (doing whatever it was he did) and moved jobless to California so Emily could pursue her acting career.

"So what are we going to do now?" I asked.

"I'll get a job, and this won't ever happen again."

"Wait. You'll *get* a job? I thought you were busy working on the next *Star Wars* movie or something."

"Didn't Emily tell you?"

"Tell me what?" I braced myself.

"Val, I lost my job six months ago. It's been tough. I've been working at a Starbucks part-time, trying to bring in something, but it's not nearly enough to pay our bills. Emily took that stupid role because of the money. Neither of us had any idea what she'd end up doing."

My initial thought was how cool it would be to work at my favorite coffee shop. Then I shrugged that inane thought off and sank further into my seat. Luke was out of work, but never a word from my daughter. "Why didn't you tell me sooner?" I asked.

"We didn't want to worry you. Something will turn up."

I wished I could be as confident as he sounded.

CHAPTER SIXTEEN

I wanted William to leave. I needed to be alone with my mom to ask about her name appearing in Doris's check register.

Plus, I had to tell Emily that her husband had just called me. The two confrontations couldn't take place together, though. I had to tackle them separately.

But William had a glass of port, and then another.

Margaret called to tell us the funeral for her mother would be on Thursday, with a viewing on Wednesday afternoon. She asked my mother if she would care to say a few words at the funeral, but my mom declined.

William, however, was more than happy to speak about Doris. When it was clear he wasn't about to beat it out of my mom's house any time soon, I asked Kit and Emily if they wanted to go out for a drive. They jumped at the idea, ran to change clothes, and reached my car before I did.

Kit suggested we go to a casino. I wasn't too keen on that, but Emily loved the idea. So after I started the car, Kit began googling casinos, and we headed down toward Green Bay.

"Emily," I said, when we were just minutes into our journey.

"Hmm?" she responded from the backseat.

"Luke called me."

There was no response. But I could tell Kit stopped googling to listen.

"He told me about losing his job," I said.

Still no response.

"Emily, why didn't you tell me? I could have helped. We could have figured something out; there was no need to—"

"Mom." Emily reached forward and put her hands on my shoulders. "We didn't want to worry you. Luke will find something. He's really smart—"

"I know how smart he is," I said. But what I thought was, *how smart* is *he to let his wife take that awful role?* "There was no need—"

"Mom, we wanted to figure this out on our own."

"Are you in debt?" Kit asked, setting down her phone. I hadn't had time to share Luke's news with her, but she caught on fast.

"No. Well, not that bad," Emily replied quickly.

I groaned. "Then why did you take that role—"

"Mom, I've told you a million times. I didn't know what the role would entail. If I'd known, do you think I would have continued?"

I had to think about that. If they really were in debt, maybe she took the job willingly. "I just wish you had let me know—"

"How much?" Kit asked. "How much do you need? To get by? I'll write you a check. A gift, not a loan. Give me a number—"

Emily slid along the seat and reached her right arm out to give Kit a hug. "Auntie Kit, there's no need for that. We are fine now."

If the lights had been on in the car, I would have caught the smile that I knew covered Kit's face. Emily hadn't called her Auntie Kit for a long time, and I felt Kit's hand squeeze my leg.

"How can you be fine?" I asked, as I tried to see Emily's face in the rearview mirror. "I'm sure the money from that movie wouldn't go far in California. Or anywhere else, for that matter."

"We have Luke's Starbucks money, and he got some severance pay when he lost his job. We're okay, Mom. Really."

"I'm writing you a check when we get home," I heard Kit say in her *that's that* voice.

"If anyone is writing her a check, it's me," I said.

Emily leaned forward and gave us each a kiss on the cheek. "We are fine. And neither one of you needs to write anything. Dad gave us some money."

"Aargh." I tightened my hold on the steering wheel. The last thing I wanted to hear was that her father came to their rescue. Everyone knows he is the most irresponsible man on earth, whereas I am always there for them. No matter what.

"Does your dad know about the movie?" Kit asked, and I was so glad she did.

"No! He'd have a cow. He was in LA on business, and he took us out to dinner. I guess it didn't take him long to figure out Luke wasn't working."

"Really?" Kit asked. Like me, she knew that if David had picked them up from a refrigerator box under the freeway, he wouldn't necessarily figure out they had money problems.

"Yes. We didn't mean to tell him. But it was sort of obvious. And when he left, I found a very generous check in my purse. Wasn't that sweet of him?"

"He's a saint," Kit said, turning toward the window to watch the road rush by us.

"Yeah, a real saint," I said.

We continued in silence. Emily sat back in her seat, and I mulled over the conversation that had just taken place. I was a little jealous that David had come through for Emily and Luke. But for the rest of the journey I concentrated on telling myself it was the very least he could do.

***

We ended up at the casino Kit had located on her phone. The three of us sat on tall stools at the bar and ordered beers from a pretty waitress who looked too young to be there.

"I'm so glad we left." Emily took a sip of her beer and wiped the creamy froth from her top lip.

There were several tables nearby, mostly filled with young men who looked as if they just got off their shift at a meatpacking or paper plant. I was amused, but not surprised, that many of them were checking Emily out. She was wearing tight jeans and a Grateful Dead T-shirt, with her hair falling in thick, silvery-blond locks down her back. Who wouldn't be checking her out?

"I think William was glad we left too," Kit said. She looked as comfortable in a Midwestern casino as she would have at the Ritz in Paris. And when she took a sip of *her* beer, it didn't leave a frothy mark.

"So, Mom, what do we think of William and Grandma?" Emily asked. A young man dressed in jeans and a Packers T-shirt walked past, his eyes never leaving Emily.

"Why? Do you know something?"

"No, of course not. Just wondering what you think. They seem pretty close."

I hadn't shared with Emily any of the stuff Kit and I had found on Doris's desk, including the note—presumably written by William—that concerned money. "He's very fond of your grandma, that much is clear. And he certainly treats her well. I just think . . ."

"He's full of shit?" Kit offered.

"Thank you *so* much for that little insight." I suppressed a chuckle. I didn't protest because I thought she might be right.

"Well, I'm gonna play some blackjack." Emily hopped down off her stool.

"I'll come with you." Kit daintily slid her feet to the floor.

"Then I guess I better come, too, and keep an eye on you both." I followed them.

For a Monday evening, the place was jammed. Emily found one empty seat at a table, and Kit and I stood behind her. Kit had switched to vodka martinis, but I held on to my original beer. I was driving, and the last thing I needed was to get a ticket for being over the limit. My mom was already going to have a coronary if we told her we'd been to a casino.

When a bald guy sitting next to Emily finally left, Kit quickly took his seat. After watching them both win and lose a few hands, I decided to walk around the place. It had an atmosphere both carefree and exciting, and I could see the temptation it presented to people after a hard day's work.

There were a dozen or so blackjack tables, all full, and closer to the back of the room were the higher-stakes games. From a table requiring a minimum bet of one hundred dollars came a big whoop, and several people began cheering. I strolled over to get a look at the winner.

I was shocked to see it was someone I knew.

***

"Tom!" I'd retreated to the ladies room and dug my phone out of my purse.

"That's me. Whaddya want, Val?" he growled. Just how I love him.

"I need you to do something for me."

"You must mean something *more*. Let me guess—you got *yourself* a part in a porno movie. *Pankowski Does*

Pewaukee?" I heard him laugh at his own joke. Well, someone had to.

"That's so hilarious, Tom. By the way, you are still working on the Emily thing, right?"

"I'm on it. What do you want *now?* I'm in the middle of a poker game here. Aces full, so make it quick."

"Okay, it's just a small thing. Can you check out a Margaret Edwards for me? She's—"

"Doris Dibble's daughter. I know."

"Good. She lives in—"

"Minneapolis. I know."

"Okay. So can you find out what she really does there? And don't say something in computers. Also, can you check out her finances?"

"PANKOWSKI! What the hell do you think I'm running, a friggin' detective agency?"

"Tom, it's important. Well, it might be important."

"Does it have anything to do with Emily?"

"Yes," I lied. Knowing Tom's adoration of my daughter, I figured he'd be more apt to do a little digging for her than for me. "Maybe. I just need to know what she does and if she's in any kind of trouble. I'm thinking financial."

"Speaking of . . . *you're* not in any kind of trouble, are you, Kiddo?"

"No, of course not. By the way, Doris's funeral is Thursday, so it looks like I won't be back until the weekend at the earliest. Okay?"

"Okay? No, it's not okay. But I doubt there's much I can do about it. While we're on the subject, have you found out anything about her house?"

"House?"

"Yeah, house, Pankowski. Big brick structures that people live in. I can understand you might not be familiar with the term since you haven't sold any recently."

"Right. Well, I'm working hard on that too."

"If you think Margaret Edwards is having money problems, it might be a good time for her to sell."

"If she even owns the house."

"Dammit, that's what you're supposed to find out."

"I know. I will. I would just like a little background on Margaret."

"And this relates to Emily how?"

"Well, it doesn't really. It's a separate issue." I'd thought better of my earlier lie and didn't want Tom to waste time digging up unnecessary stuff.

"Okay, okay. I'll see what I can find out. I gotta go."

"Thanks, Tom. Thanks for everything. For the Margaret stuff and the Emily stuff."

"Anyone else you need me to run down for you?"

"I'll let you know. And I really owe you."

"You bet you do, especially if I lose this hand." He hung up.

***

"I don't know why we have to leave so early," Emily said. "It's not even nine."

I wasn't sure, either, except it seemed imperative that we get out of the casino before Margaret spotted us. I'd watched her wrap her hands around five stacks of chips and pull them toward her. I didn't know how much they were worth, but judging from her reaction, and those of her blackjack buddies, she appeared to have hit a jackpot.

"Exactly. It's *almost nine*. Grandma will be worried. Plus, I don't want her to be on her own for too long."

"Er, she's not on her own. She's got Willy the Wonder Dog with her, remember?" Kit said.

"Well, surely he's gone by now." I steered both of them out the door to my car. I thought I spotted Margaret's Dodge in the parking lot, and I rushed them both past it.

"You're acting odd," Kit said, as we turned onto the highway. "Even for you."

"Shush," I said. "We'll talk later." Emily was in the backseat, engrossed in a phone conversation with Luke, but even so, I didn't want to take a chance that she'd hear what I had to tell Kit.

"Tell Luke hi," I called over my shoulder.

"My mom says hi." She turned the phone in my direction and hit the speaker button.

"Hi, Val," I heard him say. At least I knew she really was talking to her husband.

I watched her mute the speaker, and then she resumed their conversation.

"Now tell me what's up," Kit said. "You didn't rob the casino, did you?"

"Ha ha." I paused. "I don't want Em to hear us," I whispered, turning slightly to see if Emily was lost in conversation.

Kit nodded and then scooted forward a little bit and turned on the radio. She fiddled with the dial until she came to NPR, where a man with a droning Southern accent was describing his recent visit to the Himalayas. She turned up the volume, and in my rearview mirror I could see Emily put a finger in one ear to drown out the sound.

"Okay," I whispered, when I was certain my daughter wasn't listening to us, "you won't believe who was at the casino."

"Who? Frank Sinatra, Wayne Newton? Tell me, for crying out loud."

"Margaret. Margaret Edwards."

"With Stan?"

"I didn't see Stan. As far as I could tell, Margaret was on her own. Well, except for the other six players, of course."

"Darn it. I was hoping we'd catch those two in a tryst."

"Tryst? Who says *tryst*?"

"It's a word. I can use it. So . . . our Margaret likes to gamble?"

"I guess so. And didn't she just call us, like a few hours ago, to tell us about her mom's funeral?"

"The two are hardly related, ya know."

141

"Who? Who's hardly related?" Emily's face suddenly appeared between our seats. "Geez, Mom, are you going deaf? The radio's so loud, I can barely hear Luke."

"Sorry, honey." I turned the volume down just a smidge and waited until Emily was back in her seat, talking to Luke again.

"Another thing," I whispered to Kit. "I called Tom and asked him to check out Margaret."

"Tom?" she replied, after thinking it over a few seconds. Kit has known Tom Haskins as long as I have; we went to the same high school, and he hung out with her husband, Larry, and my older brother, Buddy. But that doesn't mean Kit and Tom like each other. "And just how do you think *Tom Haskins* can check anything out?"

"He's got a lot of connections, Kit. He knew all about Doris's company. He might just find out something useful."

"Unless one of his so-called *connections* is sitting right next to him at a poker table, I don't see him being much help."

"That's not fair. Tom gets around. He knows stuff."

"Hmm . . ." She mumbled something else I couldn't hear.

"What? What are you saying?"

"I said he couldn't find his own ass, even with a GPS."

"Who's got a GPS? What are you guys talking about?" It was Emily. She'd finished her conversation, and her head again appeared between our seats.

"Nothing important, darling." Kit gave Emily's cheek a quick kiss. "We were just saying how difficult it is for some people to find things. How's that cute husband of yours?"

***

When we pulled into my mom's driveway, I saw William's car still parked there. "Damn. I'm surprised he's still here," I said.

But that wasn't even the half of it.

I knocked on the front door, and William opened it. His grin extended almost to his earlobes, and before I could say a word, he engulfed me in a huge hug. "Ah, Valerie. Come in, come in."

When he released me, he pulled Emily into a similar hug, and then it was Kit's turn. My mom was sitting on the couch, and I swear she was sporting a smaller version of the same grin. But it quickly disappeared as she stood up. "Where have you girls been? I was getting worried."

"We just drove around and stopped for hamburgers," I said. "What's going on?"

"Well, sit down, all of you. We have some news." She gently pushed all three of us to the couch, and then she and William stood in front of us.

I noticed they held hands. It looked almost obscene. I tried to remember if I'd ever seen my mother hold my father's hand, but no memory was forthcoming.

"Emily. What does Grateful Dead mean?" my mother asked, as she eyed Emily's T-shirt.

"It's a rock-and-roll group," William whispered loudly into my mother's ear. "Nothing to worry about, my dear."

"From Europe?" she whispered back.

"No, from the good old USA," Kit said.

"Never mind about that," William said. "Your mother and I have some wonderful news."

"They're planning a comeback tour?" Kit asked, and I gave her ankle a little kick.

And then I saw it. How I had missed it when I first came into the room, I'll never know. On my mother's left hand was a ring. A big honking ring. A diamond as big as Texas.

When she realized I'd spotted it, she held up her hand for us all to see. "William Stuckey has asked me to marry him." She suddenly looked coy, sweet, and definitely happy.

"And this lovely lady said yes," William announced.

CHAPTER SEVENTEEN

Y ou didn't act very happy for Grandma," Emily said. We were in our room getting our pajamas on and straightening out our belongings that seemed to end up littered on the beds, chair, and night tables, no matter how organized we tried to stay. I'd about had it with living out of a suitcase.

But Emily was right. It was hard for me to muster up any joy at the moment. Luckily, no one else wanted to stay up and celebrate, either. We were all tired and wanted to get to bed. "Oh, Em, it's just such a change. And you know I don't like *any* change, let alone my mother marrying someone besides my dad."

"But Mom! Grandpa's been gone a long time, and surely you don't want Grandma to live alone, not when she can be *married* to William." Apparently, it was a no-brainer as far as Emily was concerned.

"I'm just tired, Emily. Let's call it a night and talk about this tomorrow."

"Well, I don't know what there is to talk about." She sounded just like she had when she insisted on going to college in California. And by the way, I'd been right about that. She'd been miserable and returned to Illinois after one semester.

I hoped I wasn't right this time too.

We said good-night and settled into our respective twin beds. I closed my eyes and thought about my mom and William. I pictured his Cheshire-cat grin and wondered how anyone could put up with that on a daily basis.

During my childhood my mother constantly complained about the way my father brushed his teeth (in her opinion, he always took too long), and she disliked the way he read the paper, working backward from the last page to the first.

I turned my thoughts to sweet memories of my dad, but soon found myself consumed with the troubling note we'd found in Doris's study, the one written by William. *Our* William, we assumed. *We need to see a sample of his handwriting*, I suddenly realized, wondering why I hadn't thought of it sooner.

Even more disturbing was my mother's name in the check register. What was up with her? Was she a blackmailer? Or worse? Did she have something to do with Doris's death, and maybe even Virginia's? I suddenly remembered how she left home to get a cherry pie during the time Virginia would have been dying. Were my mother and her fiancé in this together?

I waited until I heard the deep breathing that told me Emily was sound asleep, and then I climbed out of bed and tiptoed to the living room, where Kit was lying on the sofa bed. I sat down on the edge and peered into her face, trying to tell if she was awake. Then I decided it didn't matter. "Kit!" I hissed. "Kit, we need to talk."

She jerked, and her eyes flew open. After staring at me wide-eyed for a few seconds, she pushed up on one elbow. "Val, what on earth are—"

"I said, we need to talk."

"About . . . ?"

"About the fact that my mom might be engaged to a murderer."

"Oh, that."

"What do you mean *oh, that?*" I asked.

"I mean you seemed to think I was making a big deal out of everything." She sat upright and pushed the blanket off her. I wondered if she was having a hot flash. "*You're* the one who didn't believe anyone was being blackmailed or murdered." She was enjoying this way too much.

"Well, that was before my mom got engaged to William. And besides, I *have* been worried about my mom getting money from Doris. You know I have. I just haven't felt that meant anyone was blackmailed or murdered. But now I'm not so sure. We do have to get to the bottom of this, whatever it is. I can't let her marry William until we know who he really is. Don't you see?"

"Yes, Valley Girl, I see." Kit reached her arms around me and gave me a gentle hug. "But can we sleep on it first?" She pulled back, but her face was just inches from mine as she awaited my answer.

"Yeah, sure. Of course."

But I knew full well *I* wouldn't be sleeping.

***

I heard the squeak of my mom's bedroom door the minute she opened it the next morning. I'd been fully awake for at least an hour, and I'd been half-awake, it seemed, all night before that. I bounded out of bed and got to the kitchen before she was finished in the bathroom.

"Valerie!" she barely managed to whisper when she saw me. "What are you doing up so early?"

"I guess I take after you; I'm up by five thirty more often than not." Then I decided to stop stalling. "Mom, I have to ask you something."

She poured water into the coffeepot and reached for her coffee canister, which unbeknownst to her held Starbucks. I wasn't sure she'd heard me, but just as I started to repeat myself, she turned.

"Yes, Valerie. I noticed you seemed less than thrilled about my engagement to William Stuckey." She frowned as she wiped her hands on a dish towel and then sat down at the table, as if bracing for my opinion.

I saw that she wasn't wearing the Rock of Gibraltar on her ring finger. Did I dare hope? Knowing my mom, I decided she probably just took it off to protect it. "Well, for starters," I said, "I do have to wonder if *marrying* a man whom you call only by his full name seems the natural thing to do. I mean, do you really know William all that well, Mom?"

"Valerie, I've known him for most of my life! And he was your dad's good friend."

"Yes, but was he *your* good friend? And how well did dad know him, anyway? I mean, how much do you get to know a person playing golf?"

"Well, your father always said that was an *excellent* way to get to know someone, like if they cheat or—"

"Yes, that could certainly come in handy if you're thinking of marrying someone, I guess. But Mom, that's not what I want to talk about."

"And why *don't* you want to talk about my marrying William Stuckey, er, William? There, is that better? Why don't you want me to marry him?"

"I didn't say that, Mom. But first things first." I sat down next to her at the table. I wanted to make sure she could hear me while I kept whispering. I wanted Kit to stay asleep. Usually, her presence makes me braver, but I knew I couldn't count on my mom to tell the truth in front of my friend.

Damn. Why had everything gotten so complicated, when all I wanted to do was come celebrate Mother's Day with my mom? The words from a Bob Seger song floated through my head. *Wish I didn't know now what I didn't know then.*

"Go on, Valerie. You obviously have something to get off your chest."

"Let me get us some coffee first." I rose and poured us each a cup of the strong brew. And then I asked her. "Mom, why was Doris Dibble writing you a check for five thousand dollars every month?"

My mom swallowed her first sip of coffee and furrowed her brow. "Has Katherine put something in this coffee? It's so strong."

"No," I said. And technically, it was the truth. "Well, Mom? The checks?" I pushed.

"Valerie Caldwell, I have no idea what you're talking about."

Valerie *Caldwell?* That hadn't been my name for more than a quarter of a century.

"Okay, Mom. Here's the truth. I'm not proud of it, but when Kit and I were cleaning up at Stan's the other night, we were in Doris's study—"

"Why on earth were you in—"

"Shhh, Mom. You'll wake up Kit."

"I should wake her up. And I should give her a darn good spanking."

I chuckled, and my mom had to shush *me.* But the image of my mom giving Kit a spanking was, well, it was as ludicrous as Doris Dibble giving my mom five thousand dollars every month.

"That girl was always trouble. Any time you were with her, I had to worry what she'd be leading you into. She—"

"Mom, this isn't about Kit. This is about *you.* We were in Doris's study, uh, looking for any dirty dishes—"

"Dirty dishes in Doris's study? You'll have to do better than that, Valerie. Did you also check out the attic for stray cups?"

"Whatever," I said, even though I hated that lazy response when other people used it. "I couldn't help but see your name in her check register," I continued quickly. "She'd written you a check for five thousand dollars! So of course I looked closer, and I saw that she'd been doing that on the first of every month. What's that about, Mom?"

She had the same incredulous look on her face that had appeared when I first asked the question. And I started to believe that my mom truly didn't know what I was talking about.

"Making wedding plans?" My mother and I both jumped when Kit suddenly appeared, her voice still husky from sleep. She had a black-and-gold Japanese kimono-style robe wrapped tightly around her body, and it looked as if it cost more than a month of my wages. "What time is it, anyway?" Kit squinted at the microwave clock. "Yikes, you two *are* early birds."

"Go back to sleep," I said, hoping she heard the firmness in my voice. I couldn't believe she could joke about wedding plans after I'd told her how afraid I was for my mom. Why wasn't she *getting* it?

"Too late," my oblivious friend answered, and she reached into the cupboard for a coffee cup. Joining us at the table, she ignored my glower and turned to my mom. "So, Jean, is it going to be a lavish affair, this wedding?"

"Katherine, Valerie tells me you two were snooping in Doris's study." She was still whispering but suddenly seemed to realize the sleeping person was now seated next to her. She continued in a loud voice. "That was beyond inappropriate of you two. I've never—"

"We were just trying to be helpful to your friend," Kit said.

"What friend?" My mother gave her a fierce look.

"Doris, of course." Kit returned my mother's glare.

"And just how was snooping in her study supposed to help a dead woman?"

While I was glad to have Kit's support, I wasn't sure I wanted her to have this conversation with my mother. But I remained silent.

"It could help her get justice," Kit said. "That's all we want for Doris. If someone *pushed* her down the stairs, then we think that little fact should come to light. That's all."

I decided it was time to speak up. "Mom, I don't care about anything except *why Doris was giving you so much money.* And all those gifts," I added for good measure. "Are you in some kind of trouble?"

"Valerie, I'm going to say this one time, and then this subject is closed. I know nothing about any money, from Doris or anyone else. Doris gave me lavish gifts, that's true. She was generous with everyone that way. But I never took a damn dime from her."

Ooooh, she was swearing. The only times I'd heard my mom say *damn* in my whole life, she immediately followed it with a justification. And sure enough, here it came.

"This is enough to make a preacher swear," she said, and then she stood up and walked quickly out of the kitchen. Kit and I both flinched when we heard her bedroom door slam.

"That went well," Kit said a few seconds later. She took another sip of her coffee and idly turned the page of a Bed Bath & Beyond catalog lying on the table.

"Kit." I leaned in closer. "*Kit.*"

"What?" She looked up at me.

"We've got to find out more about William. For starters, we've got to see his handwriting—make sure he's the William who wrote Doris that note. I don't feel right about this. And it's not the marrying part; it's that I don't know enough about him. I don't care if my mom *has* known him for a hundred years. That doesn't mean *I* know him. Oh *man*. I just thought of something: he's going to be my stepfather."

"That's right, baby doll." She had returned to the catalog. "Look, they've got Calphalon on sale."

"Would you please pay attention?"

"Truly nonstick, Val. I love mine."

"How can we find out about William?"

She sighed and took another long sip of her coffee. "Ya know, you could just ask him. However, that didn't seem to work out too well with your mother just now. How about enlisting your supersleuth pal, Tom Haskins? While he's busy putting the feelers out on Margaret, maybe he could place a few calls—"

"Stop. I'm not calling Tom." I watched her smile wickedly as she turned a page. "Got any good ideas, smart girl?" I asked.

"Hmm." She reached the last page of the catalog and slapped it closed. "As a matter of fact, I do."

CHAPTER EIGHTEEN

My mom stayed in her bedroom for an hour or so and then finally emerged, dressed and fully made-up.

"Valerie, I have decided to forget our little conversation earlier. This is a happy day for me. A happy day. Understand?"

I nodded obediently. Kit was in the shower, and I was glad to not have her around for the time being. "I'm sorry," I said, although we both knew I wasn't. "I just worry about you, that's all."

"Well, I'll let you know when you need to worry. And right now, you don't. Got it?"

"Yes." I nodded. "So, what's your plan for the day?"

"I'm going shopping with Emily. You don't need to come with us. You and Katherine can take in some of the sights. I'm cooking dinner tonight for William Stuckey. I'd be pleased to have my whole family around me."

I gave her a raised-eyebrows look.

"Okay, *William*," she said. But I could see she was thinking about it. "No, William *Stuckey* it is. Get used to it, Valerie."

***

Kit's plan was simple. Rather than ask William about his past, we would ask Ruth, since obviously she had known him well enough to have a picture of him in her bedroom. Once my mother and Emily left, Kit called Ruth and asked if we could buy her breakfast. She was delighted.

But first, I had to scour my mom's place for a sample of William's handwriting. I knew it wouldn't take long. A woman who alphabetizes her canned goods would no doubt have a well-organized system for keeping cards and letters from friends.

Sure enough, in her filing cabinet inside her bedroom closet was a folder labeled *Keepsakes*. And in that folder were a number of cards from William.

"I don't know, Kit. The note to Doris was signed *Wm.* All these cards are signed *William*. And I can't really remember how the other signature looked, and how are we going to get back into Doris's—"

"This is the same." Kit nodded her head up and down and tapped the note and signature at the bottom of a valentine. "I'd recognize that *k* anywhere." She pointed to the word *kind*, written with distinctive flourishes like something out of eighteenth-century penmanship.

"He had a *k* in that other note?"

"Yes, he did. *K* as in *know*—and *kill*."

"Wow. Good memory, Kitty Kat." But then it sank in. "Damn! I didn't want that note to be from *our* William."

Kit gave me a sympathetic look and a pat on the back; and then, ever my Kitty Kat, she moved things right along. "Let's go get Ruth."

***

Ruth was standing outside waiting for us, her front door firmly closed behind her. "Whoop-de-do!" She ran down the short path from her house to the car. "This is a real treat."

Before we could even get out and offer to help her, she had opened the back passenger door and climbed in. She was wearing the red hat covered with sequins that we'd seen before. She also had on a black sweatshirt with two cat's eyes, one of them winking.

"You look nice," Kit said, turning toward the backseat and sounding sincere.

"Thanks." Ruth broke into a wide smile, and I had to agree with Kit. I was getting used to Ruth's feline-adorned outfits and would have been disappointed if she appeared catless.

"What's Jean doing today?" Ruth settled back in the seat. "I thought she might be with you."

"She's taking Emily shopping." I didn't want to mention the engagement. I felt sure my mother had a plan to break the news to her pals, one that included CNN and Fox. I didn't want to spoil that for her.

We drove to the Town Hall Café and Bakery, *another* charming eatery (weren't they all, in Door County?), and when we were seated, Ruth took off her humongous specs and cleaned them with a tiny soft cloth she had taken out of her purse. Without the glasses she looked a lot older, and I realized they were a fashion statement that worked. For her, at least.

"My mother's cooking dinner for William tonight," I said, as a clumsy attempt to bring him into the conversation.

"That so?" She returned the glasses to her face and opened the menu that had been placed before her.

"Yeah, he and my mom seem pretty close."

"You betcha." Ruth nodded. "I think I'm gonna have this omelet. It has cheese and mushrooms." She smiled at her good choice and set the menu down.

"How long have you known William?" Kit asked.

"Me? William and I have been friends for a long, long time."

"Before he moved to Door County?" I asked, just to see how she'd answer.

"Way, way before that. We worked together for a while down in Chicago."

"He was practicing medicine there, right?" Kit asked.

Ruth laughed and then took a sip of water. "Yes. You know they always say doctors *practice* . . ." She had made air quotes around the word practice and laughed again. "Seems a funny way to say it. Practicing medicine—uff da, as Virginia would say, rest her soul. Like we're waiting for them to get off their hineys and start working for real, huh?"

"Good point. It is silly. But what kind of doctor was William?" Kit persisted.

"He was the finest doctor I ever worked with. I was a nurse, you see, before I retired. And a darn good one too." I noticed she'd put more air quotes around the word *retired*, and her face grew solemn, as if the memory of it wasn't happy.

"That's not hard to believe," I said. "Did you not want to retire?"

She gently laid a wrinkled hand over mine, which was resting on the table. "At the time, no. But I haven't thought about it since. I've been so preoccupied with the cats. They keep me busy. People think cats care for themselves, but the truth is—"

"Did William retire at the same time?" Kit interrupted the cat soliloquy.

"Uh, yes. We were both in the same boat. After the business with . . . with the hospital, we decided it was time to leave it to the younger folks."

"What business?" I asked.

"It was bad, toots. But it's all in the past now. If you don't mind, I'd rather not talk about it. These days I just concentrate on my cats. They are so energetic and—"

"Look," Kit said. "The lady at the next table is having an omelet too. It looks good."

***

We dropped Ruth Greenway off at her house two hours later. We had learned nothing more about the incident at the hospital where she had worked with William, but we did learn more than anyone needs to know about raising and caring for cats, despite our attempts to silence her on the subject.

When we got back to my mom's, she and Emily were still gone.

"Do you know the name of the hospital where William worked?" Kit asked me, as soon as we were inside.

"No," I said. "All I know is, he was a good pal of my father's. It seemed like they played golf together every Saturday."

"So we know it was probably a hospital in or close to Downers Grove, right?"

"I suppose." I emptied two cans of iced tea into tall glasses and handed one to Kit. She didn't bother to hide her disdain for the drink. She always makes her own iced tea from scratch, as does my mom. But Emily, probably because of her youth, had no time to steep tea bags and was a huge fan of canned drinks. Maybe she bought them when she was out in William's car.

"Can you think of any other friends of your dad's who might also know William?" Kit asked.

I sat down on the couch next to her. "Yes, there was another guy they were both friends with. Henry Crandall. He was a doctor too. My dad and mom often played bridge with Henry and his wife, Beth. I know they still live in Downers Grove. I've sold houses in their neighborhood."

Kit looked excited. She plunked the untasted iced tea on the table. "Okay, here's what you do. Call him and tell him we're planning something for William and your mom, to celebrate their engagement. We need info on William's early career, that kind of thing."

"Are you nuts? I haven't spoken to the man in a million years. I doubt he'd even remember me."

"Come on, Valley Girl. Who could forget you?"

***

We found Henry Crandall's home number quite easily with a brief Internet search. His wife answered the phone and to my surprise did remember me. I told her the purpose of my call, and when I made her promise not to breathe a word of the engagement, she was delighted to conspire with us.

Henry wasn't home at that moment, but Beth gave me his cell number and assured me he'd love hearing from me. She reiterated that she wouldn't say a word to him herself.

Ten minutes later, armed with a fresh cup of coffee and a rough script written by Kit, I sat across my mom's kitchen table from my best friend, and we called Henry Crandall, putting him on speakerphone.

He was waiting for my call (so much for Beth's promise of secrecy), and we chatted for a while. He asked how my mother was, and then William.

"The reason I'm calling," I said, "is because we want to put together a little something for my mom and William; you know, a story with pictures, showing the highlights of their lives. But you mustn't breathe a word because they haven't announced their engagement yet."

"Mum's the word," he said, and I hoped he was more trustworthy than his wife.

"Okay," I continued. "Any idea what prompted William to retire?"

Silence.

"Dr. Crandall?"

"Valerie, you'll have to ask him about that. We all have our own reasons for doing certain things. I'm afraid I would only be giving you my opinion, and I'm not sure I have all the facts."

"Well, just a general idea, then?"

"Sorry. That's for him to say."

I realized that was all I was going to get out of Dr. Crandall, so I asked a few meaningless questions to support my story of putting something together for my mom and William. "Well, thank you so much for your time," I said, as soon as I felt I could without making him suspicious enough to call William. "I really appreciate this."

"No problem. When's the wedding?"

"They haven't gotten that far yet, but I assume it will be soon."

"Good for them. Although I must say I'm a little surprised."

"How so?"

"Just between you and me, I always thought William would end up marrying Virginia Huntley. They were quite an item. But that was before your mom moved up to Door County."

"No kidding. I had no idea."

"Yes, he took Virginia with him to a couple of medical conferences where he was speaking. They seemed close."

"I had no idea," I repeated, feeling stunned.

"How is Virginia, by the way?"

I hesitated. But remembering that he was a doctor and probably had had to deliver bad news himself a few times, I plunged ahead. "I'm so sorry to tell you this, but Virginia passed away recently."

He was silent on the other end.

"Heart attack," I added. I wasn't about to go into Kit's—and my?—suspicions.

"I'm so sorry to hear that," Henry Crandall said. "My wife will be sad. She always liked Virginia."

"One last thing, Dr. Crandall."

"Call me Henry, please. You used to come over and swim in our pool with my boys when you were little."

"Okay, Henry. Yes, I remember. How are your boys?"

"Grown and gone." He sounded rather relieved.

"Well, just one last question. Do you know Ruth Greenway?"

"Yes. Don't tell me she's—"

"She's fine. I just wanted to include her in our story. She used to work with William, right?"

"Yes," he said tersely.

"Anything you can tell me—"

"Again, my dear, you should ask them. Although I'm not sure their association is something they would want dredged up."

We said our good-byes, and I noticed Kit—who had been taking notes—had an *aha* look on her face.

She put down her pen. "Aha!" she said.

CHAPTER NINETEEN

My phone was still in my hand when it startled me by ringing. Because my peepers were perched on my nose, I could read the number on the display. "Who's calling me from Wisconsin?"

"Um, why don't you answer and find out?" Kit raised her eyebrows at me. "We *are in* Wisconsin, ya know."

"Yes, but apart from my mom, I don't know anyone up here who would have my number."

"Then answer it!" she ordered, sounding just like my mother.

I slid my finger across the bottom of my phone and then spoke into it. "Hello?"

"Val, sorry to bother you, but you're a Realtor, aren't you?"

"Yes, uh, to whom am I speaking?"

"Sorry. This is Stan Dibble. Sorry. I'm just a little stressed out. I need to sell my house, Val. I thought you could help me."

If Tom has called and badgered him, I'll kill him, I thought. But surely not. Even Tom wouldn't be that pushy just to help a fellow Realtor in Wisconsin. Unless he owed the Realtor *really* big-time.

"Val . . . are you there?"

"Sorry, Stan. I don't get the best reception here. You kinda cut out on me."

I love talking on a cell phone. Such freedom. How did we ever function without the ability to claim faulty reception to end a call on a whim or explain the silence sometimes required to mull stuff over? Like why Stan was suddenly calling me about selling his house. If it even *was* his house to sell.

"Did we cut out again?" he asked.

"There I heard you. Can you hear me?"

"Yeah, I can hear just great. Can you, Val?"

"Can I what?" I looked at Kit, and then I raised my eyebrows at her, hoping to convey that something weird was going on.

"*What?*" she mouthed.

"Help me sell my house." Stan sounded a little frustrated.

"Sorry, this phone—"

"Look, could we just meet and talk?"

"Well, sure, Stan. I suppose I can come over right now—"

"No, not here."

"Well, I don't think my mom's place—"

"No! Not your mom's. I'd appreciate it if you'd keep this on the down-low for now, Val. Let's meet at Luna in a half hour."

"Luna, yes. I'll be—"

But he'd hung up.

I looked at my phone like *how dare he?* "Well, that was a bit presumptuous."

"What?" Kit asked. She didn't like being outside any loop.

"I don't know. I really don't know. Stan wants me to meet him at Luna, to talk about selling his house. And he doesn't want me to say anything to anyone."

"Luna? What's that?"

"It's a coffee shop, Kit, but that's not the important part here."

"I know, I know. I didn't realize the house was *his* to sell. And if it is, why the secret? Anyway, how can you help him? You're not licensed in Wisconsin."

"Well, he didn't exactly give me a chance to discuss all that, now, did he?"

"I'm going with you, ya know."

"He said he wanted to keep it on the down-low, so I'm pretty sure that meant for me to come alone." I didn't tell Kit it also has another meaning in urban slang; she would only tease me for the thousandth time about watching too much *Law & Order.*

"I don't have to sit at the table with you, ya know. You can drop me off a block away. But I want to be nearby with my phone in case you need me."

"Kit, really? You're going to turn this into—"

"Yes, I am, since the alternative is I sit here alone and wait for your mom and Emily to come home with their Depends and their souvenirs."

"Kit! That's so mean. That's my mother and my daughter—"

"I was just kidding, Val. You know I love them."

"I know you love Emily."

We both laughed, and I went to my bedroom for my purse, while she grabbed hers and went into the bathroom, no doubt to make sure her lipstick was perfect.

***

I assumed Stan wanted to meet in Fish Creek to give us a little distance from his friends and neighbors in Egg Harbor. But there he sat, in a window seat at the Luna

Coffee and Gift Market in the historic Whistling Swan building on Main Street. And if the world is small, Door County is miniscule. Surely he knew he was risking being seen by *someone* he knew.

"Hey, Stan," I said as I approached. "Is this private enough? I mean, aren't you afraid we'll be seen?"

"We can say we just ran into each other. No big deal. I just don't want to be overheard by some busybody."

I sat down next to him and took the coffee he'd already bought for me. Presumptuous again. "Well, what's this all about? Is it your house to sell, Stan?" How like Kit of me, getting right to the point. But I did feel her presence down the street and could almost hear her voice in my ear, directing me.

"Gonna find out soon. The will is going to be read after the funeral. But Doris always said it was mine; she even made me promise to keep it up and told me how to word *my* will so it would stay in her family. The idea was that once Margaret got her act together, it could be passed on . . . like she was so sure Margaret would outlive me. But why would she think that?"

"Well, did you ask her?"

"No, I . . . didn't want to upset her."

"So you let her think you'd make sure the house eventually ended up with Margaret, who she assumed would have her act together by then, when you had no intention of doing anything but sell it, before Doris is even buried?"

He had *busted* written all over his face. But all he said was, "She's being cremated."

"You know what I mean, Stan."

"Things have changed for me, Val. I need the money. I couldn't afford to keep that place up, anyway. I have to sell it."

"Why do you need the money so badly?"

He sat up straight and looked surprised. "If you don't mind, I'd rather not discuss that with you. It's kinda personal."

"What do you want from me, then? I can't sell a house in Wisconsin; I'm licensed only in Illinois."

"I thought maybe you could connect me with someone I could trust to keep it on the q.t., someone licensed in Wisconsin but not from Door County. I don't want anyone to know it's being sold."

"Well, they'll find out." *How dumb* are *you?* I thought.

"If they don't find out until after it's sold, I don't care."

Okay, so maybe *I* was the dumb one. "But if it's your house to sell, they can't stop you," I felt the need to point out.

"Val, I just don't want to go there with Margaret or any of Doris's friends. The lawyer hasn't set a definite time to read the will, but that should happen soon—"

"So you're *not* sure it's even your house to sell."

"No. Yes, I am. Doris assured me. And I want to be ready to sell, so I want to call a Realtor right now. Can you help me?" Stan sounded as if he were losing patience with me.

I thought of the friend Tom had told me about, the friend in Wisconsin that he "owed." I wasn't at all sure I wanted to give Stan any help. But he could do whatever he wanted to do without me. Deciding I preferred to be in his loop—more accurately, deciding *Kit* would insist we stay in his loop—I finally answered him. "I'll get a name for you. Let me make a few calls."

I rose to leave, but he grabbed my arm—a little too urgently, I thought. "Call right now," he said. "Please."

I sat back down and looked at him, finally deciding he looked more desperate than dangerous (*although desperate people can turn dangerous*, I thought). I dug my phone out of my purse and pushed my speed-dial number for Tom.

***

"Why does he need the money so badly?" Kit asked.

"I told you, he never said."

"He refused to tell you, but you lined him up with someone anyway? You just gave away all your leverage?" Kit had been grilling me for ten minutes, and we still had another ten to go before we were back at my mom's.

"Kit, I'm not as smart—or devious—as you. Sorry. I did my best."

"You did fine. I'm just dying to know what Stan needs all that money for. In such a hurry. Ya know, I've heard Larry say more than once that when someone wants money that badly, usually it's already spent."

"You're quoting the wisdom of your husband?" I laughed a little. I know Kit does think highly of Larry, but she rarely lets on.

Sure enough, she said, "Okay, he's not exactly a financial giant. But sometimes he gets it right."

"Meaning?"

"Meaning, in Stan's case, I'm guessing he probably owes it to someone else—someone not very nice. I mean, what else would it be?"

"You make him sound like a gambler. But that would be Margaret," I said.

"It could be both of them. Or maybe . . . maybe it's as simple as—not simple for Stan, of course—but maybe it's as simple as he just has no other money."

"Yeah, maybe Doris really was only a meal ticket for him."

"Ya *think*?"

"Kit, they *might* have been in love."

The look on her face asked me if I was serious.

I turned my eyes back to the road. "Yeah, I suppose you're right."

***

Mom and Emily were back home by the time Kit and I pulled in the driveway. "What should we tell them?" I asked.

"The truth. Sort of. That we went to Luna for coffee."

Turned out they didn't even ask. They were too busy showing us their purchases, none of which were Depends *or* souvenirs. They each had practically a whole new wardrobe laid out on my mom's bed, my mother's items perfect for a Wisconsin summer and Emily's perfect for LA—year-round, of course.

"By the way," my mom said, as Emily made a turn worthy of a runway model in her new London Fog trench coat, "Ruth called, all in a tizzy. Seems they're going to read the will soon."

"The will?" I asked, stalling while I tried to decide how much if anything to tell my mom about our chat with Ruth that morning. How much would *Ruth* tell her? "Why would Ruth be involved with that—"

"The cats, of course. Doris funded those . . . creatures." The way she said it reminded me how much she dislikes cats. *Funny she and Ruth are such good friends*, I thought. But then I realized that when you reach a certain age, just *being* a certain age might form the most important basis for friendship. Especially if you've uprooted yourself, as my mom had, and left behind all lifelong friends—many of whom had subsequently died or moved away, anyway.

"Of course, the cats," I answered, but only Kit was paying attention to me by now, nodding knowingly. My mom and Emily had returned their attention to their purchases, admiring the new jeans Emily had paired with a long-sleeved striped T-shirt.

" . . . seen such a great going-out-of-business sale," my mom was saying. "Not that I'm happy for their misfortune. But I'm sure we helped them by buying all this stuff." She looked to me as if for approval.

"Sure, Mom."

But right now I was focused on Stan Dibble's apparent misfortune. Or maybe, after the reading of the will, his *fortune.*

CHAPTER TWENTY

From my mother's living room window, I watched William emerge from his car carrying a large bouquet of calla lilies. The fragrance of the flowers filled the room as soon as my mother opened the door and took them from him.

"William Stuckey, you shouldn't have," she said in a girlish voice, sounding like one of the Kardashians on steroids. I didn't like her tone or the smell of the flowers, which had always reminded me of funerals. "Valerie, fix drinks for us," she commanded, as if we drank alcohol on a regular basis.

Dinner was her famous beef Wellington; she'd taken all afternoon to prepare it. I'd done my best to keep Kit out of her way. Two women who both consider themselves to be great cooks, in the same kitchen, is definitely a recipe for disaster.

As an obvious slight to Kit, my mother had allowed Emily to prepare the salad. Romaine lettuce, mandarin oranges, and slices of red onion. I saw Kit turn up her nose as my mom carefully explained the combination to my daughter. But I'd had it before and knew it was good.

After we ate, my mom graciously allowed Kit to do the dishes. While she and Emily cleared the table, William and I took our coffee outside to the picnic table.

"So," William said, after we were seated. "I hope you are happy about the arrangement, Valerie."

"Arrangement? You mean engagement?" I didn't like that he was already planning to rearrange my mom's life.

"Ah, slip of the tongue. Of course I mean engagement. I hope everything sits well with you."

Okay, this was probably my only chance to have a *what are your intention*s chat with my future stepfather. It seemed too late, however, since the die was cast and the fabulous ring was out of its box. "I'm happy if she's happy." I sounded like an insolent child.

"Not exactly what I was hoping for." William took a long sip of his coffee. "Tell me, my dear, what are your objections?"

I turned to see Kit through the glass door. She was at the sink rinsing dishes and handing them to Emily. I almost got up to confirm with her what exactly my objections were.

"It's like this, William." I turned back to him. "I've known you for a big part of my life, and yet I feel as though I don't know anything about you." I watched him raise his eyebrows, ready to respond, and so I quickly continued. "I know you were married once, a long time ago. I know your wife passed away and you never remarried. I know you are a retired doctor. Okay, here's a question: why did you retire?"

He laughed a little before answering. "Ah, why does anyone retire? I was getting old. I didn't need the money, and I was ready to be done. Plus, I had a chance to do some speaking engagements, just enough connection with my field to satisfy me."

"I understand you worked with Ruth Greenway."

"Who told you that?"

"She did."

"It's true. Ruth and I were at the same hospital." His answer was abrupt, and his face told me that was all he was going to say on the subject.

"Okay." I decided to change courses, recalling Henry Crandall's remark about William and Virginia. "How well did you know Virginia Huntley?"

"Wait a minute. How did we go from Ruth to Virginia?"

"Just curious. A little bird told me you and Virginia were once an item."

He shook his head, and his knowing grin was planted firmly on his lips. "Not quite the truth. When I moved up here, Virginia and I did spend a lot of time together. I admired her. But we were hardly what you'd call an item."

"Did you go to out-of-state medical conferences together?"

"Valerie, where is this coming from? That was a long, long time ago. Before your mother even moved to Door County."

"Does my mother know?"

"I assume if you know, then she probably does too. It's not a secret. Just something in the past that has no relevance today. Virginia and I were close friends. But that was all. I had no intention of *marrying* her."

"Speaking of Virginia, has her cause of death been established?"

"Good question. And the answer is no. By the way, since the M.E. is a good friend of mine, I did mention your clever friend's idea of succinylcholine possibly being administered before her death."

"And?"

"And the jury is still out, so to speak."

"Hmm," was my brilliant response. I wanted to believe that if William were guilty, he wouldn't have brought up the topic of the drug, let alone suggest to the M.E. that he look for it.

"Valerie, let me assure you of one thing. Your father was a dear friend of mine. Your mother has become more than that to me. I promise that I intend to do nothing more with the remaining years we have together than to make every day as happy for her as I'm sure they were with your father."

Before I could respond, the door slid open, and my mother's face appeared. "William Stuckey," she said, "are you planning to sit out here all night? I need you to come look at this stuff Emily has found on the Internet. Wedding caterers in Door County."

William gave me a cat-that-ate-the-canary look. "It seems my bridegroom duty calls, Valerie." He rose from the table.

"Go for it." I smiled weakly.

We played happy family for the remainder of the evening. The most obvious revelation was how blissful my mom seemed. Of course, as I knew she would, she dismissed all the caterers Emily found for her, citing one reason or another. Too much emphasis on alcohol, too limited in their appetizer choice, too European.

When William finally left around eleven, we all went to bed. My mother reminded us that the viewing of poor Doris's body was the next day, and her giddy wedding mood evaporated as she said it.

***

Around midnight, after we had all been in bed for an hour or so, my phone vibrated. I was glad I'd remembered to silence it. Emily was asleep, so I shrugged into my robe and stole out of the room. I waved to Kit, who was tucked securely in her sofa bed reading. Then, phone to my ear, I slid open the kitchen door and went out to the picnic table.

"Tom?" I said. It was my second time to speak to him in one day. When I'd asked earlier on Stan's behalf for the name of a Realtor in Wisconsin, he'd quickly rattled off a name and number and excused himself, claiming to be in the middle of something. I was glad he'd called back.

"So, what's cookin' up there?" he asked.

"I gave your contact to Stan Dibble."

"Good. This could work out really well for us."

"And by us, you mean you, of course."

"I mean the business. You do still work for me, right?"

"Right." I pulled on the belt of my robe. A feeling of missing Tom washed over me. I'm used to seeing him almost every day, even if only for a few minutes. I shrugged off the thought of how much I had come to depend on him in recent years. "Anything else for me?"

"If you mean Emily's movie misadventure, I'm still working on that one. Might have to call in the big gun."

"I thought you *were* the big gun."

I heard his delighted chuckle. As smart as Tom is—and he is plenty smart—he still loves a little flattery, no matter how obvious. "Even I need a bit of help sometimes. But don't worry; I have this mess covered."

"Good." I felt relieved. With everything else going on, I had to prioritize my family concerns.

"Don't go off on a tangent, Pankowski," I heard Tom say, reading my thoughts.

"I said *good*, didn't I?"

"Yeah, but I know *you*."

Since I hadn't voiced my concerns over William, I was impressed. "What about Margaret Edwards?" I asked.

"Yeah, about her," he said. "I had some people check. Your Margaret Edwards filed for bankruptcy about three months ago."

"What about her job? She does have one, right?"

"Had one, Val; she *had* one. Her company, Reece and Habbits, a computer consulting firm—"

"What does that mean?"

"How the hell do I know? They consult. Let's leave it at that. Anyway, they fired Maggie May, and she hasn't worked since."

"No kidding? She never mentioned she had lost her job."

"But she did. Not everyone's as lucky as you, Val. Steady work with one of Chicagoland's finest real estate firms."

I wasn't sure I agreed with his assessment of our tiny company—four employees and a small office suite—but I was grateful to have my job. I looked up and saw Kit tapping on the sliding door. She had a glass of wine in her free hand and was gesturing for me to come drink with her. "I guess I better go, Tom. Thanks for finding out that stuff about Margaret Edwards."

"It wasn't so difficult."

"For you," I said, stroking his ego.

"For anyone with half a brain. This is the information age, Val."

"G'night, Tom; I'll talk to you tomorrow, after the viewing."

"Yeah, okay. Listen, one other thing. Be careful up there."

His comment surprised me. "What does that mean?"

"Just be careful. I have a feeling, okay? Don't go getting yourself all mixed up in things that don't concern you."

I heard Kit tap again on the glass door, and so I said a final good-night to Tom.

CHAPTER TWENTY-ONE

At five o'clock the next afternoon we headed for the Hahn Funeral Home in Sister Bay. Although the viewing didn't begin until four, my mother seemed to want us to be the first ones there.

I felt exhausted because we'd already driven down to Green Bay and back earlier in the day.

Since our original plan was to stay in Door County for only a long weekend, I didn't have anything even close to appropriate funeral attire. And so that morning Kit, Emily, and I went shopping.

At TJ Maxx I bought a black cropped jacket and a pair of gray pants. I found two blouses that would go well with them, one for the visitation and one for the funeral. I bought Emily two knee-length dresses also suitable for our purposes.

Kit insisted we go by a small shop she'd found on her phone, so we ended up in downtown Green Bay. After she purchased two divine suits, each one costing twice as much as I had spent on Emily and me in total, she bought us lunch at a cute café along the Fox River. That's Kit for you.

When we returned home, William was already there. He looked strikingly handsome in a dark-gray wool suit with a contrasting splash of scarlet in the silk handkerchief in his breast pocket.

My mother ordered us to get dressed. "Me first," I said, claiming the shower.

When I was dressed and ready to go, I appeared in the living room to find my mom and William sitting on the couch holding hands. I still found it repulsive, and I looked away. "Mom, what do you think?" I twirled around in my new purchases.

"I don't know why you insist on black," she answered, not letting go of William's hand.

"It's a funeral, Mom, not a fiesta," I muttered.

With Emily and Kit still occupied getting ready, I was glad to hear my phone ring from my purse on the counter. "I better get that." Happy for the good excuse to leave the lovebirds, I grabbed my purse and retrieved my cell as I made my way out to the deck.

Holding the phone before me, I could read the screen even without my glasses on. And my heart stopped. The name CULOTTA appeared with a Downers Grove number beneath it.

I sat down unsteadily at the picnic table and waited a few seconds for my heart to resume its natural beat. But then a colony of butterflies took up residence in my stomach.

Detective Dennis Culotta and I had not seen or spoken to each other since the nasty business involving the murder of Susan Reed, an employee of Kit's husband. I like to think we collaborated a little in bringing the matter to a conclusion. He probably would say I interfered—or worse.

While the phone continued to play the *Law & Order* theme song, I briefly held it to my beating chest, picturing the tall man with prematurely silvery-white hair, a tough demeanor, and the bluest eyes anyone should be allowed to have.

Finally, I felt composed enough to answer. "Hi," I said.

"Valerie? This is Dennis Culotta."

"Really?" I feigned surprise. The last thing I wanted was for him to know his name and number were still stored in my phone. "How are you?" So far so good.

"Okay. How you been?"

"Good. This is a nice surprise." It wasn't a lie.

We were both silent for a few seconds. If my phone had come with a curly cord, I would have been twirling it around my fingers by now.

"So . . . ," we both said at the same time.

"You first," I said quickly.

"Let's see . . . I've been talking to Tom Haskins. He asked me to do a little checking on something for him. A lady with ties to Door County. I remembered that your mother lives there, and I put two and two together."

"What does that mean?" I didn't want to sound offended, but an old familiar feeling I had often experienced while around him surfaced. I recalled how many times Dennis Culotta had put me on the defensive.

"I thought I'd just call and say hi. Is that okay?"

"Yes, yes, of course." *Yikes. Now I was gushing. Another familiar feeling.*

"Good. Tom just wanted some information, but it got me thinking. Knowing your proclivity for—"

"For what?"

"Let's face it, Valerie, you sometimes get a little too, shall we say, involved—"

Okay, gushing totally over. "Er, let me interrupt you for a second. How do you know Tom's request had anything to do with me?"

"Come on, Valerie. I'm a detective, not a moron. Since when did Tom Haskins have any interest in a middle-aged woman whose mother just died in Door County, where you just happen to be this week?"

His description of Margaret as a middle-aged woman was a little jarring, especially since she was about ten years younger than me. "How do *you* know where I am this week?" I asked.

"Tom told me that part."

"So you were discussing me with Tom?"

"Not really. He brought your name up."

"Well, I have no idea what you're talking about."

I heard him laugh, and I had to stamp my foot as a substitute for saying something I'd regret. I remembered his laugh so well. How his whole face lit up. How his eyes seemed to get bluer.

"Okay, okay," he finally said. "You have no idea. We'll leave it at that. I just wanted to say hello. See how you were."

"I'm fine. And I honestly can't talk now. I'm about to head out somewhere with my family." *Why had I said that?* The reality was, I had a million questions for the detective. *Was he happy, was he still employed, was he married?*

"Okay. You have a nice day," he interrupted my rambling train of thought.

Nice day! Was he freaking kidding me? I felt as if I'd been stopped for a traffic violation by a uniformed rookie. But I kept my reply calm. "I will, and you too."

"Okay," he said. Then it was awkward, as if neither one of us could quite hang up.

"Gotta go, Detective," I said, anxious to find out who would actually end the call first.

"Yep, me too."

"Okay. Bye."

"Bye. Oh, and Valerie, one last thing. You look after yourself, okay?"

"Will do, Dennis."

We both remained on the line for a few more seconds, and then finally it went dead in my hand.

***

"When is Virginia's funeral?" Emily asked. She was scrunched between Kit and me in the backseat of William's car. Mom had insisted we all go with him, like one happy family.

My mother took her eyes off William long enough to turn around and answer her granddaughter. But it didn't seem easy for her. From the moment he'd put that colossal ring on her finger, she'd become as smitten as a girl with her first crush.

"Well, Emily, I suppose Virginia's family thought they should let us honor Doris first, before giving us details of her service. One funeral at a time is more than enough to bear."

Kit leaned in front of Emily and whispered to me, "They shoulda had a double funeral."

"Katherine, they do that only if people die together, I'm sure." My mother's eyes remained firmly planted on her man, who was nodding in agreement.

"Their deaths might be connected," Kit whispered, even more softly this time.

I was relieved Mom didn't hear her, but I felt uncomfortable when I saw Emily's eyebrows shoot up in surprise. "Wha—?"

"Don't pay any attention to her," I told my daughter. "Kit, this is not the time."

"Time for what?" Emily whispered, sensing the conversation was not for her grandmother's ears.

"Time for her jokes."

"People often tell jokes about funerals and death," my mom said. So much for her not hearing us. "Don't they, William Stuckey? It can be their way of handling fear of their own mortality."

I noticed she hadn't given William time to respond, even though she'd asked his opinion, and I had a sudden memory of her with my dad. That was how most of their conversations had gone.

Was it how the conversations between David and me *had been?* I wondered. I felt a surge of uncomfortable warmth—*not* a hot flash, I assured myself. William had the heat on, even though it was seventy-eight degrees outside. Not to mention the crowded backseat and the accompanying body heat. I felt myself wanting to ask Emily if she remembered me talking right past her father like that, not seeming to care about his opinion.

Oh, what difference does it make now, I decided, as William eased his car into the funeral home parking lot.

I immediately realized why my mom had us leave so early. William drove even more slowly than she did, and the place was already crowded with people.

The first person to greet us as our group made its way up the stairs to the front doors was Stan and Doris's housekeeper, Jacqueline. Like the time we'd seen her shopping in Sturgeon Bay, gone was the sack she wore at the Dibble house.

Instead, she looked as if *she* were going to a fiesta, not a funeral. I assumed that would please my mother.

Jacqueline Bakos was wearing a formfitting dress with a white background covered in large, brightly colored flowers. The short tight skirt stopped well above her knees. A fascinator adorned the top of her head, with an orange flower and matching mesh. It contrasted dramatically with her blue-black hair, which was woven into an elegant French twist.

"My, my; are you here for the funeral?" my mother asked when we reached the top of the stairs, where Jacqueline stood in four-inch heels that were clearly no problem for her.

"What else I be here for?" she answered the unnecessary question with one of her own.

We paused so my mother could finish the conversation she'd started, and Kit looked tickled, no doubt with anticipation about just where it was going. She loves fireworks, hers or anyone else's.

But so does my mother. "I wasn't sure," she said to Jacqueline. "Your dress is so . . . so colorful. Is this how they dress for funerals in your country?"

"Hmmph. Croatia is my coun*tree*." She emphasized her words, as if it were my mother who had trouble with English. "And we don't have rules; we dress how we please."

"I can see that," my mother said. "I'm just not used to seeing you in such vivid colors."

"I'm surprised you ever notice me at all. You and your people just never got to see the real Jacqueline Bakos when Doris alive. She not like me to dress pretty. I think she jealous."

"Jealous? Doris? I very much *doubt* it." My mom raised her eyebrows, as if this were the most ludicrous statement she'd ever heard. I knew from her quizzical look and the fact that she didn't move that she was willing to wait for an elaboration.

Kit, who had squeezed in at my side, turned her head to whisper in my ear. "What woman *wouldn't* be jealous of her? Get a load of those—"

"Kit!" I said. My mother and William turned to look at me. *Damn their freakishly good hearing.*

But Jacqueline quickly reclaimed their attention. "She worry Mr. Stan think I too beautiful."

"She told you that?" My mom shook her head at what she clearly considered Jacqueline's delusions.

"Not in these words. But she make it clear I never to look good if I'm around them. Now I can dress as I please. And this pleases me."

I found myself feeling sorry for the petulant Jacqueline and her need to defend herself. I wanted to tell her to just give it up, that she'd never beat Jean Caldwell. But she didn't need my help. She smiled broadly, showing brilliant-white teeth that looked like the handiwork of an expensive orthodontist.

"Excuse us," my mom said, pushing William forward and leading us all into the funeral home.

Jacqueline grabbed my arm, pulling me back. Kit, of course, stuck by me like a conjoined twin. "You remember I tell you I hear Mrs. Doris have a big argument on the day she die?" As she said it, she rolled one hand over the other, illustrating how Doris tumbled down the long staircase. "You want to know who I overhear fighting with Mrs. Doris?"

"Yes, of course. Who?"

"I tell you after I pay my respects." She turned and headed for the door, and I took another look at her shoes. Surely those heels were at least *five* inches high.

"I thought you said you didn't know," I called after her.

"I hear the voice again. Now I know."

And then she was gone, slipping through the doorway, forging ahead of my group and most of the others in front of them. But I could see the orange flower atop her head bobbing up and down above the crowd as she made her way toward the casket. I didn't plan to take my eyes off it, or the woman wearing it.

Minnie Ebert, who was sitting on a chair at the back of the room, stood and joined us as we began to make our way up to the casket. Her heavy makeup remained intact, in spite of her constant dabbing at her eye area with a Kleenex—which, I noted, remained clean. No doubt about it, she'd mastered the trick of faux-tear wiping. I almost pointed it out to Emily, in case she wanted to learn from Minnie's acting technique.

"She looks so good. Valawee, you won't believe your eyes," she said. Her own eyes were shining behind the false eyelashes. I noted she was wearing an outfit as colorful as Jacqueline's, and I was certain my mother didn't like it one bit.

"I doubt that," Kit said to me. We were just far enough back from the others that they couldn't hear us. "Why do people always say someone looks *good* in a casket? I've never, ever seen one who does."

"Well, Kit, what do you want them to say? They look fake? They look made-up? They look *dead*?"

"How about nothing? How about they just say nothing."

"That's the opposite of what funerals are for, Kit. We're supposed to say things that comfort others."

She shook her head to show me she still didn't get it. "I thought Stan told you she was going to be cremated, anyway."

"Well, she probably is. But they can still have a viewing and funeral first. And maybe they can't cremate the body—I mean Doris—if there are any questions about her death."

"See? I told you! I'm *not* the only one who is suspicious."

"Of course you're not, not after you told William to ask the M.E. about sux."

"That was for Virginia, dum-dum."

"I know it was for Virginia, but you don't think that could make them think twice about Doris? We're not in Chicago, you know. Two deaths in Door County in a matter of days, when they were close friends, and someone suggests one of them might be *murder*, well, I think you might have stirred up a hornet's nest, Kit. And why am I not surprised?"

I was going to remind her later of the time she insisted someone had stolen her autographed Rod Stewart album from our locker when we were sixteen. She convinced the gym teacher, who rifled through five or six lockers as their owners stood by screaming *foul*, before Kit remembered she'd loaned it to Larry, her then-boyfriend-now-husband.

It was several days before Kit charmed those classmates into speaking to her again. And the thing about Kit was, she wasn't faking it. She simply turned the whole thing into a dumb-me story that seemed to amuse everyone into forgiveness.

"Hey, Minnie," Kit spoke over the murmurs of the others now. Stan had joined us, and everyone seemed more than happy to turn Minnie over to Kit.

Minnie moved away from them and closer to Kit and me. "How are you girls?" she asked, still patting at her eyes. "Isn't this just so sad? And then Virginia . . . Her service is going to take place in New York, did you know? That's where she's from."

"Hmm," Kit said. "I hope they don't rush her out of here too soon. I've got a feeling—"

"Kit, let's just pay our respects here," I said, shocking myself at how stern I sounded but still remembering the chaotic scene by our locker all those years ago. I didn't want that for Doris's viewing.

Kit ignored me, of course. "Minnie, you probably know all these people better than anyone else. Because you seem to be everyone's favorite," she hastily added, as if fearing Minnie would think she was attributing it to her age.

"I suppose that's true; I—"

"We were wondering, what do you know about William retiring up here from Chicago?" Kit quickly told her what we were supposedly putting together for him and my mom and why.

"It's still a secret." I hit Kit's arm just hard enough to remind her that my mother would not be happy that she'd told Minnie.

"Engaged?" Minnie quit wiping away fake tears. "They are *engaged*?"

"Yeah, but you can't tell *anyone* about it, Minnie," Kit said. "It would ruin it for William and Jean. But do you recall—"

"You can count on me; I don't gossip. Or pass on other people's secrets."

"No, of course you don't," Kit said. "But I was just wondering why William retired. If anyone would know, it would be you."

"Yes, I recall when he first came here. He was different from most who retire here to Door County. We're known to attract the artistic types, you see, writers and painters and such. But William seemed to be in one of those depressions you hear retired people fall prey to when they *don't* have such pursuits to follow. I didn't think that at first, of course, because I didn't know him. I just thought he was a grumpy recluse. But when I got to know him, when he came out of that depression, I figured that was—"

"Then why did he retire, if it depressed him so much?" Kit asked.

Minnie stood there a moment. Her eyes seemed to focus on something within her own mind. "Yes, that's right. Ruth Greenway had already moved here, and he helped her with her cats. I thought they were just meeting through that, but I did pick up on the fact later that they had worked together in Chicago."

Her eyes returned to the present. "How are you going to use *that* in your story? If I were you, I'd focus on Jean and William. Maybe you could even do a funny part about her stealing him away from Virginia. But I suppose that would be in bad taste now—"

"Maybe we could do it with great tact," Kit said, although we both know she is the last person to employ tact of any kind. "Tell us about it, Minnie."

"I'm sure Valawee knows the story, how Virginia and William had been quite the companions. They always said it was that and nothing more, that they just liked going to the theater and even traveling together. As pals. But none of us believed that. Especially not after Jean moved up here and it was obvious William enjoyed her company more, and definitely not as a pal. And that's when we knew Virginia hadn't thought of William as just a friend."

Minnie stopped, as if she needed to catch her breath. Or retrieve a memory. "Yes, she was quite heartbroken. I think that's why she gained all that weight. But her surgery was sure a success. Too bad—"

"So she was quite heartbroken?" Kit nudged her back on topic.

"Yes. Ruth and I might be the only ones she talked to about it, but she certainly unloaded to us one day. She said she missed his company terribly, but even though Jean kept inviting her to do things with them, she didn't need charity dates. She'd just bide her time. That's what she said. *I'll just bide my time.* I never really knew what she meant by that. William has been head over heels for Jean since she got here."

We were at the casket now and found ourselves saying how good Doris looked. Even Kit. But the word *good* was barely out of her mouth when she jabbed my upper arm and pointed her head toward the back of the room.

"Crap!" I said. Ignoring the shocked looks of the others, I followed Kit as she rushed through the friends and family awaiting their turns to have a last moment with Doris.

I knew what Kit was after. I saw the bright-orange flower heading toward the people standing by the doorway that led out of the funeral home. And I'd thought I had it in my peripheral vision the whole time.

When we caught up to Jacqueline in the parking lot, I grabbed her arm as she had mine a half hour earlier. "Jacqueline! Tell me whose voice you recognized. It's important."

She turned her head and just stared at me until I let go of her arm. "Are you sure you want to know?"

"Of course she's sure," Kit answered for me. "She asked, didn't she?"

Jacqueline ignored her and waited for my confirmation.

"Yes, I want to know. This isn't a game—"

"Your mother," she said. And before I could ask *what* about *my mother*, she spoke again. "Your mother is the one I heard arguing with Doris."

CHAPTER TWENTY-TWO

I watched dumbfounded as Jacqueline marched to her car and drove away. Then I walked over to William's Mercedes and leaned on the trunk for support. Kit was immediately by my side with a steady arm around my shoulders.

"Can that be true?" I asked her.

"Not necessarily. And even if it is, so what? Let's face it: Jean could have an argument with her hairbrush. It doesn't mean anything."

"But Kit, on the day Doris fell? Why didn't Mom even tell me she'd seen her that day? Not to mention the money Doris was giving her each month. It doesn't look good."

"I think we should just confront her—"

"I have. Well, about the money, at least, and all she did was deny—"

At that moment my mother and William appeared, with Emily trailing behind them talking on her phone.

"William Stuckey is taking us out for dinner," my mom said, waiting for William to open the car door for her. I looked at my watch; it was six thirty.

"Good idea; I'm starving." Kit opened the back door and got in. "Come, Val," she said from inside the car. "Come, sit." She patted the seat next to her, and I dutifully climbed in. Her sudden cheerfulness gave me a little hope. Of what, I wasn't sure.

We soon ended up back at William's condo, and we made the short walk around the pool to the Lake View Coves Restaurant.

Edmundo, the waiter who had served us on our first visit there, greeted us at the door. "Mr. Stuckey. A pleasure." He clutched five menus as he led us to a table.

Once again, I was surprised to discover that the dining room was more than three-quarters full.

"William Stuckey and I have made a decision," my mother proclaimed, as soon as our drink orders had been taken. "We're going to celebrate our engagement on Saturday night. We're going to have a party."

"Really?" I asked. "So soon after Doris's funeral? You think that's wise?"

"Wise? What does that mean? Life goes on, Valerie. We don't want to wait. And I assume you girls will be leaving Door County at some point. I'd like you here for the party. If that's not too much trouble for you."

"Grandma, I think it's a great idea," Emily spoke up. "Everyone is so sad; it will be nice to think about something fun for a change."

My mom smiled at Emily, but pressed me for a response. "Valerie?"

"I guess it's fine." I studied the menu. "If it's what you really want."

"For goodness' sake, I wouldn't suggest it if it wasn't what I really wanted, Valerie. I don't understand your mood."

"It's nothing, Mom. Sorry to be so gloomy."

I ordered a steak. At thirty bucks it was the most expensive thing on the menu. But as the rest of the table chatted about wedding plans, my gloom worsened.

I looked across at Emily, who was laughing at some dumb joke William had just shared. Why was *she* so happy? Her so-called career and reputation could be in ruins.

I looked over at Kit, who seemed as happy as Emily. Why wasn't *she* more concerned?

And then there were William and my mother. They both had their elbows on the table, and I watched him take and kiss her hand.

A fleeting thought of Dennis Culotta washed over me. Was I jealous? Could that be the problem? I always figured my mom would live alone as long as she was able, and at some point we would make other arrangements. Suddenly it seemed as if I would be the one who lived alone for eternity.

"Do you or don't you?" I realized my mom was addressing me when Kit gave my leg a kick under the table.

"Do I what?"

"Want dessert. For heaven's sake, Valerie, what is wrong with you?"

"Cheesecake," I said, as Edmundo removed my plate. I had taken three bites of the steak. About five bucks' worth.

"That's more like it," William said. "The cheesecake is exceptional."

***

Later, after William had returned us to my mom's and said a lengthy good-bye to his bride-to-be, we all took turns in the bathroom getting ready for bed. When Emily had retired to our room, and Kit was soaking in a bubble bath, my mom and I ended up alone in the living room. I watched her as she turned the sofa into a bed for Kit.

"I hope you are done sulking." She fluffed up the pillows.

"Sorry," I said. "I'm okay now."

"Well, thank goodness for that. I don't want you raining on my parade, Valerie."

"Can I ask you something?"

She sat down on the edge of the sofa bed and cradled one of the pillows over her tummy. "If you are going to bring up that business about the so-called checks—"

"No, it's not that. It's something else. Something Jacqueline said—"

"That girl! She is bad news. And I don't care how they dress in Czechoslovakia—"

"Croatia, Mom. She's from Croatia."

"Wherever she is from, it's not appropriate to wear bright colors like that to a funeral."

"Well, you questioned my black outfit—oh, never mind. Here's the thing. Jacqueline told me she heard you and Doris arguing on the day she died."

My mother bolted up and began fluffing the pillows again.

"I just wondered why you argued," I continued.

"For heaven's sake. Haven't you ever had an argument with Katherine? It was nothing. In fact, I can't even remember why we had words."

"Okay, so Jacqueline was right?"

"I don't know how Doris could stand that girl snooping around her house all the time. I would have gotten rid of her. And it's not as if she's any great housekeeper. More than once I saw dust on the blinds, and as for the streaks on the furniture—"

"So this argument you had—it did take place on the day Doris died?"

"I can't remember, Valerie."

"You can't remember the last time you saw one of your dear friends?"

"Okay!" she said so loudly I was afraid Emily would come out of the bedroom. "Okay. I did see Doris that day. And yes, we did have a disagreement. But it most certainly was not an argument. And before you ask again what it was about, let me just say this. It was a personal matter. Something I know Doris didn't want me to share with anyone."

"Even if it had something to do with her death?"

"Her death? Have you lost your mind? Next you'll be saying I pushed her down the stairs. Doris asked my opinion on a personal matter, but she didn't like the answer I gave her. We had words. Nothing more. We parted on good terms. Surely your little Russian friend can confirm that, since she seems to know everything that went on."

"Okay, Mom," I said quietly. "Forgive me; I didn't mean to pry."

"I think you did. You seem to have me pegged as something very sinister lately, and frankly, I don't like it. Perhaps it would be better if you left."

"Left? You mean go home?"

"Yes, that's exactly what I mean. I am sick and tired of your veiled accusations."

I thought I might start to cry. In all my years as Jean Caldwell's daughter, she'd never sounded so cold toward me, and I felt a little panicky. I rose quickly and moved in for a hug.

But the pillow was still between us, and she stood up and turned away. "Do us both a favor, and just go to bed," she said.

"Sorry, Mom." But she was way too busy whacking the hell out of the pillow to hear me, even with that fantastic hearing of hers.

***

The funeral for Doris Dibble was at ten thirty the following day. My mother's house was strangely quiet as we each got ready. Conversation was at a minimum. *More coffee? Are you done in the bathroom? Does this scarf look okay?* I was relieved when William arrived on the dot of ten to transport us.

"I'll take my own car," I said, expecting my mother to protest. But she only shrugged in agreement. Kit, of course, accompanied me, and even she was strangely quiet as I relayed the previous night's conversation with my mother.

"She nearly threw me out," I added, when I had finished my sad tale and there was no response from Kit.

"Ya know, maybe we should leave," she said.

"*What?* Are you nuts? I can't leave things like this. I don't know what my mother has gotten herself mixed up in. And as for William Friggin' Stuckey, who knows what his game is. It's all such a mess."

"Look." Kit fiddled with the air-conditioning button. It was unusually hot, and the extra heat wasn't helping either of our moods. "Don't you think the police would be involved by now if there was really anything wrong with the situation?"

"Yeah, the police. Because they're always *so* on top of things. Kit, I'm surprised at you. You were the one who started digging around, and now you seem to be—oh, I know what you're up to. You're afraid we *will* uncover something bad about my mom."

I glanced at her, and sure enough, she looked sheepish.

I patted her knee in gratitude and forgiveness. "I have to know the truth, Kit. Do *you* think everything is kosher? Do you believe my mom had a disagreement with Doris just before she died, but it had nothing to do with her death? Oh! I can't even believe I'm talking like this. But do you really think she knows nothing about her name appearing in Doris's check register every month?"

"Ya know, if it helps you any, Larry writes a check every month for three hundred big ones, and he enters Red Cross Disaster Fund in the register. But I know it's really dues to the Red Oak Country Club."

"Why would he do that?"

"Because he already belongs to two other clubs that charge an arm and a leg. It's deceitful, I know, but I write a real check to the real Red Cross at the end of the year. It's just his little game, and he thinks he's so smart. But we both know he can't outsmart me."

"Why don't you call him on it?"

"Because I rather like having something on him. I may need it one day. And really, he works hard, we can afford it, so I don't see that it does much harm. All marriages have their little secrets, Val."

In my case, that had been half-true. Whereas I really kept nothing from David, he, on the other hand, had a whole secret life going on. "So you think maybe my mother's name in the register doesn't necessarily mean the money went to her?" I asked.

"Maybe. Doris could have been giving the money each month to the blackmailer that Virginia hinted at, and she could have used your mom's name as a cover-up."

"She never said blackmail," I reminded Kit for the umpteenth time. "But I do like your idea about the fake entry in the register. I mean, think about it; my mother doesn't live an extravagant life. If she had a stipend every month, what the heck did she do with it?"

"Stipend? I thought you had to be a character in a Jane Austen novel to get a stipend."

"Ha ha. Okay, extra income; whatever. I mean, my mom's lifestyle is hardly lavish; it doesn't make sense."

"Exactly. There are a million possibilities. Okay, not a million, but more than one."

"We gotta find out," I said.

Kit had turned the air conditioner as high as it would go. I expected light snow to appear in the car at any moment. "We'll think of something. Don't worry."

CHAPTER TWENTY-THREE

Jacqueline was dressed in red. Red suit, red hat, and five-inch red pumps. From her seat, she turned and looked defiantly at my mother as we entered the sanctuary, where a large number of Door County residents were already seated.

My mother spotted The Lady in Red immediately and turned toward William. "So inappropriate," I heard her say, as we found seats.

Across the aisle I could see Ruth Greenway. Out of character for her, she was wearing a smart black pantsuit and a sweet black hat. On her lapel was a large rhinestone cat. In her own weird way, she looked quite stunning. I waved at her, and she waved back, a crumpled tissue in her hand.

Next to her sat Minnie Ebert. I could see her sparkly gold eye shadow even from a distance. Her too-blond wig was combed into a pageboy, and she was also wearing a smart black suit. For a moment I expected Virginia to complete the trio.

I became aware that someone at the front of the room was singing "How Great Thou Art," and then everyone turned toward the back of the room, like wedding guests expecting to see a bride. Only instead, the coffin appeared on the shoulders of six men. Stan was at the front on the right, and William on the left. I hadn't even known he was a pallbearer.

Slowly, they passed by, the coffin closed, poor Doris inside.

People sniffled and wept all around me, and even though I hadn't really known Doris, I felt my own eyes begin to sting. My mom, sitting next to me, gave a slight nod of her head when she saw my watery eyes, and grabbed my hand and squeezed it. I had never been so grateful for a squeeze. Especially from her.

Stan took a turn at the pulpit, and although he could hardly talk through his tears, he managed to say how he had loved his wife, how he would miss her, and how Door County would never be the same.

William was next. Fully composed, he described Doris as a strong and loyal friend who would be missed. He finished on an upbeat note, telling a funny story about Doris trying to cheat at golf. My mother laughed a little too loudly, as if we were being treated to an act by a first-rate stand-up comedian.

After a few more people took the podium, accompanied by a lot more tears from the mourners, we all watched the coffin slowly make its final journey as it silently rolled backward, reaching two black curtains that opened and then closed. Like a magic show, Hahn Funeral Home had made the lady disappear. This time for good. There wasn't going to be a graveside ceremony, maybe because the body was to be cremated.

We all made our way slowly out of the church and headed toward our respective cars. In the unhappy and slow-moving throng of people, I found myself walking behind Margaret, and I touched her on the shoulder.

She stopped and turned, putting her arms around me. "Valerie, thank you so much for coming."

"Of course," I said over her shoulder. "I'm so sorry."

"Me too; I'm going to miss her so much." She sniffed and wiped her nose with a tissue.

"Margaret, about what you said, about your mom not falling? Who do you think—"

"Val, I don't know what I think. What I do know is that my mom was a meal ticket to more people than just Stan. Given the way she threw her money around when she was alive, I'm guessing there are a lot of people who figured they'd benefit from her death, from what they expected her to leave in her will. Except for blood relatives, how can someone with money ever be sure who really loves them and who just wants their money? *I'm* the only one who truly loved her."

She paused and sighed, but I remained speechless. I had no idea what I should say. I felt a shiver of fear at the possibility that my mom was one of the people she was talking about.

Then Margaret broke the silence. "You're coming back to the house, right?"

"Absolutely. We'll see you there."

She turned, and I watched her take the steps down to the pathway leading to the parking lot.

"Looks like she doesn't have any friends here," Kit said, coming up behind me.

"I know. That's sad, isn't it?" But I was far more worried for my mom than I was sad for Margaret. "By the way, where's Stan?" I asked. "Those two seemed so chummy the other night at Doris's house."

I felt Kit put her hands on my shoulders. "Just don't you die before me, Valley Girl. I'd like at least one person at my funeral who can dig up something good to say."

I shuddered at her words. "Don't even say that, Kit. It's not funny. And don't you even think of dying anytime soon."

She laughed. "Okay. How about we go together? Kinda like Thelma and Louise."

"Yeah, and I'll drive."

***

Even though we had just come from her funeral, Doris Dibble's house was alive with people. Margaret and Stan held court in the living room, although they clearly were not on the same friendly terms they had been the last time I'd seen them together.

Minnie Ebert met us at the entrance to the spacious living room. "I made a chicken quiche and left it with that Jacqueline. I'm just waiting to see if she puts it out." She leaned in to give my mother a kiss before turning to thread her way among the groups of people, no doubt in search of her quiche.

"I wonder if she remembered to remove the Sam's sticker first," my mother said, and William gave an affectionate laugh, as if she were a naughty girl to insinuate such a thing.

From his place across the room, Stan spotted me and waved. He excused himself from the people he was talking to and headed toward me, giving a thumbs-up. "Thanks for the contact, Val." He kissed me as if we were old friends instead of having just met for the first time five days ago.

"No problem. I hope it works out for you."

"We'll see." He crossed his fingers for good luck.

"What was that about?" my mom asked, as soon as Stan left to mingle with the mourners.

"Nothing. He asked me to put him in contact with Tom Haskins, that's all."

"*Tom*." My mother smiled and forgot about Stan. "I'm going to invite Tom to our little party on Saturday."

My stomach lurched. As much as I was counting on his help from afar—okay, and even missing him—I knew his presence up here would only complicate my life. "He's always so busy, Mom. I wouldn't count on him to get away on such short notice."

She laughed and looked straight at me. "He'll come. He's like family to me."

I pictured the scene. Tom doesn't care for Door County and its cozy atmosphere. "They call it the Cape Cod of the Midwest," I remembered telling him when my mother first announced she was going to move there.

I also recalled his response. "I don't even want to go to the East Coast Cape Cod. Why would I want to go to one in the Midwest?" And when he did visit her once and only once, he claimed he caught potpourri lung or some damn thing, which took several puffs on his cigar to get rid of.

Eager to avoid further discussion of Tom, I looked around for Kit. She had disappeared, never a good sign. I excused myself from my mother, who was busy extolling the virtues of Tom Haskins to William.

"Should I be jealous?" I heard him say with a phony laugh, as I walked out of the living room into the enormous hallway in search of Kit.

I headed to the kitchen. Two women I'd never seen before stood at the counter, one of them cutting radishes into tiny rosettes. She looked up and smiled.

"I'm looking for—"

She pointed her paring knife in the direction of the back door, and I smiled and thanked her.

But it wasn't Kit sitting at the top of the paved steps leading to the lawn. It was Jacqueline.

"Hi, Jacqueline."

She stood up at the sound of her name. She'd changed out of her red designer outfit, but she looked just as good with a white blouse tucked into a slim-fitting black straight skirt. It came to just above her knees and showed off her perfectly shaped legs. She wore black patent-leather shoes, very high, very sexy.

As she sat back down again, I saw a cigarette in one hand and a tiny pillbox in the other that she was using as an ashtray. The cigarette had an unusually strong odor, and I noticed it had no filter.

"Are you working today?" I asked.

She nodded and then took a tiny puff of the cigarette. "Mr. Stan ask me. Then Miss Margaret. Those two cannot decide who I work for. But no matter; this is my last job here. I just work for this day and get double the money. It's all good."

"What will you do next?"

"I have job lined up in New York. I work for family. Very rich. Very successful. Only problem, two small kids. I am not nanny, so I make it clear to new bosses. No kids. Just take care of house."

"You don't like kids?" I sat down next to her.

She took a long drag from her cigarette and stared straight ahead at the fountain in the center of the lawn, a fair distance from us. It had a statue of a cherub with a bow and arrow aiming at something we couldn't see.

"I love kids," she said after a while.

"Well, maybe you'll have some. You are still a young woman."

"I'm thirty-eight. I lost two babies already." She said it in such a matter-of-fact way that I wasn't sure if she was giving me good news or bad.

"I'm sorry," was all I could say.

"Not for you to be sorry. You didn't cause the problem."

"Did you have a husband?"

"Of course I have husband. How you think I have two babies to lose?"

I wanted her to keep talking, but I felt like a quarterback trying to make a successful pass and constantly being intercepted by her damn attitude.

"I just meant . . . well, in America a lot of women have babies without husbands."

"Yes, you Americans are genius, all right. In Croatia we do it the old way of fashion. We find a husband first, then we have the babies." She puffed again on her cigarette, leaving a blood-red stain from her lipstick, and then she daintily tipped the ash into the pillbox.

"And is your husband in America?" I asked, still hoping for a successful pass.

"No." She turned to look at me. "He is dead. Mrs. Doris killed him."

CHAPTER TWENTY-FOUR

Ifound myself wishing Kit could be with me before Jacqueline uttered another word. And true to form, Kit suddenly appeared before us out on the back steps, right after Jacqueline had dropped her bombshell. I wondered if it would be rude to ask her to repeat what she'd just said. Does a person ask Charles Manson to run through his story one more time?

"Could you excuse us, Jacqueline?" The usually unflappable Kit sounded harried.

"I enjoy my break for seven more minutes. You may excuse yourself anytime." She reached into the pocket of her skirt and produced a soft-blue cigarette pack, and I read the word *Gauloises*. She turned it upside down and tapped the bottom, and an unfiltered cigarette emerged. Slowly, she went through the ritual of lighting it.

Jacqueline was definitely done being pushed around by our crowd. Then again, I doubted *anyone* ever pushed her *anywhere*. And her work at that house was all but done. She no doubt planned to wash some dishes and then collect her double pay. And she was going to leave the steps in her own sweet time, thank you very much.

"Val, I need to talk to you," Kit said. "Come." She turned and headed toward the back door, assuming I'd follow.

I looked at Jacqueline, who was smoking her cigarette with a smug look planted on her face, which somehow did not mar her beauty. "I'll be right back," I said. "Could we talk some more? Please?"

She shrugged. Her look suggested *maybe yes, maybe no, maybe I don't give a flying flip.*

I heard Kit's voice from just inside the door. "Valerie!"

I hurried over to her and let her grab my hand and drag me to the bathroom off the kitchen. I was more than a little frustrated at not getting to hear Jacqueline finish her story. "Kit, you interrupted something really important. She was about—"

"Just listen. I found out why Doris was so upset with Margaret."

"Why?"

"I guess Doris had gone to great lengths to help Margaret get a job. Something in compu—"

"I know, I know, something in computers. Go on."

"Exactly. And then Margaret up and quit. Worse, actually, she got fired. Because she basically left without telling the company. She just didn't show up."

"Who told you all this?"

"Margaret." Kit looked proud of herself, as if she'd elicited the truth from O.J. Simpson.

"You're kidding—"

"Not directly, ya know. I overheard her arguing with Stan."

"When?"

"Just before I came and rescued you from—"

"Where was this? Do you think they know you heard them?"

"No, of course not. Do you think I'm an idiot? I was hiding behind a bush. I had to go get something from the car—"

"Kit, you didn't even have my keys. You *couldn't* have gotten anything from the car."

"I realized that, once I was outside—okay, I saw them outside and purposely went to spy on them. Now are you happy?"

I smiled. "Keep talking. I'll let you know."

"Bottom line is you have Dumb and Dumber running this show, now that Doris is gone. Or more accurately, Broke and Broker."

"You mean Margaret and Stan?" I asked.

"Yeah, or maybe the other way around. Stan and Margaret. Not sure who's broker. Or dumber. Margaret apparently asked Stan this morning before the funeral, and then again when I was . . . okay, spying . . . for some money to tide her over just until her inheritance came through. And he told her, number one, he had no money himself until *his* inheritance came through, and number two, he knew for a fact she was getting *nothing* but a reprimand from her mother."

When someone pounded on the bathroom door, it registered to both of us that it was the *second* time someone had knocked while we'd been immersed in our conversation.

"Hold yer pants on," Kit yelled.

"A thousand pardons," came the sarcastic reply in a thick Croatian accent. "In my country women prefer to use toilet facilities one at a time."

"Yeah, in your country—"

"Kit, I gotta finish talking to Jacqueline. The news she's spilling makes what you overheard sound like a weather report about sunny skies." I was whispering, sure that Jacqueline had an ear planted firmly against the door. She'd probably heard what Kit had told me.

As I reached for the doorknob, Kit took my upper arm in her manicured hand and squeezed. "What? Tell me now."

"No time." I opened the door, but Jacqueline—in spite of the fact that I'd expected her to fall into the room after eavesdropping—was nowhere in sight.

"Don't forget," Kit said, starting to follow me.

But I turned and pushed her back into the bathroom. "You're right. You should hear this now." I relayed the conversation I'd had with the mysterious Jacqueline on the steps.

"Why did you let me interrupt you?" Kit demanded when I'd finished.

"You hardly gave me a choice."

"You could have told me to get lost, ya know."

"Well, I didn't. I never have, and I'm not about to start now."

She gave me a quick hug, and then it was back to business. "We've gotta find Jacqueline. You know she's still here somewhere. There are still dishes to be washed. And no doubt a paycheck or two to collect."

But I wondered just who was going to pay Jacqueline, since she'd been hired by Broke and Broker.

"Yeah," Kit seemed to read my thoughts. "Do you suppose she somehow found out there might *be* no paycheck?"

"Maybe."

"Let's go find out." She opened the bathroom door, and I followed her out and into the living room, where we saw Jacqueline gathering dirty plates and abandoned wineglasses.

Unfortunately, I also saw my mother standing at the entrance to the living room, arms folded across her chest. Her face looked furious.

"Hi, Mom." I smiled, attempting to walk past her, but she caught my arm and stopped me.

"Valerie, there are at least five bathrooms in this house. Is it really necessary for you and Katherine to share one?"

"You know Kit. The back of her earring came loose, and I was just helping her fix it."

"*Really*," my mom said. She might just as well have said *bullshit*, although of course she never would.

"Okay, we were smoking a little weed; happy now?" As soon as I said it, I wanted to wash my own mouth out with soap and send myself to my room for the rest of the night. "Sorry, Mom; I'm so sorry. I was trying to be funny," I hurried on. "I really was just helping Kit—"

"You think drugs are funny? Sometimes I wonder how Emily turned out to be so sweet and innocent, with you and David for parents."

We both looked across the room at the precise moment that Emily leaned forward to take a slice of cheese from a tray on the coffee table. A clear view of her cleavage flashed for a brief moment.

"It must be your influence, Mom."

I hurried away with two thoughts: the first, whether my mother had been eavesdropping outside the bathroom; the second, more important, thought was to advise Emily to stand up straight at all times.

***

I had a splitting headache by the time we returned to my mother's after the funeral and luncheon. I excused myself and retreated to the bedroom, where I lay on top of the covers; I needed some time to think.

First, I never got another chance to talk to Jacqueline alone, but I had to know how Doris killed her husband. Plus, there was the issue of what Kit overheard between Stan and Margaret.

Without saying so out loud, we were both by now treating Doris's and Virginia's deaths as related murder cases.

The scary part was that it seemed my own mother had motive, opportunity, and means (really, who *couldn't* push someone down the stairs? and wasn't she engaged to a *doctor*, who no doubt knew how to poison someone without leaving a clue?). So it seemed imperative that we prove the two women were murdered by someone *other* than my mother.

But first things first, and I realized I better hurry and call Tom before it was too late. I had to give him a heads-up so he could invent a good excuse for not coming to my mom's Cape Cod for her engagement party.

I sat up on the bed and took my phone from the bedside table. When I called Tom's cell, it went right to voice mail, so I decided to call the office. Rather than leave a message on Tom's phone, where he'd probably never retrieve it, I'd tell the efficient Billie, the one who *really* runs our little office. She also runs its owner and two other employees (Tom's nephew and me). If I turned that task over to her, I could forget about Tom and try to focus on the bigger things that were no doubt responsible for my headache.

" . . . Val, are you there?"

It was Billie, who's younger than Emily but light-years wiser. I knew *she'd* never bare her—

"Val?"

"Sorry, Billie. I got interrupted. What's going on down there?"

It seemed like weeks, not days, since I'd been in the office, getting irritated at Perry and relying on Billie up close and personal. Now it sounded like heaven.

"Things are good here," Billie said. "Tom's at a Realtors' luncheon, and Perry's off getting a facial." She cackled.

In spite of my worries, I smiled. "And what does his Uncle Tom say about that?"

"Are you kidding me? His Uncle Tom has no idea. I think he might be tempted to fire his favorite nephew if he knew."

"Perry is Tom's *only* nephew."

"Why do you think he's his favorite?"

That time I couldn't even force a half smile. "Uh . . . speaking of Tom, would you let him know my mom is going to invite him to her engagement party Saturday night? Tell him to get his excuse ready."

"Your mom's *what*?"

"Long story, Billie, and I have no idea how it's going to end. We'll have lunch when I get back, okay?"

"Can't wait."

"Me, either." I sighed. "Me, either."

CHAPTER TWENTY-FIVE

Finally, I took a fitful nap, in which I dreamed I was a spectator at a peep show in a seedy part of Manhattan; and then miraculously, as tends to happen in dreams, I was suddenly sharing a yogurt with Abraham Lincoln.

"Wake up." I felt someone shake me and heard a voice, clearly not belonging to Honest Abe.

"What? What time is it? Kit, what are you doing?"

"Jean and Emily have gone to that Pine Place restaurant to make arrangements for the party on Saturday. We're alone. Don't you love it?" In the dusk of the room her brown eyes sparkled with excitement.

I pulled myself up and rested on the headboard of the bed. "And?"

"And what?" she asked.

"You seem like you have something to tell me."

"We have a free evening. We could go somewhere, ya know. We could take a drive."

"Where?"

"We could stop in and see how poor Margaret is faring, see if she has anything else to shock us with. Or poor Stan, for that matter. Or even better, we could go visit sweet little Jacqueline and find out the rest of her sad story. The possibilities are endless without Mother Jean watching our every move."

I swung my legs onto the floor. "Speaking of Mother Jean . . ."

"Yes, what about her?"

"I am so high on her shit list right now—"

"Welcome to *my* world."

"Yes, but it's slightly different. I'm her daughter, after all. Seems like every time I open my mouth, I say the wrong thing to her. I just wish she would come clean."

"Maybe she has; ever considered that?"

"Let's see . . . she refuses to tell me why Doris was giving her a check every month, she refuses to tell me what she and Doris argued about—although she did at least admit they did—and she—"

"Ya know, you really need to move on just a little."

"Sorry if I'm boring you."

"No, honey, it's not that. I know you're upset with what you don't know. But let's see if we find out something that we do know."

"That sentence doesn't even make sense."

"I know. But you know what I mean."

Unfortunately, I thought I did.

***

Ten minutes later we were in my car parked outside Jacqueline Bakos's condo. It was a plain brick two-story that would have been considered rather nice anywhere else. In Door County, with its abundance of dwellings either adorable or magnificent, it was probably considered on the proverbial wrong side of the tracks.

I checked my watch. It was nearly seven thirty. Certainly time for the guests at Doris's house to have finished the after-funeral mourning and left. By Jacqueline's own admission, there was no real reason for her to hang around there anymore.

Fifteen minutes later we watched her pull up in front of the building. She seemed to be on the phone for a few minutes, after which she opened her car door and got out.

"So how do we do this? *Just stopping by to say hi*?" I asked Kit.

"Something like that. We say you were really worried about what she told you about Doris Dibble killing her husband, and we just wanted to be sure she's okay, blah, blah, blah."

"Right—because we are such close friends."

"Let's just hope she's in a good mood."

"Ha! Well, I guess there's a first time for everything," I said, not feeling very hopeful.

We waited another twenty minutes and then crossed the street to the ground-floor apartment we'd seen Jacqueline enter. The first thing I noticed when she opened the door was the sweet music emanating from behind her. A soft jazz combo, maybe Miles Davis or one of his contemporaries. It was beguiling.

Jacqueline had her hair pulled back into a heavy ponytail. She wore black leggings and a man's white shirt. Her feet were bare, her toenails painted a deep crimson, and she held a glass of wine in one hand. But none of those was the second thing I noticed. No, it was her smile. A real, genuine, happy-to-be-alive smile. It radiated joy, and I fought the urge to take her in my arms and hug her.

"Ladies." She stepped back so we could enter her home.

"We were just passing by." Kit took in the surroundings. The room was casually furnished. Nothing too pricey, but nothing too shabby, either. A brown overstuffed couch and a modern glass coffee table, the IKEA kind.

"I'm glad you stop here. Come celebrate with me. I can offer you wine. It's Portuguese, so not too bad. At least as good as your California wine."

We both ventured fully into the room, while Jacqueline disappeared behind the counter of the small kitchen and poured two more glasses. "I won't ask how you find out where I live. Not so difficult, I think, for Americans to know everything about everyone in such a small place as this Door County."

"What are we celebrating?" Kit stood in front of a framed pen-and-ink drawing of two small children. It hung alone on the wall facing the couch. Its solitary position showcased its beauty, which was as captivating as Jacqueline's newly smiling face.

"My husband do that." She nodded toward the drawing and then handed a wineglass to Kit.

"It's excellent," Kit said.

"Yes. He was very talented. Please, sit." She handed me my wine and then sat on the floor in front of the glass coffee table with her legs positioned in what I'd grown up calling *Indian style*, but which Emily's preschool teacher had, with political correctness, called *crisscross applesauce*. "Here's to my new life." She raised her glass in a toast.

"So that's the celebration?" Kit sounded utterly disappointed.

"Yes. My work here is finished. I leave for New York on Wednesday." She pronounced it with three distinct syllables. Wed-nes-day. Her accent, which up until now I had found slightly grating, suddenly seemed enchanting.

"Well, here's to you, Jacqueline," I said. "I hope you will be very happy."

For a moment, her smile disappeared, and it seemed to take sheer will on her part to bring it back. "Yes, I think I will be. Let's say I will try my damnedest."

"Jacqueline." I placed my glass gently on the table. "Earlier today you told me Doris Dibble killed your husband." I watched closely, but her expression didn't change. "I hope you won't think I'm prying, but when you hear something like that, it's upsetting."

"You want explanation?" She rose and disappeared for a few moments, during which time Kit and I gave each other quizzical looks but didn't dare speak. We silently agreed we didn't want to say anything that might shut the suddenly talkative Jacqueline up.

She returned with a worn leather satchel. Folding into the same position on the floor that she'd held earlier—how *did* she do that so smoothly?—she unlatched the bag and took out some newspapers. Carefully, she laid one of them on the table.

It was not an American newspaper. "It is in Croatian, so I don't expect you to understand it," she said. "Three pages devoted to this subject. In your *USA TODAY* there were nine lines written on the same topic, hiding on page eight."

She dug around and finally produced a tiny piece of paper, presumably taken from the American newspaper. She laid it on the table and turned it around so we could both see it.

SIXTEEN DEAD IN SHIPYARD ACCIDENT, the headline announced. I had to strain to read the dateline: *Locktia, Croatia*. I couldn't read anything that came after that, not without my glasses, and they were tucked away in my purse that I had left on the floor by the front door. Somehow it seemed in bad taste to retrieve them and break the momentum that Jacqueline had created. I noticed she was softly rocking back and forth, her hands on her tummy, as if she had a stomachache.

"Tell us what happened," Kit said quietly. She had kicked off her shoes and was sitting beside Jacqueline on the floor, one hand resting protectively on her new friend's back.

"A terrible time. My husband, Toska, was manager of shipbuilding project in Locktia. They build big ocean liners for Edwards Industries. The only real work to be found there. Many, many times Toska tell his boss that condition there is not safe. Like you say here, corners are cut to save money and time, making it dangerous for people who work there. But they need jobs; they have families. My husband write a personal letter to Mrs. Doris Dibble. He tell her straight what her company is not doing to protect people, that she is responsible. He write whole thing in English, so she knows what is going on in her name in Locktia."

I left my seat on the couch and joined Jacqueline and Kit on the floor.

Jacqueline was rocking even harder now, tears rolling down her velvety cheeks. "Doris Dibble never write back. Instead, my husband is told by his boss that he no longer have job. Toska protests. He tells everyone he knows about the bad business. About danger at the workplace. He has a lawyer friend, and together they make a law case against Edwards Industries."

She stopped rocking, wiped her cheeks with her fingertips, and took a big gulp of wine. I noticed Kit was running her hand up and down Jacqueline's back.

"What happened, Jacqueline?" Kit asked. "Tell us what happened."

"A date is set to go to court. We get several letters and phone calls telling us to stop. But Toska say no. He will continue to bring problem to authorities. One day Toska is driving our two children to school. They are five and seven. Our car is tiny. It would be considered a toy in America. Like a golf cart. But another car, a big, heavy one, like a military jeep, is stopped at the corner of street. It waits until Toska drives by and then rams into him. Witness tells us it knocks Toska's car over and over several times, with Toska and the children inside. Finally they are dead."

The room was silent. The lovely music had stopped.

I spoke first. "But how could Doris be—?"

"These men work for Edwards Industries. They are very important in Locktia. If shipbuilding moves to another place, it's very bad for the town. Toska was trying to make it safe, for everyone. Two weeks after he and our children died, there was an accident, just as Toska knew there would be. Sixteen men died because equipment not safe. Several big steel bars fall onto platform. All men are killed. Just like my Toska."

"Did you ever discuss this with Doris? Did she know what happened to your family?" Kit asked.

"She don't know who I am. That it was my husband who write to warn her. But she knew all about accident."

"How can you be sure?" Kit asked. "As CEO of such a large company, she couldn't be aware of everything that happened all over the world."

"I found letter Toska wrote. In that study of hers where you were searching around."

I was too stunned to talk. But Kit asked, "Why didn't you confront her with it?"

"That's strangest part. I meant to. It was my plan all along. It was the reason I came here. But things change. And now I don't have to."

I waited a few seconds, and then I just had to ask. "One more thing. You said you heard my mom arguing with Doris on the day she died. Did you hear what they were arguing *about*, Jacqueline?"

She wiped her tears away again, and then she replied. "No. Why you not ask her?"

"Good question," I said. But the better question was *why wouldn't my mother answer it?* "We better get going, Kit." I rose from the floor, and the others followed suit.

I collected my purse from the spot by the front door. "Well, good luck to you, Jacqueline."

She reached forward to give me a hug.

"Yeah, good luck in New York," Kit said, but no hug was forthcoming. "Be careful there. It's gonna be very different in The Big Apple."

"I'm sorry your little Door County is turned upside down." Jacqueline took a step back after she opened the front door. "I have enjoyed my time here. But two suspicious deaths in a week. Maybe that Big Apple will be safer, huh?"

She gave us a radiant smile again, the same one she had greeted us with. I had a feeling she was gonna swallow The Big Apple whole.

***

"Let's stop somewhere and get a drink," I suggested to Kit, after we'd driven only a few minutes. I wasn't ready to face my mom just yet.

"Good idea. Look, there's a bar over there." She pointed to the establishment that had, in fact, inspired my suggestion. "Pull over."

I swerved into the well-lit parking lot on the side of the road. Inside, we took one of the small tables toward the back.

"Whew!" I said, as soon as we had placed our order. A gin and tonic for me, a vodka martini for Kit. "That was hard to hear, wasn't it?"

"Yes, it certainly was."

"But?" Even in the semidarkness I could tell Kit had something on her mind.

"Ya know," she said, "it does sort of shine a light on Jacqueline as the one most motivated to push Doris down the stairs."

"And Virginia?"

"Who knows? Maybe she saw Jacqueline do it, or found out she did it. I'm not sure about that one."

We both sipped our drinks, and then my phone started ringing in my purse. When I pulled it out, I saw Tom's name and picture on the screen. "Oh man, it's Tom."

"Get his credit-card number. I feel like getting drunk, and he can foot the bill."

"Yeah, funny." I slid my finger across my phone screen to reply. "Tom?"

"Hey, Val."

"I'm taking this outside; I can't hear him in here," I said to Kit, rising from my seat. It wasn't quite true, but I felt better talking to Tom without her expressive reactions to every comment.

"Okay, that's better," I said, once I was out in the parking lot. "Look, my mom is going to invite you to this damn engagement party of hers, and I just wanted to let—"

"She already did."

"What?"

"Yep. She had Emily call me."

"Wow." I was truly impressed with my mother's cunning. She knew Tom wouldn't say no to Emily. "Well, you certainly don't have to—"

"What the hell are you talking about? I wouldn't miss it. I need to check out your new stepdaddy." I could hear him chuckle, and if he'd been in arm's reach, I might have socked him. "I'll be there," he continued. "I've got a buddy who's gonna fly me up there."

"Really, Tom, you don't have to do this—"

"I want to, Pankowski. It'll be nice to see Jean again. I assume her intended has got some dough?"

"I have no idea. He's a retired doctor; that's all I know."

"I thought you'd known him for years."

"Well, do we really know anyone?"

"Please; spare me the psychobabble. Is he a good guy?"

"My mom seems to think so."

"Isn't that enough, Kiddo? You sound like she's marrying a serial killer."

Could be, I thought, *or maybe* he's *marrying a serial killer*.

"One more thing," I heard Tom say, just as I was ready to end the call. "I hear the Dibble will is being read tomorrow morning—"

"What? How the heck do you know *that*?"

"Doris Dibble's lawyer is an old friend of mine. He let it slip. Anyway, at least we'll find out who owns the property."

"You are amazing, Tom—"

"I know."

"I didn't mean in a good way. Anything else you wanna tell me?"

"Nope, that's about it. Except that your stepdaddy is the executor of the will. But you probably knew that already."

"Of course. Everyone knows *that*." I ended the call, not sure who I was suddenly so mad at.

CHAPTER TWENTY-SIX

I crammed my phone into the pocket of my jeans—
not easy to do because my jeans were growing
tighter with each day in Door County—and went
back into the bar.

As soon as my eyes adjusted to the darkness, I realized
Kit was not at our table.

Before I could worry about that, I heard her raucous
laughter coming from even farther back in the large room.

For the first time, I realized there was a pool table back
there. A hanging light cast a glow across the green felt. I
heard the crack of the pool balls hitting each other, followed
by more raucous laughter, this time too deep to be Kit's.

I went past our table and right to the four pool players,
two of whom were young enough to be Kit's sons and the
other a girl young enough to be the daughter she never had.
And the fourth player was Kit herself.

"Hey, Valley Girl, meet my friends." She rattled off
some names I knew I'd never remember—or even try to—

and then laid her pool cue at a diagonal across one corner of the table. "Thanks, guys; this was fun."

They mumbled similar sentiments, but I noticed their attention had already returned to their pool playing, far more exciting, no doubt, than a couple of boring old dames.

If they only knew we were actually a little too exciting for our own good.

"So what'd ol' Tommy Boy have to say?" Kit followed my lead and sat back down at our table.

"Somehow he found out the will's being read tomorrow. And William's the executor."

She rolled her eyes, as I'd known she would. "How the hell does—"

"Who knows? But the really big news, the bad news, is that he'll be here Saturday, for my mom's damn engagement party."

She took a big gulp of her martini. "Your mom and *William's* party."

"Yes, my mom and *William's*. Unless you know something I don't, and she's broken up with him to marry Russell Crowe." I took a sip of my drink, one of only a few sips I was going to allow myself since I was driving.

"Okay, calm down. Ya know, I was thinking while you were outside—"

"You were? It looked like you were playing pool."

"I can do both, ya know. And why are you so pissed off all of a sudden?"

"Sorry. I just hate the thought of Tom coming up here. Having to see him and my mom fawn over each other— yuck. I hated it in high school, and I'll hate it Saturday night."

"Hmm. Your mother did always have a thing for Tom, which is surprising since he's such an asshole."

Ugh, I thought, dreading how I'd not only have to deal with my mom, but also have to run interference between Kit and Tom. "Yeah, she really latched onto Tom when Buddy left home," I said. "I guess because he came around so much and has always treated her like a queen, he worked a way into her heart. I know she likes to think of him as another son."

"Fine. I get that. But don't try to tell me again that Tom's only a *brother* to *you*."

"Kit, don't go there." I sighed. She is always teasing me about Tom being more than a friend. As if that big lug could ever evoke romantic feelings on my part. "Tom gave me a job. He's my boss."

"Like you couldn't have gotten a job *anywhere*."

She also says *that* a lot. And I'm touched by her confidence in my abilities. But the truth is, Tom gave me a job when I'd been out of the job market for eons. I'd started working at his real estate firm with no experience and little self-esteem.

"Okay." She was obviously bored with the topic. "So what should we do now? The evening is still young."

"I don't feel that young. How about we call it a day and go back to my mom's? Veg out. Watch one of your movies."

"That does sound tempting. I mean, how often can I drag you away from *Law & Order* to watch an old film? But we gotta make use of this time to investigate."

"But *what*? Investigate what?"

"I don't know, but *something*. Someone. Think. What's our next logical move?"

"Logical? *You*?" I chuckled. Then I grew quiet and thought about her question. Seriously.

But Kit came up with the answer first. After a brief pause, she pushed back from the table and stood up. "Let's go, pardner."

"Where?"

"To Ruth Greenway's."

***

"I still say it's too late to be showing up on someone's doorstep," I said to Kit, as I parked in front of Ruth

Greenway's dollhouse-like residence. Hers definitely fell into the adorable category of Door County abodes, not the magnificent.

"You worry too much."

"Well, she's had a hard day, with the funeral of her friend and all. And it's not like she's a teenager. Old people—"

"This old person, you might recall, showed up on William's doorstep a few nights ago at about ten o'clock."

She had me there. I put the car in park and opened my door, but Kit was already halfway up the curving sidewalk by then. I could smell the lilacs that surrounded Ruth's front porch and wondered what we could possibly learn about a potential murder—*murders*, plural—from a sweet old lady who loved cats and fragrant flowers.

I was about to find out.

By the time I joined Kit on the porch, Ruth was standing at her open door looking startled. And definitely ready for bed, in a long cotton nightgown. The white fabric was covered with tiny cat paw prints. I elbowed Kit in her side.

This was the first time I'd seen Ruth without some kind of head covering, and now I could see why. She obviously used the same stylist as Donald Trump. "Sure, you gals can come in," I heard her saying to Kit. "But what on earth—is Jean okay?"

"Yes, yes, my mom is fine," I assured her. At least three cats scurried out as we entered her house.

"And William?" she asked. "Is William all right?" Beneath the Trump comb-over her forehead furrowed into wrinkles of concern.

"Actually," I said, although Kit and I hadn't planned it, "William is what—er, who, whom?—we want to talk to you about."

Kit gave me a *what the hell* look, as if to point out that it was no time to worry about correct grammar. Then she followed Ruth to the couch, stepping over a large ginger tabby on the way. I joined them, eager to find out where the conversation would go.

I watched Kit carefully inspect the couch cushion before she sat down. I gave her the same *what the hell* look she'd given me, hoping to convey that it was no time to worry about cat hair.

Deciding to get it started, I spoke as soon as I took my seat in the chair next to one end of the couch, near Ruth. She was so close to me, I took her hand, as if to pull her through the questioning that was about to take place. "Ruth, I need to talk to you about William."

"About William? Why?"

"Well, he's about to marry my mom, and I'd just like to know more about him."

She withdrew her hand from mine. "Hot diggity." She sounded happy, but not surprised.

"Did my mom tell you?"

"No; Minnie Ebert let it slip."

"*Really,*" I said, recalling Minnie's declaration that she wasn't one to pass on other people's secrets. I was a little angry at her, choosing to forget that I'd just blabbed myself. "Do me a favor," I continued. "Please don't mention it until my mom tells you herself. She's kinda touchy about that stuff."

"It's safe with me, sugar pie." Ruth's eyes twinkled.

"Thanks, Ruth. Now about William."

"What's to know? William is the salt of the earth; your mother couldn't find a better man. She's a lucky woman, toots." She stroked the fur of a black-and-white cat that had leaped onto her lap. I heard purring, and I wasn't sure if it was Ruth or her cat.

"Well, I've heard that he retired up here, shall we say, rather abruptly? Do you know anything about that?"

I remained quiet, waiting until Ruth finally tore her eyes away from the cat and looked first at Kit, as if to learn if she really had to answer my question, and then at me. "Can you keep a secret?" Again, she looked at Kit and then at me.

"Of course we can." I glanced at Kit to back me up.

"Yes, of course we can," Kit concurred.

Ruth nodded, as if deciding whether it was wise to go on. "Marmalade!" she suddenly blurted out.

"Marma . . . ," Kit said, her eyes going from Ruth to me as she circled her index finger on one side of her head.

"Marmalade, stop that this minute," Ruth said, and we followed her gaze across the room, where an orange tabby, presumably Marmalade, was busy scratching the hem of the heavy curtains covering the front window. "She's not used to having guests," Ruth explained. "She acts up. Such a naughty girl."

"She's cute." Kit smiled, which almost made me choke. *Cute* is generally not in Kit's vocabulary, but the shredding of the draperies seemed to do it for her. "But back to William," she said, "and your secret."

"It was so long ago. And totally forgotten, I thought. But now . . . with all that's happened . . ." Ruth kept stroking her cat's fur, murmuring, "Oh, Baby, Baby." I hoped it was the cat's name and that she wasn't about to break out in a Justin Bieber song.

"What? What's happened?" Kit urged kindly.

Ruth looked shocked, as if Kit had just asked her if the world was round. "Two of my friends have died. *That's* what's happened." She sounded like the teacher Kit and I'd had in sixth grade, Mrs. Roundhorst, the one who could always make us feel as dumb as dirt.

"Of course; I'm so sorry," said Kit, the duly chastised student. "I just didn't know what that had to do with—"

Ruth sighed so heavily, it shut Kit right up. No mean feat. "William's my hero. He stood up for me when no one else would. And it cost him his job," Ruth continued. "Wooee," she added for good measure, employing the unique lingo I'd grown rather fond of.

Kit and I sat there, waiting for her to continue. And after more stroking and murmuring and purring, she did just that.

"I worked in oncology, you see. Cancer," Ruth said, still the teacher, making sure we understood. "It was a painful business, and not just for the patients. It was so hard to watch their suffering." Stroke, stroke, murmur, murmur, purr, purr. "Really, it was unbearable. And it wasn't like nowadays, with all the good hospice care at home and in centers. No, we really had to watch people go through so much pain before they finally passed."

"Aha," I heard Kit say, and I gave her a *be quiet* look.

Ruth seemed not to have noticed the lightbulb going on in Kit's head. And then mine.

"So sometimes I did what family members and hospice workers are now more free to do. I helped my dying patients along, with more frequent and stronger doses of morphine. Anything to alleviate their pain. And if it made them die hours—or even days—sooner, so *what*?" She glared at me and then turned her angry expression toward Kit.

"Hey, don't blame me," Kit said. "I'm on your side. We still treat our sick animals better—"

"Well, that's a slippery slope we don't need to go down right now," I said.

"So you're saying," Kit got us back on track, "that you—"

"I'm saying I was accused of mercy killing. They didn't have enough to actually charge me, legally, but they forced me to quit. That was back when they could get away with such strong-arming."

"And William? Where does he fit in here?" I asked.

"I didn't tattle on him back then, and I'm not going to start now." Ruth looked smug at the knowledge of what a loyal friend she was, so I didn't say what I was thinking: *well, you just* did *tattle on him.*

"Was he forced out too?" Kit asked.

"No. I *said* I didn't tattle on him. But he quit out of loyalty to me, I guess. Insisted he was ready to retire, anyway, although he was really too young for that, still in his fifties. But I think he's been happy. And I know I've been happier. They *allow* me to do for my animals what I wasn't allowed to do for people: keep them from suffering. That's my whole reason for being, to prevent suffering."

Thinking of that slippery slope, I found myself wondering if William had slid down it. Maybe it wasn't that big a stretch, after helping people in pain to die more quickly, to help along, say, a Virginia with a poke of a needle, if he felt the circumstances warranted.

But what could those circumstances have been?

***

It was pitch-dark as we drove back to my mom's, having left Ruth and Baby as soon as we realized she either had no more information to share with us, or she wasn't giving it up.

After a few moments of silence, I spoke. "Well, that was enlightening."

"Ya know, I'm not so sure. Did she really give us anything? I mean, anything to help us decide who would *want* Doris or Virginia dead?"

"Well, she gave me enough to be even more wary of my mother's fiancé."

"Val, you can no more stop your mom from marrying William than she could have stopped you from marrying David, and we both know she would have loved nothing more than that."

"I bet I can stop her if I prove he's a murderer."

"Is that what you're trying to do, prove William murdered them?"

"What do you *think* I'm trying to do?"

"I thought you were trying to find out *who* killed them, not trying to pin it on William just so your mom won't marry him."

"I am, Kit. I just got hopeful there for a minute that I could kill two birds with one stone." I cringed at the figure of speech but continued. "If I could prove my mom didn't do it and prove her fiancé *did*, then she'd be off the hook and also wouldn't marry him."

"And why are you so against that? They could have a really good life, ya know."

"Because he's not my dad. I guess I'm just being selfish."

"Yeah, Valley Girl, you are." But her tone of voice, if not her words, was sympathetic.

Before I could wallow in the shame that Kit's confirmation should have created in me, we were back in my mother's driveway. I noticed right away that William's car was there, which meant he and my mom and Emily were as well.

And, observant detective that I was, I also noticed the sheriff's car parked next to William's.

CHAPTER TWENTY-SEVEN

My mother and William were sitting on the couch—holding hands again, for Pete's sake. Emily was curled up in one armchair, and in the other sat an overweight man wearing what looked like a sheriff's uniform two sizes too small for him.

"Ah, ladies," William said, as soon as we entered the house. He disentangled himself from my mother's hold and rose from the couch, giving us each a hearty kiss on the cheek. "Marv, let me introduce you." William turned to the guy who was now struggling to get up out of the chair. "This is Valerie Pankowski, Jean's daughter. And her friend Katherine James."

"Pleased to know you." Marv was finally free of the furniture. He took two giant steps in our direction, his meaty palm extended.

"Marv is the sheriff," my mom said, from her place on the couch. "He's here on official police business."

Really, Mom? I thought, but didn't say. I didn't think he'd come to organize a wedding shower.

"Just wanted to see the doc," Marv said. "Had a bit of a nasty shock from the medical examiner concerning Virginia Huntley—"

"Yes," William said. "Seems like our sweet Virginia did not die of a—"

"Heart attack," my mother finished his sentence before he could. "Now they think she was deliberately killed."

"*Murdered?*" I said.

"Deliberately killed by persons unknown," my mother continued, purposely ignoring my outburst.

"Isn't that the same thing?"

"Valerie, why do you always have to be so dramatic?"

I sat down on the arm of the chair where Emily was curled up. "Wow, that's just horrible. How do you know?"

Marv rubbed his large belly. "Seems like they found a needle mark on her neck. She was injected with something to simulate a heart attack. Or *cause* a heart attack. Hmm. Not sure which. But terrible, terrible thing. Virginia Huntley was a fine woman."

I looked at Kit, who had moved to the kitchen area and was visible across the dividing counter. "Any idea who might have done it?" she asked.

Marv turned toward her. "No, ma'am. Not yet. But we'll catch whoever did; I can promise you that."

"It was good of you to let us know." William approached the door, clearly expecting Marv to follow his lead.

"No problem." Marv hooked his thumbs into his belt loops and pulled his pants up a notch. A wasted effort, by the way. "I know you and Virginia were good friends. I'm just checking with everyone who saw her on the day she died."

"Of course." William was at the front door, his hand actually on the doorknob. "As I said, I was supposed to give her a ride over to the Dibble house, but she never answered the door, so I assumed she wasn't home. If only I'd tried to get in—"

"Oh, William Stuckey," my mom said. "Don't go feeling guilty. There was nothing you could have done to save that poor woman."

William looked over at her and sent a sweet smile. "I guess not." By now he had actually opened the front door, even though Marv hadn't made a move toward it. William turned his gaze from my mother to the large sheriff. "If there's anything we can do, just let us know."

"Yep. Like they say, I know where you live." Marv chuckled. "I guess I'll be on my way." He took two steps and reached the front door. "You know, Doc, I'm kinda surprised you let this one slip by you."

"How so?" I asked, before my future daddy had a chance to.

The sheriff's eyes never left William. "Doc here was one of the best in the business, so I hear tell. I'm surprised you didn't think of something like this yourself."

William placed a hand on Marv's heavy shoulder, all but pushing him out the door. "I've been out of the doctoring business a long while," I heard him say. "Such a thing never occurred to me." He pulled the door closed behind them. I could hear their voices coming from the driveway, but not what they were saying.

I got up and went to the limited privacy of the kitchen and took Kit's arm. "He's lying," I whispered. "He told me he mentioned that sucky stuff to the M.E."

"Yeah, I caught that too. Didn't he tell you the jury was still out?"

"Well, it looks like they came back in," I said.

"I know, right?" We gave each other startled looks, and then Kit spoke again. "I wonder if Marv's as dumb as he acts. Maybe he's onto our William."

***

After William returned to the house and we heard the sheriff's vehicle drive away, my mom jumped up from the couch.

"My goodness," she said, as William took her in his arms. "Do you think Marv will ever figure it out?"

"He has a whole police department to help him." It wasn't clear if William thought that was a good or bad thing.

"Do you think we should postpone—"

"No. Definitely not. Everything's in place. All the arrangements are made. You and I are celebrating our engagement, no matter what."

Emily had entered the kitchen area, and the three of us stood behind the counter watching the loving couple. It looked like the final act of a Mexican soap opera.

"Te amo, Juana."

"Te amo, Guillermo."

"Grandma is so lucky," Emily whispered, in English.

***

The next day was a busy one, the day before the party. My mom spent most of the morning on the phone, calling and inviting friends to her little shindig. *Sorry it's such short notice. Yes, it was a big surprise. Please, no gifts.*

When she had called everyone in Door County she wanted to invite, we all drove to Green Bay to buy something to wear to the party. My mother insisted that William was paying for everything, so we should choose whatever we liked, as long as it was tasteful and appropriate. In other words, as long as it was something *she* liked.

As executor of Doris's will, William was at the lawyer's office, in his official capacity.

"I wonder what Stan thinks of William as the executor," I said to Kit, who was sitting in the backseat with me. Emily sat in front with my mom, who was driving her car at a dangerously slow pace to Green Bay.

"Not to mention her daughter," Kit said.

"No kidding. There's just something about William—"

"Yeah, he flat-out lied to Marv and couldn't wait to shove him out the door as soon as we arrived. And by the way, your future stepfather drives more slowly than your mom," she added, as if that were the worst crime he could be guilty of.

"Well, doesn't it bother you?"

"Of course. Slow drivers can be worse than speeders."

"No. I meant—"

"I know what you meant," she said. "We just have to find out why William lied to Marv. Don't worry; we will."

Our voices had raised above a whisper, and I saw my mom strain her neck a little to see us in the rearview mirror. "What are you girls talking about back there? You will what?"

Kit leaned forward to respond. "Have an awesome time shopping, Jean."

"Well, for heaven's sake, let's all stay together. I don't want to waste time searching for you if you wander off."

Kit sat back in her seat. "Yes, Miss Hannigan," she whispered.

***

We decided William had more money than we did time, so we went straight to Kit's favorite little—and very posh—shop in downtown Green Bay.

My only pleasure was finding an expensive dress, something I would never have purchased if I hadn't had the luxury of Daddy Warbucks's American Express Card.

Kit insisted on paying for her own outfit, a simple LBD that looked classy on her slim figure. She probably had ten just like it in her closet back home.

My mother chose a deep-purple silk dress and matching short jacket that accentuated her blond hair. She looked really pretty when she came out of the dressing room to show us.

I talked them all out of having a late lunch in Green Bay, preferring instead to go back to my mom's and relax. William was coming over for dinner later, and I planned to talk myself into a better mood by then. As Kit had said, it was what it was, and maybe it wasn't such a bad thing. I just hoped I wouldn't be visiting one of them in prison any time soon.

But my mood turned even more sour when we pulled onto my mom's road and could see William's Mercedes parked in her driveway. He was sitting inside the car, obviously waiting for us, and my mom's pleasure at seeing that did nothing to lift my spirits.

"Look! William Stuckey is here," she said.

"*Now* she speeds up," I whispered to Kit, as we pulled into the driveway and parked behind him.

"Let it go," Kit whispered back.

I watched him get out of his car, and I saw my mother's face break into a wide grin. I don't recall her ever being so happy to see my father.

"Here's my girls." He opened the driver's door and extended a hand to my mom.

"William Stuckey, this is a lovely surprise. I thought you'd be tied up all day."

He bent to kiss her cheek. "Me too, but it all took less time than I'd thought it would."

"So they read Doris's will?" Kit asked. I thought she might say *who got what*, but she didn't.

"Was it awful?" my mom asked.

"It was . . . interesting. Let's go inside, and I'll give you the gory details."

***

We had to wait until my mother and Emily had hung up their new purchases. Then my mom returned two calls from people who had left messages. Next she heated water to make tea, before disappearing into the bedroom to change clothes. (Why? She simply exchanged one pair of cropped pants for another.) When the tea was done, she finally joined us at the table.

Then I addressed William. "Can you tell us what happened?"

"I don't see why not," he said. "It's going to be big news soon."

"Okay, let's hear it," Kit said.

He took the cup of tea my mom offered him and smiled up at her. "It was somewhat of a surprise."

We all remained silent, waiting to hear the big news as eagerly as if we had actually been recipients of Doris's fortune.

"Well, for heaven's sake, tell us, William Stuckey." My mother was the first one to come out of the daze we all seemed to have fallen into. "You are being very mysterious."

"Actually, it was Doris who was mysterious," he said. "I don't know her motives; she never shared them with me. But it was a shocker, I can tell you."

He took an agonizingly slow sip of the tea. Finally, he spoke again. "She left a sum of ten thousand dollars each to Stan and Margaret."

"*No*," my mother said. "That's all?" She put her hand to her heart as if she were having an attack. It occurred to me that with Doris gone, her monthly income had come to an end.

"Yep. That's all. But here's the humdinger. The remainder of her estate, including her house here, her condo in Palm Beach, and all the assets of her company went to—"

"Who?" my mother asked. "Wait; don't tell me she left it to those ridiculous cats. I can't believe—"

"No, no, my dear. The cats have to fend for themselves, I'm afraid. It was Jacqueline Bakos. She left everything to her. And believe me, no one was more surprised than Miss Bakos."

"She was there?" my mother asked. "Why would she even be there?"

"She was invited by Doris's attorney. Which, as it turns out, was for good reason. She's now a very rich woman."

My mother stood up, looking alarmed. "There must be some mistake. Why would Doris do such a thing?"

"Why, indeed," William agreed.

***

Later, when my mother and Kit were once again battling it out in the kitchen, and Emily was reading in the bedroom, I enticed William outside with a glass of wine.

"Did you girls have fun shopping?" he asked.

"Yes. And thank you for being so generous."

He waved a hand in the air, indicating it was nothing.

"Can I ask you something?" I had decided to use our little time alone to level with him about some of my fears. It would have been better if Kit were with me, but through the glass door I could see her sitting at the kitchen table with her glasses on and a recipe card in her hand.

My mother stood over her, waving a long wooden spoon in the air. They appeared to be having a disagreement about something, probably whether shrimp should be cooked in or out of the shell. I had absolutely no opinion on the subject.

"You can ask me anything," William said. "In fact, I wish you would. I'm still getting a bad feeling from you, Valerie, and I don't like it. I want to clear the air."

"Okay, why did you lie to the police officer or sheriff or whatever Marv is?"

"Ah." He took a sip of wine. "I knew you caught that. How can I say this . . . In our field, or my previous field, we doctors don't like to interfere with each other's work. I did mention the drug that Kit asked me about to the medical examiner, but this is a very serious matter. I didn't want to steal his thunder. It was for him to find, not me. It was just better if it appeared that he came up with it on his own. A professional courtesy."

"Hmm," I said. "Okay, what about this?" I took a sip of wine before continuing. "Why did Doris make you executor of her will? It seems a bit strange to me, when she had a husband—"

He raised a hand to stop me from speaking, and I expected him to say *ah* again, but he didn't. Instead, he laughed. "Valerie, you might think you know everything that goes on up here—"

"On the contrary, I don't think I know enough."

"Doris and I had a unique relationship. Many of the people up here in our little social group are, shall we say, not overly sophisticated. But Doris was a special woman, highly educated. We clicked on many levels."

He's a snob, I thought, *and he feels superior to his Door County buddies*. At least that explained his appeal for my mother. She's the biggest snob I know.

"We were really close friends," he continued, looking sad. "In fact, Doris was the one I confided in about my feelings for your mother."

"Ah," I said. Was that a new family trait I'd already picked up?

"Yes. And she encouraged me to pursue Jean. In fact, she even picked out the ring. She found it and purchased it for me."

"What?" I asked. "You didn't buy that gorgeous ring yourself?"

"No, no, that's not what I mean. I had planned on giving Jean a family heirloom. A ring that had belonged to my mother. I showed it to Doris, and she nearly fell over— sorry, poor choice of words. What I mean is, she told me Jean would never want that old thing, and she made it her mission to find something more suitable."

He gave a wry chuckle, as if at the memory. "She purchased it on a trip to Amsterdam," he continued. "As you probably know, they are quite famous for their diamonds. I wanted to fly over there and get it myself, but she sent me a text with a picture of the ring she'd found, and she insisted on buying it while she was there. I felt a little strange, but she talked me into it. Naturally, I told her I'd reimburse her as soon as she returned."

"Hmm," I said. At least no *ah!* "That must have been some reimbursement." I figured he'd dropped at least ten grand on the thing.

"What does the cost matter? Doris was certain that Jean would love it, and she was right. By the way, Doris enjoyed the intrigue of the whole matter. It was exciting for her. She and Stan didn't exactly have what you would call a romantic relationship, so I think she was living a little vicariously through Jean and me. She insisted the whole business be kept secret, so no one else knew. Just the two of us."

"And you paid her back?" I asked.

"Of course, Valerie. A necessary evil." He chuckled. "But seriously, you think I wouldn't pay for my fiancée's ring? What kind of man do you think I am?"

I had to think about that for a few seconds because I recognized his words from the note we had found, signed *Wm.*, in Doris's study: *a necessary evil.* Could he merely have been referring to the blasted ring?

After listening to his explanation, I really wanted to believe he was a good man; I'd known him for most of my life, and my mother appeared to be completely smitten with him. But I still couldn't get the right words out. "I think we should go see how they're getting on in the kitchen," I said instead.

We both turned to look through the glass door.

Kit was standing by the sink, her arms crossed over her chest, a defiant look on her face. My mom sat at the table, carefully peeling the shells from a large bowl of innocent shrimp (uncooked, by the way). She looked very pleased. Clearly, the great shell debate had gone her way.

"If you think I would join those two when they are trying to outcook each other, then you must think I'm a fool," he said.

"No, I don't think you're a fool. That's one thing I am certain of."

CHAPTER TWENTY-EIGHT

If I was surprised to see Margaret and Stan at the engagement party, I was *shocked* to see Stan appearing so . . . well, accepting of inheriting only ten thousand dollars. In our last conversation, he had seemed frantic to sell the house he assumed—in spite of their prenup—would be his.

Margaret was a different story. Acceptance wasn't the word that came to mind to describe her reaction.

We had arrived at the party place early—William and his entourage of women—and we found absolute perfection awaiting us. My mom looked disappointed.

William had convinced her to hire everything done. Obviously, he didn't know her well enough to be marrying her if he thought the word *delegate* was part of her vocabulary. She'd planned to go two hours ahead of time, by herself, "just to make sure everything is right." But William insisted we'd all go with her, and then we'd need to go only *one* hour early.

I was growing used to my mother giving in to William's insistence. Still, every time she did it, I was reminded of my dad, who hardly ever insisted on anything. On the rare occasions that he tried to, he was quickly shot down by my mother.

We took seats at a high bistro table in the bar area near the banquet room. William, looking elegant in his dark-navy double-breasted suit and yellow silk tie, ordered champagne. He insisted we have a private toast before the other guests arrived. I thought I'd be doing well to toast to the uncertain event *once*.

But before William had a chance to raise his glass, our attention was turned toward a large man with a booming voice who burst through the archway. "Here you are!"

It was Tom Haskins. My friend, my boss, my whatever. He has a knack for entering a room and completely taking it over, his presence filling the entire space and reducing everyone else to mere bystanders. He was dressed impeccably, as always, this time in a gray suit hand-tailored to fit his sturdy body. His silk tie with a dash of red and his chunky gold cuff links added just the right flourishes.

"Tom!" my mother squealed, as she hopped off her high stool like a limber teen and ran into his open arms.

Tom's infectious lopsided grin was a welcome sight. I might not have been thrilled that he was invited, but I was glad to see him.

"Tom!" Emily joined her grandmother in throwing her arms around him.

It wasn't the first time I'd seen him enfolded by more than one woman, and I could almost see his bald head growing bigger with all the female attention.

I felt awkward in my straight-skirted dress as I lowered myself off the stool. Taking a deep breath, I went to where they were still enjoying their group hug and reached in to give him a pat on the back. "Hi, Tom."

William approached Tom in a leisurely manner. "William Stuckey," he said, sounding like my mom. He extended his hand to Tom, forcing my boss to remove himself from the embrace my mother still held him in.

Tom held his hand out to William. "Tom Haskins. Nice to meet you, William. And welcome to the family." He threw a smile my way, with a gleam in his eyes. I knew that meant he thought my concerns were unfounded.

I returned to our table, where Kit was still sitting, and eventually Tom walked over to us and gave me a long, hard hug. "I think this guy looks pretty safe, Kiddo," he whispered in my ear.

"Ha," I whispered back. "What do *you* know?"

He finally released me and gave Kit a curt nod as he scraped a stool over from a neighboring table.

"I went to Jean's house first, and when no one was there, I figured you guys would be here." He snapped his fingers and then pointed to my champagne flute, motioning to the waiter to bring him a glass of what we were having.

"He's so *bright*," Kit said out of one side of her mouth, cocking her head in my direction. "Like a *star*."

"Speaking of space objects, how the hell are you, Kit?" Tom asked.

"So much better now that you're here."

I was beginning to get that uncomfortable feeling I always get whenever those two start to bait each other, and I was groping for something totally benign to distract them when my mother (God bless her) marched over to do it for me.

"Why are you just sitting here, Valerie? Make yourself useful." Well, *almost* benign.

"Whaddya need, Jean?" Tom took a full glass of champagne from a passing waiter.

"Not you, silly. You're a guest. Valerie, run into the kitchen and make sure the staff look presentable. I think I noticed one of the waitresses wearing brown shoes. And Katherine, would you please check with the person at the front door and make sure there are enough valets. I hate it when you have to wait for someone to take your car keys."

Tom looked at his Rolex. "Just about party time. Everything in there looks lovely, by the way. Thanks to you, Jean, I'm sure," I heard him say, as Kit and I prepared to depart to opposite ends of the building to perform our unnecessary tasks.

My mother merely smiled, and I knew she was sorry she *hadn't* had more to do with it. But she didn't mind taking the credit, anyway.

When I returned from my mission thirty seconds later (no brown shoes spotted), Tom raised his glass, and the rest of us joined him.

"To the happy couple," he said, triggering a chorus of "here, here."

How like him to take charge of the first toast. I thought I saw a look of dismay flash across William's face, which pleased me.

When Kit returned from her own useless assignment, she took a sip of her champagne and then belatedly raised her glass to the happy couple.

And indeed, the couple *did* look happy. Very.

And then the party almost ruined it.

***

The first two people to arrive were Ruth Greenway and a woman I'd never seen before, although she did seem vaguely familiar.

Ruth looked adorable in a green velvet jacket and slim black pants. Perched on her head was a cream-colored cap with matching sequins covering the brim. I had become so accustomed to her huge glasses that I barely noticed them. I did notice, however, a small gold cat pin on the lapel of her jacket. I'd go so far as to say it was tasteful.

The woman with her looked to be in her late twenties, tall and slim, with honey-colored hair that came to her shoulders. She wore a conservative navy-blue suit, with a starched white blouse underneath.

"Ruth! Stephanie!" My mom rushed to the women and gave them a joint hug. "Stephanie, I'm so glad you were able to join us."

"Wouldn't miss it," Ruth answered for both of them. "Wowzers, that's some rock." She took my mom's hand and held it up to her face, inspecting the ring closely, like a jeweler.

"I want you to meet everyone." My mother shook her hand loose and clutched Stephanie's arm, turning her toward us. "This is William Stuckey, my fiancé. And this is my daughter, Valerie. My granddaughter, Emily, is around somewhere. Katherine, go find her."

It wasn't lost on anyone that my mother had failed to introduce Kit, but I saw my friend smile slightly as she extended her hand to Stephanie. "Kit James, friend of the family."

"Nice to meet you." Stephanie smiled back, and then I realized she was related to Virginia. The same facial features, only younger and fresher.

"Stephanie is Virginia's niece," Ruth confirmed my assumption.

"Grandniece, actually." Stephanie smiled again and then turned back to my mother. "Thank you so much for the invite."

"My dear, it's so good to see you again. I just wish it were under better circumstances. You know how much I loved Virginia. We are all devastated."

"Yes." Stephanie's smile disappeared. "It's horrible. And right after poor Doris. I'm glad we at least have something good to celebrate. Congratulations, by the way. William, do you remember me?"

"I never forget a beautiful blond," William answered, which made me want to throw up. Hadn't he used the same corny line on Kit when we'd first arrived in Door County? "I had no idea you were in town," he added.

"Yes, I came to make arrangements for my aunt."

"I'm so sorry," I spoke up.

"These things have to be done," William said. "If you need help with anything, anything at all, you let me know. I am at your disposal."

"Everything's under control, thanks. Ruth has kindly offered to let me stay with her for a couple of days."

"That's good," Kit said, and I could see her scanning Stephanie's dark suit for cat hair. "Where are you from, Stephanie?"

"I live in New Orleans."

Kit nodded. "Nice city."

"Yes, I like it. I'm originally from New York. My family lives there—in Elmsford, where I'm making arrangements for my aunt's . . . for Aunt Virginia."

"What do you do in New Orleans?" Kit asked.

"She's a top salesperson for fancy jewelry down there," Ruth said.

"Good heavens, Katherine, how many questions do you plan to ask poor Stephanie?" my mom said. "Please go find Emily, like I asked you to do ten minutes ago."

Before allowing herself to be dismissed, Kit glanced at her watch to make her point. "Definitely not ten minutes," she said, "and I'm sure Stephanie doesn't mind a few social questions."

"Let me get you a drink," I said, trying to defuse the awkward situation my mother was busy creating. I took Stephanie's arm and led her toward the bar. "Please excuse my mom; she's a little stressed out, what with losing two dear friends and then this last-minute engagement party."

Stephanie smiled. "I'm not bothered a bit. I'm just glad I came tonight. I wasn't planning to, but Ruth insisted."

"I'm glad you did too. I didn't know your aunt well, but she seemed like a lovely person."

"She was. I'll miss her a lot."

"Were you close?"

"Yes. Very. We spoke on the phone a couple of times a week, and she was always so encouraging to me. She made me feel there was nothing I couldn't do."

I saw her eyes moisten over, and I put an arm around her shoulders. "This must be so hard for you."

"Yes, it's hard. But she lived a good life, and she was very happy here. Except for losing Doris, of course. That really upset her. Especially under the circumstances."

"Yes, of course."

At the bar, I ordered a glass of pinot grigio, and Stephanie asked for the same.

"She was so troubled by what she saw," Stephanie said.

I recalled Virginia telling us how she caught Doris crying and how Doris said she felt ashamed. I nodded in sympathy, wrapping a napkin around the stem of my glass.

Stephanie took a deep breath and then continued. "I advised her to go to the police—"

"The police? Have you spoken to them?" I wondered if she'd been told yet the real cause of her aunt's death.

"No, but I'm going to. By the way, is Margaret here yet? Can you point her out to me?"

"What's a girl gotta do to get a drink around here?" It was Ruth. She put an arm around Stephanie's waist and gave her a glowing smile. "Everything okay, toots?"

"Everything is just fine," Stephanie assured her.

When I scoped out the room, which was quickly filling up, I saw my mother on the far side, waving at me like a crossing guard directing children safely from one side of the street to the other.

"Valerie, come here," I heard her call. "I want you to meet my dentist."

"Excuse me," I said to Ruth and Stephanie. "We'll talk later, I hope."

***

At least seventy-five people had arrived to celebrate my mom's engagement to William. I figured he was probably responsible for most of the friendships, having lived there longer, and my mom probably met most of those people through him. Well, however she'd met them, they appeared to be keepers: warm and welcoming and oh-so-happy for my mom and William.

Even Stan seemed to leave his troubles at the door to revel in someone else's good fortune. He approached us as soon as he arrived, looking dapper in a gray suit, different from the one he'd worn to the funeral. "You got yourself a good one, William." He reached up to slap my mom's fiancé on the back. I was impressed with his happy demeanor, considering he'd been rendered homeless and had only a mere ten grand in the bank.

William looked almost guilty, maybe because Stan no longer had a good wife. "Thanks, Stan, I appreciate—"

As if a director had whispered to him in a nonexistent earpiece, Stan removed his hand from where it still rested on William's back and gave my mom a quick kiss on the cheek. Then he bolted halfway across the room to another circle of partiers.

And then I saw why.

Margaret had arrived. And she was headed our way.

She appeared still dressed in mourning: a black straight skirt, black silk blouse with three-quarter-length sleeves and covered buttons, and black shoes that were as flat as Jacqueline Bakos's favorite footwear was high. Only the small gift bag that swung from her hand as she walked offered a touch of color. It was deep purple, with lavender tissue paper spilling over the edges.

But the look on her face told me the first word out of her mouth wasn't likely to be *congratulations*.

CHAPTER TWENTY-NINE

There must be something you can do," Margaret said, as soon as she reached William. She looked up at him with an expression that was a mixture of panic and fury.

"I told you, dear, I'm just the executor. That means I execute the wishes of the deceased, er, your mother. You can contest the will, I suppose. You'd have to consult an attorney."

"You're damn right I'll consult an attorney." Margaret turned to leave and then seemed to suddenly remember her manners. "Congratulations. Where shall I put this?" She held the gift bag out in front of her as if it were a smelly fish.

My mother reached out to take the gift. "Why, Margaret, you shouldn't have. And with all you have to contend with—"

"Are you kidding me?" Margaret gave a shrill laugh that sounded like a half sob. "My mother would kill me if I didn't give you a gift."

No one said the obvious: her mother was in no position to kill anyone.

"Yes, your mother was always more than generous," I heard my mom say, as I watched her usher Margaret to a chair at the next table over. They sat down, and my mother set the gift bag carefully on her lap before putting an arm around Margaret's shoulders and saying something we couldn't hear.

"That's a tough one." William drew my attention from my mother and what I figured would become her latest project: the grieving orphan.

"What was that all about?" Tom had arrived, bringing with him the faint aroma of the cigar he'd been enjoying out on the deck. Of course smoking wasn't allowed, even out there, but I knew Tom would assume that pesky rule didn't apply to him.

And then the unthinkable happened.

As the four of us watched, in curiosity and then in horror, Margaret yanked herself out of my mother's embrace and stood up, wobbling from the fast movements in spite of her flat shoes (was she perhaps drunk?), and then she lashed out angrily. " . . . a lot of money . . . you've got some explaining . . . check register . . . damn suspicious . . . ," we heard Margaret hiss when her voice occasionally rose from its almost whisper.

Like wooden soldiers, we all slowly edged a little closer to the table where they sat, so we could hear better. I was getting scared.

My mother merely sat there, with her lips forming a silent "O" of shock.

We were now close enough for William's long legs to reach the table in a couple of strides. Putting himself between them, he took Mom's arms and helped her to a standing position. Then, in a commanding voice, he said, "That will be quite enough, Margaret. I know you're upset, but this is not the time. You will start behaving right now, or you will leave."

I saw Margaret's wild-eyed look transform into a dazed expression as she looked at William and then at me. I decided she didn't seem drunk. She seemed drugged. She gave us an angry look and wandered unsteadily off to another table.

I felt Kit at my side now and Tom's presence right behind her. Well, maybe I didn't feel his presence so much as I smelled his unlit cigar that I knew he was vigorously chewing on. He always does that whenever he is mad or worried.

"What the hell . . . ," he and Kit said in unison.

I turned to see them both looking chagrined that they'd found themselves united in something. But then we all focused on my mom, who looked stunned. I had to hand it to Margaret; at least she had managed to shut my mother up.

"She's completely out of line," William said. "Disgraceful behavior."

"She's crazy, Grandma," Emily said.

"Yeah, she's nuts," Kit added, for good measure.

"She's drunk," Tom concluded. "Forget about her." It was like telling someone to ignore the thunderstorm rolling in off Lake Michigan and have fun on the beach.

I looked around the room for Margaret. She was a few tables away from us, talking animatedly with two women I didn't recognize.

And Kit was poking me hard in the ribs.

"Ouch! Wha—"

"Shhh." Kit nodded her head and spoke with her eyes.

I followed her gaze and spotted Margaret's purse on the floor by the chair she had been occupying only moments earlier.

"Yeah?" I gave Kit a look of confusion.

She rolled her eyes in exasperation, reached down and picked up Margaret's purse, and walked swiftly toward the archway that led out of the party room.

I looked at my mom, who was being comforted by William, and decided she would be taken care of (although I knew memories of her engagement party would never be among her favorites).

Tom was busy with Emily, his arm around her waist, saying something that elicited laughter from her (as well as from the pretty waitress who was hovering next to them with a tray of champagne flutes).

So I followed Kit, catching sight of her just as she went out the door into the parking lot.

I picked up my pace and pushed through the same door. "Kit! What are you doing? That's stealing," I said, when I finally caught up.

She was rummaging through Margaret's purse and didn't answer me until she found what she was looking for: a set of keys. She dropped them into her own bag and then snapped Margaret's shut. She thrust it at me and said, "Return this to where it was and do whatever you have to do to get William's car keys."

"What in—"

"Val, we don't have time. I'll explain while we're driving."

"Driving where?"

She gave me a look that convinced me I should just follow her orders.

When I returned to Kit, I waved William's keys in the air, feeling rather proud about how efficiently I'd talked him into handing them over.

"Impressive, Val. Way to go. I hated to think how we were going to talk the valet out of his key."

We located William's car, which luckily had been parked at the end of a row of equally luxurious automobiles, so we could easily drive it away. Kit got into the passenger seat as I put William's keys in the ignition.

"Just tell me where we're going," I said. "And tell me why."

"Are you kidding me? Do I have to spell everything out?"

"I guess so. Where to?"

"To Doris's house, of course. Where else? Don't you see? Your mother was practically accused of murder back there."

"Hardly murder. Blackmail, maybe."

"Ha! Whatever it was, Margaret isn't going to stop with telling just your mom about her suspicions. We have to prove she's innocent."

"But how?"

"We have to search that study again, especially Doris's computer. And *especially* we have to look for something that connects Doris to Virginia—some reason they'd both be dead within a day of each other." Then, as if to close the sale, she added, "Ya know, if the police listen to Margaret about your mom having anything to do with Doris's death, they'll look at her for Virginia's too."

And of course I knew Kit was right. I just wondered if we could get back to the party soon enough to make the lie I'd told William believable, that Kit had forgotten her cell and was expecting an important call from Larry. I also wondered what we were going to do if Margaret discovered her keys missing before we could get them—*somehow*—back into her purse.

"Details," Kit said, reading my mind.

"How do you—"

"I know you are making a list in your head of all the things that can go wrong. They are details, Valley Girl. We can do this. By the way, has Tom put on weight or what?"

"He looks exactly the same to me."

I wasn't sure if I'd even uttered that comment out loud. At that moment, I just had to drive. We were across the peninsula from Stan's house. It wasn't as far as it sounded— less than ten miles—but the winding roads slowed me down more than Kit liked.

"Can't you go just a little faster?"

"No, I cannot. And this had better be worth it or else . . ." I said it like the warning I meant it to be, even though I had no idea what the *or else* would be.

But Kit didn't give me a chance to say more. "Yes, it sure as hell better be," she agreed. "Or else your mother is in a heap of trouble."

***

When we crept into Doris's house, I was struck by how cold it felt. Or maybe it was just *I* who was cold, from fear. After all, it was a warm May evening.

We both stopped in the hallway and looked up at the long staircase facing us. The huge house seemed twice as large with no other people in it.

"Plan?" I asked Kit.

"None that I know of."

"So we make it up as we go along?"

"Good girl. Now we *do* have a plan."

We took a brief look around the first-floor rooms. In one corner of the dining room was a suitcase, the small carry-on kind. Emerald green, with a black patent-leather strap. "Margaret's or Stan's?" Kit asked.

"Surely Margaret's. Where would Stan be running off to? He does live here."

"Or did. I'm sure Jacqueline will kick him out."

"Right." I laughed nervously and followed Kit through the dining room into the kitchen. It was deserted.

"Okay, we don't have a lot of time." Kit turned quickly and headed back toward the hallway in the direction of the study. As we passed the grand staircase again, I tried not to think of Doris tumbling to her death.

The double doors to the study were closed, so Kit gingerly turned the brass handles, and we entered the room. It didn't appear altered since our last surreptitious look around. Except for the papers on the desk. There were even more of them than before, and they looked as though they'd been hastily read and thrown down.

"You start in the desk drawers," Kit said. "I'll go through these papers."

"What about the comput—"

But she was ahead of me, having hit a button on the computer tower under the desk before I finished my question. "What are the chances it needs a password?" she asked.

"I'd say pretty darn good." I was kneeling on the floor, where I'd pulled out a heavy drawer stuffed with manila folders. Each had a label handwritten on it.

"Okay," Kit said, "if you were Doris Dibble, what would your password be?"

"Hmm. She didn't have a pet. She might have used a variation of Margaret."

"Larry's password is now a secret."

"Don't worry. You've cracked his code before."

"No, you don't get it. That's his password: *a secret*."

"That's cute."

"It's cute if you're Harry Potter."

I laughed, but only for a second. "Here's something," I said. I'd pulled out a folder marked *J. Bakos*. I sat back so I could more comfortably peruse its contents: a copy of Jacqueline's passport; several letters and documents in a foreign language; and a résumé, in English, with JACQUELINE BAKOS typed at the top of the page. "Now this is interesting. Jacqueline's résumé. It looks like it was typed on a typewriter."

"Anything good?"

"Well, she worked in a hospital in Zagreb for a year. That must have been after her husband—"

"Sounds about right. She's got the bedside manner. And ya know, if she worked in a hospital, she might know how to give an injection."

"Yeah, that's what I'm thinking, although it doesn't say what she did at the hospital—just that she worked there." I returned the résumé to the folder and shoved it back in the drawer. "But I can't help but feel sorry for her," I added.

"Hmm. I wouldn't waste too much time on *that*. She's a rich woman now."

"Well, that still doesn't bring back the husband and kids she lost."

Kit had her fingers poised over the keyboard. "We may have a little problem if we can't access this computer. Why do we need passwords, anyway, to get into our home computers?"

"So that people like us can't gain access." I flipped through some more folders.

"Who remembers passwords? How do you remember yours?"

"I keep all my passwords and log-in stuff in a book in my kitchen drawer. What about you?"

"They're stored in my cell phone." Her fingers still hovered.

"Okay," I said. "Try this. All caps. DOOR COUNTY IS FOR LOVERS."

"What the hell?" she said, as her fingers hit the keys.

As soon as she pressed Enter, she gave me a smile.

I closed the folder in my lap labeled *Passwords*. Then I stood from my kneeling position and looked over Kit's shoulder at the computer screen. A picture of Doris and Stan filled it. They were sitting at a table outside a restaurant. It was sunny, and they were both smiling and holding up wineglasses in a toast to whoever was taking the picture. They looked happy, which made me sad about Doris all over again.

"Look, here's a shortcut for Wells Fargo." Kit moved the mouse over the logo of the bank. "Check that folder and see if we have a log-in for it."

I picked up the folder again and began to search. The room's silence engulfed us until it was shattered by the *Law & Order* theme song. I grabbed my purse and reached in to silence my phone. But when I saw Tom's name on the screen, I hit the *talk* button.

"PANKOWSKI! Where the hell are you?"

"Tom." I knelt back down. "I'll be back in a little while—"

"I've been trapped by some broad who's given me the history of cats. Get back here and save me. Where the hell are you, anyway?" he asked again, and that time he waited for my answer.

"We had to go back to Mom's to get Kit's phone—"

"Oh no. You're with *her*?"

"Well, of course. Who did you think I was with? By the way, is Margaret still there?"

"Which one is Margaret?"

"Margaret's the petite brunette who was upset—"

"And drunk," Kit added.

"Okay, she's a little drunk—"

"There's plenty of drunks here. And I'll be joining them soon if you don't hurry back."

"Okay. We're on our way. Promise. Go outside and smoke a cigar."

"Where the hell do you think the cat lady accosted me?"

I smiled as I turned my phone off and dropped it back into my purse. I returned to the folder in my hands and searched for a Wells Fargo log-in. "Here it is."

As I read the information aloud, Kit keyed it in. A couple of clicks later and she was on the page that listed the transactions. "Okay, good," she said. "Whew, her checking balance is really high. You'd think she'd have found a better place to park this much cash."

"I think that was just walking-around money for her. Look for checks made out for five thousand dollars, and then we'll see if they're really to Jean Caldwell."

"I know what to do, Valley Girl. I'm not a complete idiot."

I was back on my feet, leaning over Kit, my nerves making me shaky and nauseous, as she continued to click. When an image of a check, presumably written in Doris's hand, filled the screen. I was afraid to look. But I did.

Suddenly I had to lean on the back of the chair for support. But it was because I was shaking with relief. My mother's name did not appear on the check. Instead, it was made out to something called *Locktia Edwards Industries Obitelj Reljef Fond.*

Kit quickly closed it and opened the next five-thousand-dollar check. Again, instead of my mother's name, the same words appeared. And on it went. A check for five thousand dollars written the first of every month. And none of them made out to my mother.

"I guess we don't need to be fluent in Croatian to figure this out," I said.

"Nope." Kit leaned back in the chair. "Looks like your mom was not the recipient of the monthly checks. This seems more like blood money to me, considering Jacqueline's sad little story."

"Who cares? The important thing is, my mother was telling me the truth. She didn't know anything about these checks. And obviously, Doris didn't want anyone else to, either."

"Yep. But funny William didn't mention her leaving anything to them in the will."

"She didn't want anyone to know, dum-dum," I said, turning one of her favorite nicknames for me back on her. But I could hardly say the words without laughing hysterically. I was giddy with relief. "Let's close this down and get out of here."

Kit exited the bank page and hit the shutdown button at the corner of the screen.

I gave a deep sigh. "Oh, I'm so happy."

"And we didn't get caught." Kit hit the button on the computer tower under the desk.

"Not quite," said a voice that was neither of ours.

Kit and I both looked up to see Jacqueline Bakos standing in the doorway.

"In my country, when people break into someone's home, it is the serious crime. I think you two are caught with the red hands."

CHAPTER THIRTY

And just what color do you think *your* hands are?" Kit demanded, after taking in the sight of Jacqueline. "Something tells me *you* don't have permission to be here."

"What you mean? This is my house now. I'm surprised you didn't know."

She was correct, of course. Although it didn't seem quite right.

"Kit, let's go." I waved William's car keys in the air in an attempt to get her attention. It felt as if I were enticing a dog to go out for a walk. But this pooch wasn't going anywhere.

I really didn't want us to have any further conversation with Jacqueline. I'd learned all I cared to know: my mother had no motivation to kill Doris. Or, I was sure, Virginia.

But I should have known Kit was in too deep to leave it at that. She ignored me, her gaze riveted on Jacqueline. "It most certainly is not your house yet. There's probate and title work and—speaking of red—a hell of a lot of red tape before you can call this place home." Kit sounded as if she knew what she was talking about, and even though I was the Realtor, I was ready to defer to her.

Jacqueline seemed to make the same assumption and lost just a little of her bluster.

Still, she had the temerity to join us by the desk. "I would say I have more rights than the two of you with your busy bodies. Why *are* you here? Why you go through Mrs. Doris's stuff—again?"

"Because we didn't find what we were looking for the first time. And now we have." Kit's tone implied that was justification for our breaking and entering.

I decided that was the perfect segue to convince her to leave—the house *and* "the case." "Kit, you're right. We did find what we were looking for. Now can we just go?"

"What about you? What are *you* looking for?" Kit asked Jacqueline.

"I'm leaving," I said, taking a couple of steps toward the door, hoping Kit would follow me. But she remained at the desk.

"I don't have to explain myself," Jacqueline said.

"Did you know Doris was planning to leave everything to you?" Kit asked.

"How would I know that? I'm not the snoopy."

"You don't seem exactly shocked," Kit continued. Of course neither Kit nor I had any idea what Jacqueline's initial reaction had been to becoming an heiress. She might have dropped her sullenness and performed a break dance, for all we knew. But Kit had grabbed my attention.

"Did you know Doris was giving money every month to a Croatian fund for the families of the men killed in the shipyard?" I asked.

Jacqueline didn't speak for a second and even looked a little surprised. "I have no ideas," she finally said.

"Very generous of her, don't you think?" I continued.

"Five thousand bucks a month," Kit added.

"Ha. Five thousand bucks! That was nothing for her. She spend ten times that on one of her dinner parties. You Americans. You think money is only thing important in the world. But money doesn't bring back my family. Nothing does. Everyone in Wisconsin could die, for all I care. I still don't have my family."

She walked over to the desk and began arranging the loose papers into a neat pile, as if they were hers. "I want you to leave now," she said, not looking at us, but concentrating on the tidy stack she was building.

"Don't you feel any remorse over her death?" Kit asked, from her seat behind the desk.

"Mrs. Doris get exactly what is coming to her."

"Phew. You're a piece of work," Kit said.

Jacqueline looked up from her task, her face defiant. "You are right for once. I am piece of work. I work hard for her. I do my job; I show her respect. I never ask her for anything other than wages she pay me. I never beg her for money, like . . ." She shook her head.

"Like who?" Kit urged.

"Makes no difference now. Money is all mine. And no check going to Croatia is big enough to cover damage she caused."

"*Who* begged her for money?" Kit asked again.

Perhaps assuming—correctly—that Kit wasn't going to let that go unanswered, Jacqueline obliged. "Ruth, Margaret, you-name-it; they all beg. As if she not already busy enough giving her friends lots of presents and money for damn cats—ha!"

Jacqueline looked as if something had just dawned on her. "They probably think she take care of everyone in will too." She laughed, but then her look turned angry. "But always she give her husband tiny amount to live on. He make about the same amount of money as me."

"He wasn't a prisoner. He could have left anytime," Kit said, her tone of voice implying *what the hell does that have to do with anything?*

I suddenly remembered something. "The suitcase in the dining room. Is it yours? Are you still heading to New York?"

"It belong to Margaret. I know nothing about it. And where I go now is not the business of you." She laughed as she said it, but there was no humor in that laughter.

The slam of a door in the hallway changed the subject for all of us.

Jacqueline looked alarmed and turned to leave the room, but before she could reach the doors to the study, we heard a man's voice.

"Darling, I left that damn party as soon as—" Stan Dibble stopped talking when he reached the doorway. He looked quickly from Jacqueline to Kit and then to me. "What the—"

"These two have been doing the rummage through your wife's things," Jacqueline said quickly. "I catch them in the act. Why you return from fun party—"

"Now see here," Stan quickly interjected, ignoring Jacqueline's attempt to undo the kink his sudden appearance had no doubt put in their plans. "This isn't what it seems." He moved across the room to put his arm around Jacqueline. Bad move.

Aha, I literally thought. Of course someone as lovely as Jacqueline (when she wasn't skulking around) would be irresistible to Stan, who was, after all, married to someone old enough to be his big sister if not his mother.

"Really?" Kit asked. "Do you always refer to your housekeeper as *darling*?"

"It's none of your business what I call anyone. Whatever you came here for, you should just leave now."

"So," I said, having another *aha* moment. "Selling the house so quickly was not really for your benefit, but for your girlfriend here. Nice going."

"And it wasn't too upsetting to get only ten grand in the will," Kit added. "You will be more than busy helping your former housekeeper spend her fortune."

"You are out of the line," Jacqueline said between clenched teeth. "You have no idea. Mrs. Doris an evil person. She responsible for many deaths in my country. And she treat her husband like the lapdog."

"Yeah, he's a dog, all right." Kit finally rose from her seat at the desk.

"One thing," Stan said. "We didn't have anything to do with Doris's death, if that's what you're thinking, and we had no idea she was leaving almost everything to Jacqueline. I was sad to lose my wife, but I was planning to leave her anyway. Jacqueline and I are moving to New York."

Kit just stared at him for a moment, and the look of disgust on her face told me she didn't trust him any more than I did. She finally joined me at the study doors, but before we closed them behind us, we watched Stan pull Jacqueline into his arms. Over his shoulder we could see a smile on her beautiful face. Clearly, it was for our benefit. And suddenly her face no longer seemed quite so beautiful.

***

Clutching William's keys, I scurried toward his car parked in the driveway. Jacqueline's tiny Volkswagen was parked between William's Mercedes and Stan's Jaguar, looking like the chubby baby of the two high-end vehicles.

"Weren't you getting afraid? I mean if they *did* kill . . . ," I said, turning toward Kit. Only she wasn't behind me. "Kit?" I called, looking back toward the house and noticing the front door ajar.

Fear coursed through me, and before starting back up the sidewalk, I took my phone out of my purse and hoped I wasn't too shaky to push 9-1-1 if necessary.

But then Kit emerged from the house and ran toward the car. In one hand was the small green suitcase we had seen in the dining room. She held the other hand up to her mouth, shushing me with her index finger pressed to her lips.

I hurried to start the car. "What in the world are you doing—"

"Drive." Kit cradled the small suitcase on her lap, looking entirely too pleased with herself for our own good. When she decided it was safe, she issued another order. "Here," she said. "Pull over here."

I eased William's car onto a little apron that looked like the beginning of a driveway by the side of the road. It appeared to lead nowhere, however, instead stopping at the edge of a thick woods. I put the car in park but left it running. Just in case.

"Okay. Now what?" I asked.

"Now what? Are you kidding me?" She had already opened the passenger door and stepped out, placing the suitcase on the seat she'd vacated. "We check it out, of course." She had her hand on the zipper.

"It's stealing, Kit," I told her for the second time that night.

"Whaddya mean, stealing? We just borrowed it. We'll return it; don't worry."

"Still stealing."

"We need to find out who it belongs to—"

"It's Margaret's; Jacqueline told us that—"

"Uff da." Kit laughed. "Who can believe anything she says? For all we know, Jacqueline herself stole this suitcase."

"And that would make sense how? For goodness' sake, open it if you're going to."

"You're right; this is Margaret's suitcase."

"How do you know for sure?"

She gave me a triumphant look. "It has *MME* right here." Sure enough, she pointed to the letters embroidered in a slightly darker shade of green than the suitcase itself. "Plus, this little thing." She reached into a clear plastic slot on one side of the bag and pulled out a small white card. "Here's her business card." She held it up for me to see: *Margaret Michelle Edwards.* And then she unzipped the suitcase.

I slid over the seat and pulled open the top to get a closer look.

It was neatly packed, and on top of a bed of clothes lay a plastic Ziploc bag. It contained various items, including makeup remover, moisturizer, and a battery-operated toothbrush.

"Look." Kit held up the bag. "Crest Whitestrips. I did notice Margaret has very white teeth."

"Forget her teeth. Keep looking." I should have added the word *gently* because Kit was anything *but*, as she began to rummage through the clothes.

"Nothing interesting." She had tossed the top layer on the seat and sounded as disappointed as I felt. Then again, especially once we knew the suitcase was Margaret's, I hadn't been all that hopeful that we'd find any answers.

"What the—who the hell travels with a turtle pillow?" Kit held up a soft-looking part-stuffed-animal-part-pillow.

"She's our age," I said, as if that explained it.

But it obviously didn't satisfy Kit, who continued to hold it and look at me quizzically, as if for a better explanation.

I sighed. "Well, not all of us can get comfortable on any ol' pillow. We need a little extra, or we get used to—"

I stopped talking as Kit gave the pillow a little shake that conveyed more disgust than understanding. Then she gave the turtle pillow another shake, and both of us heard the slight rattle.

"Something's in there," I said. "Look, it has a zipper. Open it."

Kit quickly reached into the green fluff and yanked the zipper down. Then she reached in farther and pulled out a second Ziploc bag. We both stared at it.

"Holy crap," I said.

"Holy shit," Kit seconded.

The plastic bag contained two syringes and a couple of vials, each labeled succinylcholine. There was also a printed sheet of paper folded in half.

Kit waved the bag in front of my face. I saw on the sheet of paper the words HOW TO ADMINISTER.

"Caught ya," she said. And she wasn't talking to me.

***

Although I hated to enlist the help of William, as soon as we were on the road again, I called and asked him to meet us at the entrance to the party venue. He didn't ask me why and in fact seemed happy to accommodate my request.

When we pulled up, he was standing at the front door, chatting with one of the valets. As soon as he saw his own car, he walked around to the driver's side and then leaned in when I lowered the window. "Ladies, I thought you'd been in an accident." He looked relieved.

"Get in," Kit said from the passenger seat. "We have something to show you. We need your medical opinion."

William, clearly flattered, followed Kit's instructions and opened the back door. "This is all very mysterious. Is someone ill? I don't think I'm quite up to another problem, not today of all days. Jean will wonder where I am and—"

"Get a load of this." Kit tossed the plastic bag into the backseat, where it landed on his lap.

"What have you got here?" he asked. For once he wasn't grinning, and for the first time I saw him take a pair of glasses from his inside jacket pocket and put them on.

"We were hoping you'd tell us," Kit said. "And don't open it. Fingerprints, ya know."

"My, my." William held the bag up to his face and read the visible words on the sheet of paper inside. "This looks bad."

"Ya think?" Kit said.

"I *think*," he said, "we need to call Marv."

CHAPTER THIRTY-ONE

I still can't believe we didn't get a referral on that house," Tom Haskins said. It was Monday morning, and I was back at work, sitting across from my boss in his office at Haskins Realty. It was hard to believe all that had happened in the last ten days.

I slid down in his visitor's chair and stretched my legs out before me. "Well, you might still be able to work your charms on Jacqueline Bakos."

"Did I meet her?"

"No. You would have remembered."

"What's she like?"

"She's clever. She's exotic. And she's quite beautiful."

"*I* sure as hell didn't meet anyone matching that description up there in Cheeseland." I watched Tom take a cigar from the leather pouch on his desk and go through the ritual of lighting it with a gold Dunhill lighter. "She sounds fun," he said, after blowing out a cloud of blue-gray smoke. "My kinda woman."

"She'd eat you alive for breakfast."

He chuckled. "Like I said, she sounds like—"

"Boss." At the sound of Billie's voice, I sat up straight and turned to see her at the door. "You got a call. Martha Somebody. Line two."

"Take a message. I need to finish up with Valerie."

Billie gave me a smile. "Good to have you back, Val," she said. "Lunch later?"

I nodded and smiled back, and she closed the door.

"So." Tom took another puff. "Finish your story."

"Tom, I gave you all the gory details on the phone. Weren't you listening?"

"Geez, you call me when I'm barely off the plane, barely awake, with the plot of some wacky murder. It was like an episode of that show, the one with the old broad up in Maine or somewhere—"

"Are you referring to *Murder, She Wrote*?"

"Whatever. Just tell me what the hell was going on up there in Wisconsin. Who bumped off who? Who got the money? And why the hell were you even involved?"

I sighed. "Okay. I'm telling you one more time. But pay attention. It gives me a headache just thinking about it."

"So you'll take an aspirin later. Talk."

"Okay. Margaret Edwards pushed her mother down the stairs."

"She admitted it?"

"Kind of. She claims it was an accident. They got into a fight about money. As you yourself told me, Margaret was out of work and in a lot of debt. She came to Door County a day earlier than planned, determined not to stay with her mom—they were already in a fight. And she says she was also eager to get away from her problems in Minneapolis.

"Anyway, she went to see Doris, who repeated that she was not going to fund her any longer. She wasn't even going to pay for her daughter's stay in the hotel, calling it a typically foolish waste of money on Margaret's part. Still, Margaret insists she barely touched her mom as they argued, but poor Doris took a header down the stairs. They just happened to be standing at the top, Doris was wearing slippers, and her foot seemed to, well, slip."

"An accident, huh?"

"I believe her. I don't think she went there with the intention of murdering her mother."

"And what about this Vanessa?"

"Virginia."

"Okay, Virginia. What about her?"

"Well, that's the main reason I believe Margaret. She *admits* to killing Virginia—no accident. Plus, I guess Virginia arrived at the house just in time to see the whole thing. Doris and Margaret were arguing and didn't hear her ring the bell or enter the house."

"And you know this how? Because Margaret the murderer told you?"

I gave Tom my best *get real* look. "No, because Virginia told her niece. In one of their phone calls, she told Stephanie—that's her niece—what she'd seen. The bad thing is that I was talking to Stephanie at the party, and she mentioned how upset her aunt was by what she'd seen."

"*That's* the bad thing? Don't you think it's all kinda bad?"

"Well, yes, of course. But I assumed Stephanie was talking about her aunt witnessing Doris crying and seeing the checkbook. We never got far enough in the conversation for her to tell me Virginia had actually seen Doris fall."

"Okay, so if it was an accident, why didn't they just call the police?"

"Well, first off, Margaret left as soon as she heard Stan arrive, before he had a chance to even see her. Virginia was busy calling 9-1-1 and of course just figured Doris and Margaret would make up the next day, that surely the accident would bring them both to their senses. So she didn't say anything to Stan, or to William when *he* arrived."

I really was getting a headache, not to mention a heartache, just relaying all I'd learned in the past thirty-six hours. But Tom sat patiently waiting, such a rarity that it spurred me on. "Then when Doris died, Virginia figured she'd talk Margaret into going to the police and telling them the whole truth. She was certain Margaret would agree—later, if not sooner—since Virginia herself could vouch for the fact that it was an accident."

"But Margaret refused?" Tom sounded incredulous. "I'd think anyone with half a brain would consider this elderly lady a credible eyewitness. Talk about overkill."

"No, Margaret agreed to go to the police. But then she had second thoughts. She says she believed her mother was going to leave her a fortune, she didn't know she'd been all but taken out of the will, and she wasn't about to risk prison when she had all that money to spend."

"When were you doing all this talking to Margaret, by the way?"

"The sheriff let my mom see her; Mom thought that's what Doris would want her to do. I guess Doris had confided in my mom about cutting Margaret off due to her irresponsible lifestyle and spending habits. My mom advised her against that, urging her to try to help Margaret get into counseling. And even though it was Doris's choice, my mom feels so bad, like maybe if she'd been able to convince her . . . Anyway, I went along with her to see Margaret, for moral support."

"That it?" Suddenly Tom wasn't so patient.

"Well, Margaret told us she had doubted the authorities would believe her because of her record—another thing that made her mom so furious—for some bad checks and minor thefts—"

"Yeah, yeah—"

I ignored his know-it-all attitude and continued. "And she has some sketchy acquaintances, too, including one who was able to help her get a legal drug illegally."

"And *you* discovered the part about the drug?"

"Well, Kit and I."

"That broad—"

I interrupted him because I wanted to assume he was talking about Margaret, not my best friend. "We found all the paraphernalia in Margaret's suitcase."

"What about Stan the Man? Where'd he figure into all this?"

"Hmm, that's the interesting part."

"Go ahead; amaze me."

"Yes. Turns out he and Jacqueline were having an affair. It kind of surprised me that he didn't have anything to do with the murder, I must admit. But not Kit; she said he didn't have the—"

"Yeah, she'd be the one to judge, having a pair the size of soccer balls herself."

"I'll continue, if you're done."

He pretended to zip his lips closed.

"Stan was never sure how much money Doris would leave him, if any, since they did have a prenup," I said. "So for a while after Doris died, he played nice to Margaret, probably hoping she'd share with him if she inherited it all. But of course he was in love with Jacqueline."

Tom grunted, his impatience breaking open the zipper on his lips. It was his turn to give *me* some information. "By the way, did you know Stan and Doris met on the Internet?" he asked.

"Someone mentioned that, but no one seemed to know—"

"Yeah, that's how they met. A bit of a scam on Stan's part, I hear. He owes some money to some not-very-nice guys in New York." Tom's tone of voice made it sound like the conclusion to his report. He lit his infernal cigar again, giving me time to absorb his little nuggets.

"How d'you know *that*?"

"I know. Let's just say he better keep low for the next decade because as sure as bears shit in the Wisconsin woods, those boys are gonna want to collect."

"I wouldn't worry about that. Remember, he's got the newly minted Miss Moneybags in his pocket now."

"He's a bum. He made some shaky deals before your Doris Dibble married him. If you don't settle your debts, Valerie, they carry over. You get in a little deeper each time. He'll learn that the hard way."

I made a mental note to make sure I paid my dry cleaner the next time I picked up clothes. Mr. Wu had let me slide on my last two pickups, and I owed him nearly fifty bucks. I certainly didn't want to end up dead on a motorized rack with a bunch of clothes.

"And your mom," Tom said. "What the hell was that about Doris writing checks to her, but not really to her?"

"Well, we can only guess at motivation since Doris can't tell us why. But I assume she wrote my mom's name because she didn't want anyone—like her housekeeper, Jacqueline—to see who they were really for. Kit said Larry has done the same—"

"I've no doubt. If I were married to Kit—"

"You're not. End of subject. The important thing is that the money was going to some Croatian charity and from there to the families of the men killed in the shipyard accident. Doris must have felt very guilty about it. She never came clean to anyone, but she obviously did care about the plight of those people."

"And you figure she knew who this Jacqueline Bakos really was?"

"Of course. Why else would she leave everything she owned to her? But I'm not sure Jacqueline knew she knew. I just hope Jacqueline does something good—"

"She could start by putting that house on the market and sending the listing my friend's way—"

"Would you get over the house? It's not ours to worry about. And frankly, if I never see Jacqueline Bakos again, it will be too soon."

"Okay, okay. I'm over it. But you still haven't explained why you got so involved."

I sighed heavily. If he'd been listening at all . . . But it was easier to repeat myself than to argue. "Because I thought those checks were made out to my mother. So I had to clear her name, and by the time we did, well, we were so close to—"

"How are you feeling about her getting married to the doc?"

For once, I was grateful for Tom's impatience. I didn't want to explain Kit's and my motivation. Some things are inexplicable. Especially to insensitive types like Tom.

"I feel okay about my mom marrying William. No, more than okay. He adores her and will take care of her."

I chuckled, as I recalled William telling us before we left that he thought he was *never* going to get to propose to my mom, the way we kept thwarting him. Like when Emily accompanied them on their walk around the premises of Lake View Coves and also when we returned earlier than he expected from our trek to buy a plunger.

"So it's all good?" Tom asked.

"My mom and William, yes. But there's something else far more important I need to talk to you about."

"Yeah?" He flipped the ash from the end of his cigar into a beautiful Waterford ashtray. "Let's hear it, Kiddo."

"You are a beast, Tom Haskins. What do you *think* I want to know?"

"Okay. You will be happy to learn that *Blood Over Ice* won't be winning any Academy Awards. In fact, it will never see the light of day. Distribution—and believe me, there wasn't gonna be much distribution to speak of—has been nixed. Emily can go on with her career, fully clothed, I hope. In fact, she's gonna get a call from a legit film studio, who may or may not have a good role for her."

I knew if it had been anyone else but Tom Haskins giving me that news, I would have rushed around his desk and given him a hug. And then I thought *what the heck* and did it anyway.

"Watch the suit." He gently pushed me away and brushed the lapel of his jacket. But I noticed the satisfied grin on his face.

"Tom, I can't thank you enough." I took a step back. "I knew you could do it. I'm not even going to ask how."

"Let's just say that some of the same big boys that could make Stan Dibble's life hell are gonna do the opposite for our little Emily."

"Okay." I walked backward to my side of the desk. "But Emily won't be in anyone's debt, will—"

"No way. And she'll never even know."

I hated to think who might be behind Emily's return to fully clothed roles, but I had to ask. "Tom, this doesn't put you in an awkward situation, does it?"

He laughed heartily before responding. "You kill me, Pankowski, you really do. You think I'm working with the *mob*?"

"Well, I'm not sure. You sound so—"

"I have some legitimate friends, too, you know."

"Well, of course, I know that. I just didn't think they stretched to California."

"Valerie, this is the electronic age. You don't have to actually *be* in California to make things work out there. Besides, I enlisted the help of a local boy. You even know him."

"Who?"

"Guess."

"Santa Claus?" I felt silly with relief over Emily's reprieve.

"Not even close."

"Then who?"

"Your old friend Dennis. Dennis Culotta."

Lethal Property

I hate being the first one in the office. It forces me to hang around waiting for Billie to arrive and work her magic with the cappuccino machine. But she is the only one in our office of four people who can produce the delicious coffee capped with creamy, white froth. Prepared to wait, I set my purse down and switched on my computer just as my phone pinged, announcing two new texts.

First one was from Billie. *Hang tough, Val. On my way. Be there in five. Traffic snarly.*

Second one was from Perry. My fellow Realtor and nephew of Tom Haskins, the owner of Haskins Realty, where we attempt to sell houses every day. *Running late. Sorreeeeee. Be there in a jiff. Don't touch anything on my desk. Puhleeeeze. Love ya.* This was followed by three smiley faces.

I immediately crossed the four feet of space separating our desks for a look-see. Apart from an oversize coffee cup bearing a picture of the sultry Jessica Rabbit, I saw nothing out of the ordinary.

I picked up a framed photograph of Perry and Tom. Perry looked handsome and absurdly young, for a thirty-year-old. He had one arm around his uncle's shoulders and was grinning like a model for a teeth-whitening product; Tom was scowling.

Nothing new there.

"Hey."

"Billie! Good morning." My workday could begin.

Billie Ludlow is barely five feet tall, with silky chestnut hair cut to just below her baby face and a smile that sometimes takes my breath away. A twentysomething, she is the office know-it-all (but in a good way).

"Won't be a second, Val." She rushed past me to the back of the small office and the tiny kitchen.

"Good girl," I said, opening the middle drawer of Perry's desk. Impressed by the neatness of the contents, I quickly closed it. "Wonder Boy is running late. By the way, he told me not to touch anything on his desk. What's that about?"

"Oh, you know how our Perry loves drama."

"You don't think he meant this, do you?" I took a sheet of paper from his otherwise-empty in-box.

"What have you found?" Billie raised her voice above the hissing sound of steaming milk.

"Has Perry joined a choral group?" I called back, studying the flyer that touted the superior voices of the Hinsdale Male Chorus sponsored by McVaughn Chevrolet.

"Sounds about right," I heard Billie say. "Gee, his uncle will be proud."

Feeling wicked, I could hardly wait for Tom Haskins to learn of his young nephew's latest undertaking. I put the flyer back in the box and turned toward Billie just as my phone rang. "Haskins Realty, Valerie Pankowski speaking. How may I help you?"

The caller was a man interested in viewing a house he had seen on our website: 3396 Lavender Lane. Four bedrooms, two and a half baths, spacious backyard, and on the market for just under two months.

"May I have your name?" I asked, pen ready.

"Gardner. Jim Gardner."

"I know that house well, Mr. Gardner; it's really lovely." That wasn't untrue. Apart from its fragrant address, the house was in perfect condition for an older home and located in a quiet, upscale neighborhood. "What would be a good time for you?"

"How about five? Is that too late? I'll be tied up most of the day."

"Yes, five would probably work. I'll check with the owner."

"Could I meet you at your office and we drive together? I'm not familiar with this part of Chicago. Or any part of it, really. I'm transferring here, and I'm in town for just two days."

"Sure. Obviously, you've seen the house online; it's a nice size, more than three thousand square feet."

"Yes, perfect. I have a wife and three children back in Utah."

"Your wife sent you ahead to scout for a home, is that it?"

3

"Exactly. I've seen a few already. But I think I'm going to really like this one. So, I guess I'll see you at five?"

"I'll be here."

***

Perry arrived at the office thirty minutes after Billie and I had enjoyed our first cappuccino. He came in with his usual fluster, cheeks red, as if he'd run from a parking lot half a mile away rather than the spot a few feet from the front door where he always parks his Corvette.

"Greetings, Val. Hola, Billie. Is Uncle Tom here yet?"

I strained my neck to look over Perry's shoulder through the glass front of the office and saw the three cars parked there. "Let's see. Did you notice his Mercedes?" I asked.

Perry actually turned and checked it out, as if he really might have missed his uncle's mammoth automobile, roughly the size of an ocean liner.

"No. I don't see it."

"So, my guess is that he isn't here, unless he hitched a ride from downtown."

"Good," he agreed with my assessment. Then he plunked down in his chair. Perry is gorgeous. Like a red setter is gorgeous. But if you want your dog to fetch the stick, and then balance it on his nose, you're better off with a Labrador.

"So," he said, taking a six-inch mirror from his desk drawer and grabbing a quick peek at himself. "This is good. I don't want him to think I was late. Has he called? Is he coming in today? You haven't been poking around my desk, have you, Val?"

"Absolutely not. I'm insulted you would even ask me that. And by the way, you do know that male choruses are fronts for money laundering, don't you?"

***

It was nearly twelve thirty when I looked at my watch. I'd had a busy morning. Two new clients had called, and I'd set up showings with both of them. Lower interest rates had turned the market a little to one side, the good side, and although it wasn't completely back to where it had been, business was much better.

From my cell phone, I dialed Kit James, my best friend for more than forty years. Kit is what they call a homemaker, and what I call damn lucky. I had the same homemaker title myself once, when David and I were married. But after our only child, Emily, entered high school, I asked my lifelong friend Tom Haskins if I could work for him part-time. It seemed like a fun distraction.

Then after David and I divorced, and I left the Big House and moved to a tiny apartment, finances dictated my job could no longer be just a distraction. It had to become my livelihood.

"Whatcha doing?" I asked Kit.

"I'm looking at my neighbor's house across the street. She had it painted this morning."

"So, you are literally watching paint dry?"

"Val, the color is all wrong. Why didn't she check with me first?"

"Huh? Why should she check with—"

"It's a hideous, barfy, sea-foam bluey-green. Remember you used to have a car that color?"

"I was nineteen, for Pete's sake. How do you even remember—never mind. Wanna meet for lunch?" I asked, steering the subject away from my first car, which, I realized upon reflection, had been a little barfy.

"I have a lot to do today—"

"C'mon, take a break. What's so important? I have a Perry story."

"I do have that date with Yuri, my Israeli lover. But I could squeeze you in before."

"Does he have a friend for me?" I slipped my purse strap over my shoulder and headed toward the door.

"How do you feel about eye patches?"

Kit has been married to Larry for about thirty years. A good guy. She has impeccable taste in everything, including husbands.

"I can live with an eye patch," I said. "Let's meet at Berto's Deli. It's close. Don't want to wear you out for Yuri."

I heard Kit sigh. "As if I have the energy for a lover. Okay. But first I gotta drop Larry's pants off at the tailor. See you in twenty minutes."

Who was she kidding? She has enough energy for ten Yuris.

***

"Where's that listing sheet I stole from Parson's Realty?" It was Tom Haskins yelling from his desk. His private office is the only room in our little facility that has an actual door. "I gave it to Perry."

"Never saw it," I yelled back.

"And just where the hell *is* Perry?" Now Tom was standing in his doorway. He is a large man, attractive if you like rugby players with bald heads. He removed the unlit cigar from his mouth and pointed it my way. "That list has a lot of information not on the Web yet. I went to considerable lengths to get it. Perry was supposed to study it and get it right back to me. And where the hell is he?"

"Don't know, Boss. Look on his desk. Check the in-box. I see something there; maybe that's your precious list."

"What're you up to today?" he asked.

"Today? It's nearly four thirty," I reminded him. "I was here early, but I do have a guy coming in a half hour to see the Lavender Lane place."

"Good. Good deal. That place is a peach." I wondered how he knew that, since he rarely checks out the listings personally. "There's a pond two streets over. Ducks and stuff. Make sure you drive the guy by it." Okay, so maybe he does check out some things. "I need that list, Val."

"Look in Perry's in-box," I said again, eyeing the lone flyer, urging him to take a peek.

"What does he need an in-box for? Do you have one?"

I tapped my temple with my index finger. "Mine's in here," I said.

"You got that list in there?"

"No, you gave it to Perry. Remember?"

Tom walked over and placed two hands on the edge of my desk, leaning forward. He turned slightly toward Perry's desk. "I don't see it."

"Are you blind? There's something in there."

"Just one sheet of paper."

"Well, maybe that's it. At least check it out."

"Nah. That's not it."

"You can tell without looking at it?"

"Yes, I can."

My desire for Tom to learn about the Hinsdale Male Chorus sponsored by McVaughn Chevrolet was overwhelming. "Okay," I said, rising, "*I'll* see what Perry's got there."

But Tom put a hand on my shoulder. "Val, I think we both know that's not a real estate list."

"Then what—"

"Some damn boys' choir. You know it, I know it, and pretty soon every poor bastard in Hinsdale is gonna know it. But hey, nice try."

He walked away chuckling to himself, drawing on the unlit cigar.

"Okay," I said, following him and stopping to lean against his door frame, arms crossed. "Was there ever even a list?"

"Ha! If there was, d'you think I'd give it to Perry?"

I could hear his chuckling grow even louder as I closed his door and returned to my desk.

***

By five forty-five I was alone in the office. Billie and Tom had both left, and Perry had never returned from wherever it was he'd been all afternoon. I picked up my cell to call Daphne Travister, the owner of the Lavender Lane house, and cancel the appointment. It was bad manners to call her so late, but I'd been sure Jim Gardner would show. When my cell rang before I could dial, I answered with relief.

"Ms. Pankowski, Jim Gardner here. Sorry I didn't call sooner, but I was in meetings and couldn't get away. Is it too late to see the house?"

"I don't think that will be a problem. Let me check with the owner and find out. Stay where you are, and I'll call you back in two minutes."

***

The neighborhood looked as inviting as always, with its towering trees and well-manicured lawns. I went a little out of my way to drive past the pond Tom had mentioned. It was very pretty, and there were indeed a handful of ducks floating peacefully on the still water.

Daphne Travister had told me on the phone that she didn't mind our coming late, but she wasn't prepared to leave the house again. No problem, I assured her. Sometimes it is even a plus to have the homeowner around during a showing.

"Come in, Val," she greeted us at the door. She was in her early sixties. A tall, slim woman, recently retired and planning to downscale to an apartment for seniors. Her short gray hair looked freshly permed, and she wore no makeup.

"Daphne Travister, please meet Jim Gardner; he's—"

"Embarrassed to be so late. Thank you for letting us come."

"Not a problem. Please, take as much time as you need. I'll be in my bedroom if you have any questions. Although I think Val knows as much about this house as I do." She smiled and patted my arm as she said it.

We watched her disappear down the hall and then heard the door close, along with sounds from a television.

"Okay, Mr. Gardner—"

"Jim, please."

"Okay, Jim. Shall we start in the kitchen? It was remodeled four years ago. All appliances will stay. Granite countertops—"

"Does Daphne live alone?"

"Hmm."

Instead of responding, I studied my clipboard with the specs of the house. I never answer personal questions about my clients. "The schools are excellent. That much I do know."

"You have children, Val?"

"I have a married daughter who lives in California. She's in her twenties. But many of my clients have children in school here. How old are your kids, Jim?"

"School-age." He had wandered over to look at the backyard through the large windows in the eating area of the kitchen. "This is lovely," he said.

"Yes, it's very nice," I agreed.

"Why, thank you."

We both turned to see Daphne in the kitchen entrance.

"I'm so sorry to be in your way," she said. "I just need to get my medication; I should have taken it at six. It's in this cupboard." She opened the door and took down a pill container.

"Nothing serious, I hope," Jim said, closing the door after her.

"No. Just an antibiotic for a chest infection."

"Can I ask you a question?" Jim smiled, leaning back on the counter, his hands in his pockets.

"Of course; anything you like."

"Your yard is magnificent. I'm gonna go out in a minute and take a better look. Do you have a service to take care of it?"

Daphne looked pleased with the compliment. "Good heavens, no. I do it myself."

"That's hard to believe; it's a big job."

"I know. But I don't mind. My husband did it before he died; we both enjoyed gardening. It's my exercise."

"You're doing a great job. Val was just telling me about the schools. I have three children. Little monsters, but we love them. How about your children? Did they go to school here?"

"I don't have any children, Mr. Gardner."

"Jim, please."

"Okay, Jim. My husband and I weren't blessed that way."

"They can be a trial, that's for sure."

"But still a blessing."

"Of course. So, you're planning to move to one of those places for seniors?"

I wondered where Jim Gardner had picked up that information, and then my eyes fell on a leaflet on the counter advertising Morning Sun Community, a luxury residence for seniors.

As I looked at it, Jim picked it up. "This looks very nice," he said.

"Yes, I'm lucky they had an opening."

"So you're retired?"

"Yes. Happily so."

"Good for you. Tell me about your neighbors here. Nice?"

"Yes. I don't know any of them really well. Most of them are a lot younger than me, and some are new to the neighborhood."

"I think we should let Daphne get back to her TV show," I said. "Come, Jim; let's go outside and see the yard."

"Yes. Good idea."

Once outside, I watched him carefully walk the perimeter of the yard, which was enclosed by a fence. "The only access to the yard is through the garage or kitchen door," he said, more to himself than to me.

"Looks like it," I said.

He was done in a few minutes, and we returned to the kitchen. Then I led him through the rest of the house, including a quick look in Daphne's bedroom, and he asked very few questions; but I noted that he carefully studied the living space and opened many closet doors.

"Okay," he said when the walk-through was complete ten minutes later, "this is very nice. Shall we say good-bye to Mrs. Travister?"

"Daphne, we're leaving," I called down the hall.

She opened the bedroom door and stepped out. "It was so nice to meet you, Jim. I do hope you'll consider this house. My husband and I were very happy here for many years."

"I can tell," Jim said. "And I'm gonna call my wife as soon as I get back to my hotel."

Daphne gave me a twinkly smile and walked us to the door.

"Make sure you lock up after us," Jim said. Then he gave the dead bolt a quick twist.

***

I drove Jim Gardner back to my office, intent on discussing some financial information. But he said he didn't have time to talk money; he had plans for dinner and would contact me soon. I couldn't gauge whether or not he liked the house; he was hard to read. Before driving away, however, he did give me a business card with home, cell, and office numbers in Salt Lake City. He also said he would give me a call.

But he never did.

***

Two days later I heard on the evening news, which I had switched on for background noise, that a woman was found dead in her Downers Grove home. Described as elderly and living alone, she was recently retired with no next of kin. A friend had stopped at her house to go on their daily mall walk and discovered the body. The deceased's name was Daphne Travister. When I heard it, I said a silent thanks to TiVo and rewound it, paying closer attention to the details.

That's when I heard the newscaster say the police suspected foul play.

Patty and Roz
www.roz-patty.com

About the authors . . .

Now a proud and patriotic US citizen and Texan, Rosalind Burgess grew up in London and currently calls Houston home. She has also lived in Germany, Iowa, and Minnesota. Roz retired from the airline industry to devote all her working hours to writing (although it seems more like fun than work).

Patricia Obermeier Neuman spent her childhood and early adulthood moving around the Midwest (Minnesota, South Dakota, Nebraska, Iowa, Wisconsin, Illinois, and Indiana), as a trailing child and then as a trailing spouse (inspiring her first book, *Moving: The What, When, Where & How of It*). A former reporter and editor, Patty lives with her husband in Door County, Wisconsin. They have three children and twelve grandchildren.

No. 1 in
The Val & Kit Mystery Series

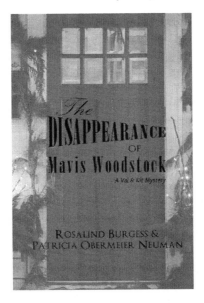

The Disappearance of Mavis Woodstock

Mavis Woodstock (a vaguely familiar name) calls Val and insists she has to sell her house as quickly as possible. Then she fails to keep her scheduled appointment. Kit remembers Mavis from their school days, an unattractive girl who was ignored when she was lucky, ridiculed when she was not. She also remembers Mavis being the only daughter in a large family that was as frugal as it was wealthy. When Val and Kit cannot locate Mavis, they begin an investigation, encountering along the way a little romance, a lot of deception, and more than one unsavory character.

What readers are saying about . . .
The Disappearance of Mavis Woodstock

FIVE STARS! "Best book I've read in a long time; couldn't wait to go to bed at night so I could read this book and then couldn't put it down. TOTAL PAGE-TURNER . . . Cannot wait to read the next book in this series!!!"

FIVE STARS! " . . . well-written mystery . . . first of The Val & Kit Mystery Series. The two amateur sleuths, Val & Kit, are quirky, humorous, and dogged in their pursuit of righting what they felt was a wrongful death of someone they knew from the past. It's full of humorous, cagey, and a few dark personalities that keep you on your toes wondering what or who would turn up next. . . . a fun, fast read that is engaging and will keep your interest. . . . A tightly woven mystery with a great twist at the end."

FIVE STARS! "I thoroughly enjoyed this book, laughing out loud many times, often until I cried. I love the authors' style and could so relate to the things the characters were going through."

FIVE STARS! "This was a fun read! The story was well put together. Lots of suspense. Authors tied everything together well. Very satisfying."

FIVE STARS! "Enjoyed this tale of two friends immensely. Was shocked by the ending and sad to find I had finished the book so quickly. Anxious to read the next one. . . . Keep them coming!"

FIVE STARS! "Mysteries are sometimes too predictable for me—I can guess the ending before I'm halfway through the book. Not this one. The characters are well developed and fun, and the plot kept me guessing until the end."

FIVE STARS! "I highly recommend this novel and I'm looking forward to the next book in this series. I was kept guessing throughout the entire novel. The analogies throughout are priceless and often made me laugh. . . . I found myself on the edge of my seat. . . . The ending to this very well-written novel is brilliant!"

FIVE STARS! "I recommend this book if you like characters such as Kinsey Millhone or Stone Barrington . . . or those types. Excellent story with fun characters. Can't wait to read more of these."

FIVE STARS! "A cliff-hanger with an I-did-not-see-that-coming ending."

FIVE STARS! " . . . well written, humorous . . . a good plot and a bit of a surprise ending. An easy read that is paced well, with enough twists and turns to keep you reading to the end."

FIVE STARS! "Very enjoyable book and hard to put down. Well-written mystery with a great surprise ending. A must-read."

FIVE STARS! "This is a well-written mystery that reads along at a bright and cheerful pace with a surprisingly dark twist at the end."

FIVE STARS! "I really enjoyed this book: the characters, the story line, everything. It is well written, humorous, engaging."

FIVE STARS! "The perfect combo of sophisticated humor, fun and intriguing twists and turns!"

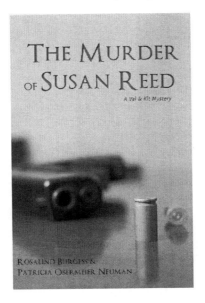

The Murder of Susan Reed

When Kit suspects Larry of having an affair with one of his employees, Susan Reed, she enlists Val's help in uncovering the truth. The morning after a little stalking expedition by the lifelong friends, Val reads in the newspaper that Susan Reed was found shot to death in her apartment the night before, right around the time Kit was so certain Larry and Susan were together. *Were* they having an affair? And did Larry murder her? The police, in the form of dishy Detective Dennis Culotta, conduct the investigation into Susan's murder, hampered at times by Val and Kit's insistent attempts to discover whether Larry is guilty of infidelity and/or murder. As the investigation heats up, so does Val's relationship with Detective Culotta.

What readers are saying about . . .
The Murder of Susan Reed

FIVE STARS! "Having thoroughly enjoyed Val and Kit's adventures in *The Disappearance of Mavis Woodstock*, I was both looking forward to and a bit nervous about reading its sequel. No need to worry. This is a terrific follow-up with the two ladies back with a bang together with some characters we already know and a batch of new ones. I had a great time going along with Val and Kit as they put the pieces together to solve the murder of a young woman known to them. The book is superbly plotted and very well written, with a little romance thrown in. A good whodunit should keep the reader guessing right to the very end, and this one really did the job for me."

FIVE STARS! " . . . takes you on a ride through the sometimes serious, sometimes hilarious relationship of Val and Kit. . . . The two have a . . . knack at solving crimes. It revisits your own high school friendships and takes you on a trip to catch a killer!"

FIVE STARS! "This book was great; kept me changing my mind about who did it. . . ."

FIVE STARS! "This is the second book in the Val & Kit Series. I really enjoyed both books and look forward to their next one. You won't be disappointed—it is a fun read that makes you hate to put it down. Never quite sure what will happen next."

FIVE STARS! "This second book in the series was as great as the first. It's a well-written, fun story about longtime friends who can't help but stumble into trouble. I enjoyed getting to know Val and Kit better and look forward to the next book!"

FIVE STARS! "I couldn't wait to get this Val & Kit adventure after reading the authors' first book, and I was not disappointed. As a fan of this genre . . . I just have to write a few words praising the incredible talent of Roz and Patty. One thing I specifically want to point out is the character development. You can completely visualize the supporting actors (suspects?) so precisely that you do not waste time trying to recall details about the character. . . . Roz and Patty practically create an imprint in your mind of each character's looks/voice/mannerisms, etc."

FIVE STARS! "Even better than the first! Another page-turner! Take it to the beach or pool. You will love it!!! I did!!!"

FIVE STARS! "Great writing. Great plot."

FIVE STARS! "Once again Val & Kit star in a page-turner mystery!"

FIVE STARS! "I loved this book and these two best friends who tend to get in trouble together. Reminds me of my best friend and myself."

FIVE STARS! "Ms. Burgess and Ms. Neuman are fantastic writers and did a great job with their sophomore effort! I enjoy their writing style and they really capture the genre of cozy mystery well! I highly recommend their books!"

FIVE STARS! "Val and Kit's interactions and Val's thoughts about life in general were probably the best part of the book. I was given enough info to 'suspect' just about every character mentioned."

Lethal Property

In this fourth book of The Val & Kit Mystery Series (a stand-alone, like the first three), our ladies are back home in Downers Grove. Val is busy selling real estate, eager to take a potential buyer to visit the home of a widow living alone. He turns out not to be all that he claimed, and a string of grisly events follows, culminating in a perilous situation for Val. Her lifelong BFF Kit is ready to do whatever necessary to ensure Val's safety and clear her name of any wrongdoing. The dishy Detective Dennis Culotta also returns to help, and with the added assistance of Val's boss, Tom Haskins, and a *Downton Abbey*–loving Rottweiler named Roscoe, the ladies become embroiled in a murder investigation extraordinaire. As always, we are introduced to a new cast of shady characters as we welcome back the old circle of friends.

What readers are saying about . . .
Lethal Property

FIVE STARS! "Rosalind and Patricia have done it again and written a great sequel in The Val & Kit Mystery Series . . . full of intrigue and great wit and a different mystery each time. . . . *Lethal Property* is a great read, and I did not want to put the book down. I do hope that someone in the TV world reads these, as they'd make a great TV series. . . . I cannot wait for the next. Rosalind and Patricia, keep writing these great reads. Most worthy of FIVE STARS."

FIVE STARS! " . . . Val and Kit—forever friends. Smart, witty, determined, vulnerable, unintentional detectives. While this fourth installment can be read without having read the first three books (in the series), I'm certain you'll find that you want to read the first three. As has been the case with each book written by Rosalind Burgess and Patricia Obermeier Neuman, once I started reading, I really didn't want to stop. It was very much like catching up with old friends. Perhaps you know the feeling. . . . Regardless of how long the separation, being together again just feels right."

FIVE STARS! "My girls are back in action! It's a hilarious ride when Val is implicated in a series of murders. We get a lot of the hotness that is Dennis Culotta this time around. . . . Also, we get a good dose of Tom too. But the best part of *Lethal Property*? Val and Kit. Besties with attitude and killer comedy. The banter and down-to-earth humor between these two is pure enjoyment on the page. Five bright and shiny stars for this writing duo!"

FIVE STARS! "Enjoyed reading *Lethal Property* as well as all by Roz and Patty. Written in a way that I felt connected with the characters. Looking forward to the next one."

FIVE STARS! "OK . . . so I thought I knew whodunit early in the book, then after changing my mind at least 8-10 times, I was still wrong. (I want to say so much more, but I really don't want to give anything away.) Just one of the many, many things I love about the Val & Kit books. I love the characters/suspects, I love the believable dialogue between characters and also Valley Girl's inner dialogue (when thinking about Tina . . . hehe). I'd like to also add that (these books) are just good, clean fun. A series of books that you would/could/should recommend to anyone. (My boss is a nun, so that's a little something I worry about . . . lol) Thanks again, ladies. I agree with another reviewer . . . it IS like catching up with old friends, and I can't wait for the next one."

FIVE STARS! "Reading *Lethal Property* was like catching up with old friends, and a few new characters, but another fun ride! I love these characters and I adore these writers. Would recommend to anyone who appreciates a good story and a sharp wit. Well done, ladies; you did it again!"

FIVE STARS! "As with the other books in this series, this can be read as a stand-alone. However, I've read all of them to date in order and that's probably the best way to do it. I'm to the point where I don't even read the cover blurb for these books . . . because I know that I'll enjoy them. This book certainly didn't disappoint. Plenty of Val and Kit and their crazy antics, a cast of new colorful characters and a mystery that wasn't predictable."

No. 5 in
The Val & Kit Mystery Series

Palm Desert Killing

When one of them receives a mysterious letter, BFFs Val and Kit begin to unravel a mystery that spans a continent and reaches back decades. It also takes them to Palm Desert, California, a paradise of palm trees, mountains, blue skies . . . and now murder. The men in their lives—Val's favorite detective, Dennis Culotta; her boss, Tom Haskins; and Kit's husband, Larry—play their (un)usual parts in this adventure that introduces a fresh batch of suspicious characters, including Kit's New York–attorney sister, Nora, and their mother. Val faces an additional challenge when her daughter, Emily, reveals her own startling news. Val and Kit bring to this story their (a)typical humor, banter, and unorthodox detective skills.

What readers are saying about . . .
Palm Desert Killing

FIVE STARS! "Have fallen in love with Val and Kit and was so excited to see there was a new book in the series. It did not disappoint. Val and Kit are true to form and it was fun to get to know Kit's sister."

FIVE STARS! "Each book in this series is like hanging out with your gal-pals! The characters, Val and Kit, are very well developed."

FIVE STARS! "I love all of the Val & Kit mysteries! Great reading! Lots of laughs and suspense with Val and Kit."

FIVE STARS! "Everyone needs a pal like these two!! Love Val and Kit! Can't wait for their next adventure!!"

FIVE STARS! "Love the authors, love the characters. This series gets better and better!"

And if you want to read about the mystery of marriage, here's a NON–Val & Kit book for you . . .

Dressing Myself

Meet Jessie Harleman in this contemporary women's novel about love, lust, friends, and family. Jessie and Kevin have been happily married for twenty-eight years. With their two grown kids now out of the house and living their own lives, Jessie and Kevin have reached the point they thought they longed for, yet slightly dreaded. But the house that used to burst at the seams now has too many empty rooms. Still, Jessie is a *glass half-full* kind of woman, eager for this next period of her life to take hold. The problem is, nothing goes the way she planned. This novel explores growth and change and new beginnings.

What readers are saying about . . .
Dressing Myself

FIVE STARS! "Loved this book!!! Another page-turner by talented Burgess and Neuman, my new favorite authors!!! I loved reading this book. It was very heartwarming in so many ways!!! Ready to read the next book from this writing duo!!!"

FIVE STARS! "I love these authors. I love the real feelings, thoughts, words, actions, etc., that they give to their characters. I love that it feels like a memoir instead of fiction. I love that it depressed me. I want to say so much more about what I loved, but I don't want to give too much away. A classic story that draws your emotions out of you to make you root for it to go one way, then in the next chapter, make a U-turn; just like the main character. It makes you reflect on your own life and happiness. It makes you check your husband's e-mails and credit card statements. I simply love your writing, ladies. Can't wait for the next one."

FIVE STARS! "I couldn't put it down! Great book! Maybe I could relate with the main character too much, but I felt as though she was my friend. When I wasn't reading the book, the main character was constantly on my mind! The ending was unpredictable in a great way! I think the authors need to keep on writing! I'm a huge fan!"

FIVE STARS! "Wonderful book! A fast read because once you start, you just cannot put it down; the characters become like your family! Definitely a worthwhile read!"

FIVE STARS! "Delightful! I so enjoyed my time with Jessie. I laughed with her, and ached for her. I knew her so well so quickly. I'll remember her story with a smile. I hope these authors keep it coming. What a fun read!"

FIVE STARS! "Love these writers!! So refreshing to have writers who really create such characters you truly understand and relate to. Looking forward to the next one. Definitely my favorites!"

FIVE STARS! "This book is about a woman's life torn apart . . . A lot of detail as to how she would feel . . . very well-written. I have to agree with the other readers, 5 stars."

FIVE STARS! "What a fun read *Dressing Myself* was! . . . I have to admit I didn't expect the ending . . . It was hard to put this book down."

FIVE STARS! "Great, easy, captivating read!! The characters seem so real! I don't read a lot, but I was really into this one! Read it for sure!"

FIVE STARS! "Loved it! Read this in one day. Enjoyed every page and had a real feeling for all of the characters. I was rooting for Jessie all the way. . . . Hope there's another story like this down the road."

FIVE STARS! "It has been a long time since I have read a book cover to cover in one day . . . fantastic read . . . real page-turner that was hard to put down . . . Thanks, Ladies!"